THE WAY WE WERE

SHANDI BOYES

COPYRIGHT

Editing: Mountains Wanted Publishing.
Cover Design: SSB Designs
Model: Andrew
Photography: Lindee Robinson Photography.

WANT TO STAY IN TOUCH?

Facebook: facebook.com/authorshandi

Instagram: instagram.com/authorshandi

Email: authorshandi@gmail.com

Reader's Group: bit.ly/ShandiBookBabes

Website: authorshandi.com

Newsletter: https://www.subscribepage.com/AuthorShandi

ALSO BY SHANDI BOYES

* Denotes Standalone Books

Perception Series

Saving Noah *

Fighting Jacob *

Taming Nick *

Redeeming Slater *

Saving Emily

Wrapped Up with Rise Up

Protecting Nicole *

Enigma

Enigma

Unraveling an Enigma

Enigma The Mystery Unmasked

Enigma: The Final Chapter

Beneath The Secrets

Beneath The Sheets

Spy Thy Neighbor *

The Opposite Effect *

I Married a Mob Boss *

Second Shot *

The Way We Are

The Way We Were

Sugar and Spice *

Lady In Waiting

Man in Queue

Couple on Hold

Enigma: The Wedding

Silent Vigilante

Hushed Guardian

Quiet Protector

Enigma: An Isaac Retelling

Enigma Bonus Scenes (Two free chapters)

Twisted Lies *

Bound Series

Chains

Links

Bound

Restrain

The Misfits *

Nanny Dispute *

Russian Mob Chronicles

Very Unlikely *

False Start *

Short Stories - Newsletter Downloads

Christmas Trio *

Falling For A Stranger *

One Night Only Series

Hotshot Boss *

Hotshot Neighbor *

The Bobrov Bratva Series

Wicked Intentions *

Sinful Intentions *

Devious Intentions *

Deadly Intentions *

DEDICATION

For my Family. . .
No, not the crazy bunch you're thinking about.
My real family—you guys!
I love you xx

I hope you enjoy Ryan's story.

Shandi xx

CHAPTER 1

Back Then

Savannah

𝒜 sense of familiarity hits me when I spot the "Welcome to Ravenshoe" sign on the horizon. When you grow up in the same town your entire life, you usually run for the hills the instant you reach adulthood. I had considered doing that many times during middle school. It wasn't because I hated my life; I just wanted to save Ryan from his.

My plans changed when Ryan and I lost contact. Then they were blasted to the next stratosphere a little over two years ago.

My dad is a brilliant man who is fighting an unimaginable disease. I thought his forgetfulness was from a broken heart. I had no clue it was something so mammoth.

Alzheimer's. My father—the light of my life—has Alzheimer's.

Now he's half the man he used to be. This cruel and debilitating disease is taking him away from me more quickly than I would like. I went from curing his broken heart to healing his head within weeks. It is quite dramatic how swiftly his disease has progressed. Within weeks of my mom leaving, little signs appeared. He'd forget his keys or his beloved cell phone. Once he even drove to Hopeton instead of his new office in Ravenshoe. For an ordinary person, this wouldn't be a big deal. But for an extraordinary man like my dad, I knew it was more than a broken heart.

I don't care how old I become, I'll never look at my dad as anything less than a superhero. No matter what my mom and I wanted, he provided. He gave us the world, only to have it brutally stripped away from him. My father adored my mother. Their story is remarkably similar to Ryan's and mine. They were friends until their final year at Ravenshoe High saw them taking a route neither saw coming.

My father has never handled jealousy well.

When his best friend—who just happened to be a girl— gained the attention of his male friends, things progressed between them very quickly. Although I don't know the full details of their transition from friends to lovers, the general gist is that they attended a friend's eighteenth birthday with dates in tow, then left with each other. The stuff in the middle is a little blurry. Not just for me but for my parents as well.

I want to act surprised by the last confession, but I'm not.

My parents were born during the Vietnam era. "Haze" is a good word to describe their senior year.

They had the ideal relationship—well, so it seemed on paper. They married within weeks of their graduation from Ithaca University. They founded their financial conglomerate within months of their return to Ravenshoe, and I joined the ranks a few years after that. Financially, things were bumpy the first few years...until my dad struck gold.

Against my mom's wishes, he invested every dime he had in a little unknown computer company. The return on his investment was astronomical. The figures cited on business records for the past ten years would blow your mind. But do you know what? My dad remained humble. The fancy house he has lived in for the past eleven years wasn't for him. It was for his queen—my mother. She wanted their living conditions to reflect the princely funds in their bank account. She desired eight bedrooms that no one would use and a six-car garage when we only owned two vehicles.

She wanted the world, and my father gave it to her.

And what did he get in return for his provision? She cheated on him.

That day—god, I'll never forget it. Little girls always favor their fathers over their mothers, but I worshipped my mother just as much as my dad. I wanted to be her when I grew up... until I heard her shouting Ryan's dad's name at the top of her lungs.

My first thought was fear; Ted is a violent man. It was only when I walked into the laundry room mere feet from the back patio where Ryan and his friends were mingling did I realize

3

my worry was unfounded. She wasn't screaming in distress. She was shouting in ecstasy.

I froze, a better reaction beyond me. I was confident what I was witnessing couldn't be true. Don't get me wrong, I was nearly thirteen and knew the vile act they were committing without experiencing it firsthand; I just didn't want to believe it.

My father could have picked any woman to stand by his side; he chose my mom because he worshipped the ground she walked on. He would have never selected an adulterer.

The trip back from Ryan's house that afternoon was awkward. My mom was quieter than usual. I guess having your twelve-year-old daughter walk in on you in a compromising position with a man who isn't your husband would be traumatizing for any woman.

She knew me so well she could tell I knew about her affair without me speaking a word.

"It will *never* happen again," she promised.

Her voice was so raw I believed her in an instant. She wasn't just my mom. She was a woman I'd admired for years, so how else was I supposed to react?

I soon discovered not only was my mom a cheat, but she was also a liar. I'm unaware of how long their affair had gone on before I busted them, but I do know it continued weeks after she promised it would stop.

Every time I smelled Ted's aftershave on her skin, I threatened to tell my father about her cheating ways. I cautioned my mother on numerous occasions that I wasn't going to let her destroy a man as admirable as my father. She never heeded my warnings. She knew I didn't want to be the one to break my father's heart, so she had no reason to fear.

She was right. I was a coward.

Perhaps if I had told my dad earlier, he wouldn't have walked in on them the afternoon he arrived home early to surprise my mom on their anniversary. Then maybe—*just maybe*—he'd still be the man he once was.

It is silly for me to believe a broken heart was the origin of my dad's disease, but it's hard denying the facts. He never forgot a single thing in the weeks leading up to my mom leaving. Not one. I don't care what the doctors say; that is not a coincidence. My mother's deceit didn't just break my father's heart; it destroyed his brilliant brain as well.

I scrape my hand across my face to gather a handful of tears that fell while reminiscing before snagging my cell off the passenger seat of my car. After checking that no wetness is visible on my inflamed cheeks, I flip open my phone and snap a quick picture of me cruising past the "Welcome to Ravenshoe" sign to send to Ryan.

I loathe people seeing me cry. It isn't just because I feel weak; I also hate how people respond to it. One tear and forgiveness that should never be issued is given. How is that logical? Having a hormonal bitch rampage that scorned every person you've ever known excused in an instant with a quick sob is bullshit. If anything, you should take their rant as gospel because it is usually in these situations that people show their true selves. If you want to know someone's real colors, watch them during a crisis. You'll see everything you want to know.

One afternoon was all it took for Axel to reveal his true self.

5

Annoyed at his father's request for him to attend the twelfth birthday party of an associate's daughter, he arrived at my house with muddy boots and an even dirtier attitude. I detested him on sight, and we hadn't even been officially introduced. He walked through my home like a king, not the least bit worried about the mud he was tracking across the wooden floors. He even laughed when he noticed our butler, Charles, mopping up his mess.

What did Ryan do when he spotted the mess Axel had made? He helped Charles clean it up. He didn't do that to express his gratitude for a fun afternoon. He did it because he knew what cleaning up other people's messes felt like.

The night before had been rough for Ryan. Not content with the "mediocre meal" his wife made him, Ryan's father threw it in her face. If that wasn't humiliating enough, he tossed her food onto the floor and made her eat as if she were an animal. Ryan begged his mom to return to the table, but no matter what he said or did, she followed Ted's command to the T.

At that instant, I knew my juvenile infatuation was no longer childish. I was in love with Ryan. I had always had a strange fascination with him that couldn't be satisfied by friendship, but I never knew it was true love until that moment. I should have. He has always been an admirable man, even when he was only a boy.

As my car glides down streets I know like the back of my hand, I glance down at my phone, hoping for a return message. I've been messaging Ryan on and off for the past eighteen hours. He has yet to return my contact.

That is so unlike Ryan.

Unless he's working, his replies are prompt. He hates waiting on people, so he never makes anyone wait on him.

Sighing at his lack of response, I drop my cell back onto the seat opposite me and continue my travels. There's a little niggle in my tummy advising me to turn left on Traitor Avenue instead of my usual right, but I shut it down, blaming a tedious commute for the knot sitting firmly in my stomach.

I shift my eyes sideways when my journey has me passing a house I know all too well—unfortunately. Axel's family mansion is only half a mile from mine. It stands proudly on a parcel of land my father used to own. I don't know if that transaction brought our families together or another foolish business decision.

I also don't know what happened to the impressive amounts in my father's business records. Around the time he sold land he intended to hold until Ravenshoe's economic boom demanded top dollar for the smallest capital, Axel's family came into our lives. As Ryan likes to say, "When you put two and two together, you can only reach four."

I reached four.

I haven't seen Axel since he disclosed he was responsible for Col Petretti's missing millions. Gah—the gall of that guy. He played me like a fiddle, recognizing my desperation had blinded me.

With my father's illness progressing at a rate faster than I could have ever fathomed, his business affairs soon piled up. I'd never had an interest in following in my parent's footsteps, but when your lack of business knowledge raises the risk of your

SHANDI BOYES

demented father losing his home, your priorities change rather quickly.

To begin with, I hid my father's disease from his associates. That barely lasted a month. They soon discovered that the brilliant man usually at the helm of their operation wasn't the same person uploading reports via the internet. The only person not smart enough to recognize the change was Col Petretti.

His accounts arrived every Monday morning like clockwork.

For the first few weeks, they were delivered by his right-hand man. But a change in the delivery schedule came with a variation I had never anticipated. Axel arrived every Saturday night within minutes of me returning from Bob's Burgers. Unlike his predecessor, he didn't hand the papers to me and go on his merry way; he lingered like a bad smell.

I don't forgive easily, so for the first four weeks, I degraded Axel in the same manner he treated Charles years earlier. Unfortunately for all involved, Axel is as determined as I am stubborn. Within a month, our conversations shifted from one- and two-word replies to brief sentences. By the time another month passed, we were somewhat friendly.

He was a wolf wearing sheep's clothing, but since he failed to interrogate me on my father's whereabouts as his predecessor had done on numerous occasions, I let my guard down. I was an idiot.

I didn't stumble upon the missing millions as my love of accounting flourished like Axel's feathers do when he struts like a peacock. Axel pointed the blunder out to me.

I won't lie; I was devastated. I called my mom every name under the sun while pacing in my den. From the pittance she left in our savings account, I knew there was no way I could repay the money she had stolen. Right at the time my father's displacement issues began playing out, I was thrown a curveball. I wasn't even holding a bat.

When Axel suggested his proposal, I thought it was perfect. He needed a well-known local girl to get his parents off his back about his philandering lifestyle, and I needed a lifeline to stop me from drowning.

Once again, I was a gullible idiot.

Axel couldn't care less what his parents thought; he just wanted a scapegoat at the ready if his plan went awry. I was his pawn. By helping me fudge the records to hide my mother's apparent theft, I shifted the burden of guilt from his shoulders to mine. My fingerprints were all over the ledger, and my handwriting was additional proof of deceit. If Regina hadn't suggested that Ryan wear a wire, I'd most likely be spending my college years behind bars.

I did everything Axel asked as he genuinely seemed worried about my well-being. He's a good actor—even the jealous boyfriend routine he played like a pro. There was just one issue: his performance didn't end once we were away from prying eyes.

Axel wasn't just intimidated by Ryan. He hated him. I often wondered if he could sense the natural connection Ryan and I always had. Even though we hadn't been within one hundred feet of each other in years, the electricity that forever bounced between us could be felt for miles. I could feel it. Ryan could feel it. Even Axel couldn't deny it.

The truth came out when Axel disclosed the reason for his parents' separation. Just like the dissolution of my parents' marriage, Ryan's father was responsible for Axel's parents' demise. But instead of Axel's mother suffering the kickbacks of her cheating ways, his father did.

Axel's dad is an everyday guy. He doesn't have millions of dollars in his account or an infamous last name that opens doors to him. He simply fell in love with a woman who had a mobster for a brother.

Axel may not have the Petretti name, but he has their blood.

Although I don't give two hoots about Axel or anyone in his family, Regina keeps me updated on his whereabouts. The last update I was given was that he was working with the authorities on their inquiries. Though peeved by the delay in the trial, in all honesty, I'd rather pretend it never happened. Who wants to have their stupidity broadcast for the world to see? My family has always been private. I want to keep it that way.

My thoughts switch from negative to positive when I spot my family home peeking over the horizon. I'm glad after everything my dad has been through the past four years, he can still call this place home. It may have a mortgage on it the size of Ben Hur, but his name is still on the deed.

There was one point earlier this year when I thought that would change. The two weeks following Justine's eighteenth birthday were the lowest days of my life. With my betrayal stinging Axel's ego more than his heart, he demanded the remaining money I owed by the end of the week.

I was blindsided and desperate. I didn't have the means to amass over four hundred thousand dollars within days. I barely had two nickels to rub together. Axel knew this; that is why he demanded what he did.

"Stay away from Ryan, Savannah, and we will continue our current payment plan," he said with a sigh as if he was helping me instead of hurting me.

I wanted to say no—I was screaming "no" on repeat in my head—but one glance into my dad's tormented eyes forced me to agree to Axel's request. My dad had no one on his side. I had to pick him over everyone—even Ryan.

That killed me.

It stung like a thousand bees when I stood behind the door, listening to Ryan knock on repeat and not answering him. I wanted to let him in and explain what was happening, but I also wanted my dad to spend his final years in a familiar environment. He lost his wife; he didn't deserve to lose his dignity as well.

My foot slips off the gas pedal when my car enters the long circular driveway of my family home. It isn't the moving truck parked at the front that has me backpedaling. It is the person standing on the stoop, directing over a dozen men.

It's been years since I've seen her, but I'll never forget her glossy honey hair and peachy red lips.

It is my mom.

CHAPTER 2

Savannah

After parking my car next to three men taking a breather from my mom's demanding aura, I curl out of my car. I feel like I'm dreaming. My mind is hazy, and my steps are sluggish. This can't be happening. Not now.

You'd think my first response to seeing my mother would be excitement. It isn't. It is angered confusion. What is she doing here? And why is she moving our belongings out of our house instead of returning the ones she wrongly left with?

I count to ten while rounding the back of the truck half-loaded with the possessions I've stockpiled over the past nine months. My long drive must be wreaking havoc with my composure, causing me to hallucinate—what else would instigate such weird delusions?

My mind isn't playing tricks on me. The back of the truck is laden with my favorite belongings. There's even a handful of items I purchased for my dad. His disease requires familiarity, so as much as I wanted to rid his bedroom of the disaster my mom's brush with interior design caused their room, I couldn't. Much to my dismay, the hideous fur rug and mismatched floral cushions had to stay.

The workers have barely sucked down their hand-rolled cigarettes when my mother claps her hands together, demanding they return to work. She commands them with the same pompous attitude she used on our house staff in the years leading to her disappearance.

She's the captain. They are her soldiers.

"Who do you think you are? You have no right to waltz in here after three years and act like you own the place," I snarl, taking the stairs of my family home like I'm Rocky Balboa climbing the stone steps at the Philadelphia Museum of Art.

The anger in my voice shocks me. I always anticipated being grateful upon discovering my mother is alive, but all I feel is anger. I went to hell and back when she left, and now, just as all the pieces are falling into place, she returns like a bat out of hell, ruffling more feathers than settling them.

No! I won't let her ruin this for me. I won't let her ruin this for *us*.

"Does Dad know you're here...?" I stop talking when bewilderment bamboozles me. "Does he even know who you are anymore?"

My mom takes a sharp breath as a mask of shock and anger slips over her face. Her response replicates mine to a T. I'm equally pissed and traumatized.

With her mouth gaped, she stares at me like I'm a mirage. I don't know where she thinks I've been. Unlike her, I belong here. This is my home.

"Savannah..." she whispers in a breathy moan, half-startled, half-stern. "You're home early. We weren't anticipating your return until tomorrow."

"We?" I ask, clearly confused. "There's no *we*, Mom. There is *us*. Me and Dad. Not you."

The confusion on her face is pushed aside for sternness. "Oh." Her eyes reveal she wants to say more than she just did. "I'm sorry you feel that way," she eventually settles on, her words not matching the deep groove between her blonde brows.

"Where's Willis? Dad needs familiarity. He's been with him for nearly a year." I skirt past her to enter the foyer of my home. "Willis?"

I'm left windless for the second time in thirty seconds when my eyes absorb the shell I used to call home. Everything has been stripped. It is even emptier now than it was when I sold every possession we owned the week after Justine's party. I wanted out of my agreement with Axel, so I did everything in my power to get out.

If only it had been enough. Axel had me over a barrel, and he knew it.

Not recognizing a single face, I charge for the curved stairwell I've slid down more times than I've climbed.

"Dad!" I shout, my frantic stomps matching the thumps of my heart. "Daddy!"

My mom shouts my name, but my strides remain strong.

Even with half a dozen men removing childhood memories from my home and making a ruckus, my dad hears my shout.

"Ruth?" he calls back, his voice echoing out of his room at the end of the hall.

Tears drop onto my white cheeks as I increase my strides. His voice—thank god. I was afraid my mother's return would coincide with me never hearing it again. I was petrified he was gone.

"Daddy," I choke on a sob when I enter his room.

He's at the foot of his bed, his face as tormented as ever. "What's happening, Ruth? I don't understand." His words sound as exhausted as I feel.

The last six months have been tough on us both, but with Willis agreeing to be his full-time caregiver, the transition wasn't as daunting as expected. My father may not remember my name, but he has never forgotten my face. That means we've racked up a lot of Skype minutes since I left for Cornell six months ago.

My dad's shirt absorbs the moisture slipping down my cheeks when he tugs me under his arms to comfort me. The wild beat of his heart causes more tears to topple from my eyes. He's as scared as me, but acting brave not to startle me.

This is the man I know and love.

"I don't know what is happening," I admit, my voice showcasing my bewilderment. "But I'll find out. I promise you I will find out."

My pledge has barely left my mouth when my dad stiffens. His fingers dig into my arm when he spins me around, sheltering me from the person I hear scuffling across the hardwood floor with his body. My tears flow more freely. Even with his mind destroyed by a horrible disease, it can't stop his protective nature. It is as naturally engrained in him as it is in Ryan.

"Thorn," whispers a tormented voice, one I would have given anything to hear years ago but will give anything to silence now. "You know me. You just don't remember."

My spine straightens, expecting my father to react negatively to my mother's remark. Displacement issues are my dad's biggest trigger, but being told he can't remember is a very close second. He can handle prompts, but if you straight up tell him he can't do something, you're set for trouble.

My stomach continues receiving blow after blow. My dad doesn't react as I am expecting. He doesn't scream, yell, or even clench his fists. He doesn't do a single thing. This is as abnormal to me as seeing my parents in the same room.

My mom smiles, pleased by his lack of aggression. "Every rose has its thorn. Just like every thorn needs a rose. I'm your Rose, Thorn."

The wind is knocked from my lungs, shocked by the sweetness of her voice. It is brimming with love and admiration, a stark contrast to the one she used when placing the blame for her extramarital ways on my dad's shoulders years ago. She wanted the world but couldn't understand that he had to work relentlessly to give it to her. She used his absence as an excuse, failing to see that he wouldn't have worked sunup to sundown if she weren't so greedy.

"I still remember the first time you said that ..." She sighs as if recalling fond memories. "...and the millions of times that followed."

I shake my head while pulling away from Dad's grasp. The extra beat his heart gained during her disclosure reveals a truth I don't want to face. He's remembering her—the woman who betrayed him time and time again.

I lift my eyes to an equally unique pair. "You can't believe her, Dad. You don't know what she did. How she hurt you."

My lungs hunt for air when he stares at me, somewhat confused. I grab his hand and run it down my cheek like he always does. "It's your Ruth. You can trust Ruth."

I stare into his eyes, allowing mine to speak the words my mouth will never be able to say. Nothing's changed. I couldn't tell him years ago about her deceit, and I can't today either. I will not break his heart for anyone's benefit, not even mine.

I inhale my first breath in what feels like minutes when my dad briefly nods. "There's my Ruth," he mutters as his thumb traces the indent in my cheek.

"Yes. Here I am," I reply, nuzzling into his hand.

Hating that the torment in his eyes grows from spotting the moisture brimming in mine, I aid him into his bed. My mom's breaths are so ragged I hear every inhalation. She isn't gasping for air because she is surprised by our closeness—there isn't a father/daughter bond in the world that can compare to the one I have with my dad—she's just shocked seeing the man she once loved stare at her as if she's a stranger.

I can imagine her pain. I pray every day for that day to *never* arrive. The day my dad forgets who I am will be my most painful day. I wouldn't wish that pain on anyone. Not even the woman who broke his heart.

"Savann—"

"No," I interrupt my mom, my tone stern like I am the parent in our dynamic. "Not in here. You have no claim to anything or *anyone* in this room."

Pretending I can't see my dad's confusion growing from my mom calling me my real name, I smile at him before asking, "Orange juice?"

His eyes light up like a Christmas tree. "Please." His love for his favorite drink is all over his face.

"I'll be right back."

I kiss the edge of his mouth before spinning on my heels and making a beeline for the door. I don't glance over my shoulder to ensure my mom is following me. The deep sigh she releases before saying goodbye to my dad tells me everything I need to know.

She isn't here for him. She's not even here for me. That only leaves one thing on her list: money.

Once I'm halfway down the hall, I spin around to face my mom. Her lips twitch like she's preparing to speak, but I beat her to the task. "What do you want? If you are here for money, I hate to tell you we have even less now than we did when you left us the first time—"

"I'm not here for money, Savannah," she interrupts, shocking me with the sincerity in her voice.

I was so sure she was here for money I didn't prepare another defense. "Then why are you here? Why now?"

When she steps closer to me, I hold my hands out in front of my body, demanding she stop. I'm not falling for her tricks again. If she wants to continue her lies, she can do it while looking me in the eyes.

She stares at the ceiling for several seconds before lowering her eyes to mine. They are glistening with tears but nowhere near the number in mine. "I'm not who you think I am. I didn't leave because I don't love your father. I love him more than you'll ever know—"

"Yet, you still cheated on him. Again and again," I argue, unwilling to go down without a fight this time.

I'm not the naïve teenager she battled during our last confrontation about her adulterous ways. I am a grown woman who won't tolerate her belittling my father any more than she already has.

When my mother shakes her head, denying my claims, I scream, "I saw you!"

"You saw a woman doing anything to claw herself out of hell," she fights back, yelling.

"Did you see him? Did you look into his eyes and see the man on the inside pleading to be set free?" I ask, pointing to my father's room. "You saved yourself from hell by sending him in your place!"

My mom steps closer to me, her face as haunted as mine, her lips as hard-set. "If I didn't leave when I did, you would have lost us both, Savannah. What would you prefer, one parent suffer or both?"

I glare at her like she's insane. She can't honestly believe she is the victim in all of this. My father lives in a nightmare. Can you imagine waking up every day and not recognizing the people surrounding you? If that isn't bad enough, your body doesn't understand the prompts your brain is relaying, and over time, even remembering how to sip orange juice is above your means. My father is suffering enough for both of them. Things can't be any worse.

I'm dragged from my somber thoughts when my mother mutters, "What happened to your father wasn't an accident. It was deliberate. I'm just glad I got out when I did." She peers at Dad's door without a bit of remorse on her face, too revolted to comprehend empathy.

My mother is saved from witnessing the lengths I'll go to protect the ones I love when a deep voice at my side pipes up. "What your mom is saying is true, Savannah. It may not be what you want to hear, but it is honest."

"What...why...?"

Now I have even more sympathy for my father's condition. I can hear the words I'm trying to articulate in my head, but seeing a man I never expected to see standing in my hall has me swallowing my words.

"Axel, what are you doing here?" I ask, my voice brimming with suspicion.

Did I fall asleep during my commute? Nothing about this evening is making any sense.

I shoo away Axel's hand when he tries to brush a tear off my cheek. "Don't touch me," I snarl, my bewilderment not strong enough to leash my anger. "You're not allowed within five hundred feet of me. If you don't leave this *instant*, I will have you arrested."

My head slings to the side when an accented voice assures me, "That won't be necessary."

A balding man with shoulders as broad as my height flashes his FBI badge. I don't need to see his identification to know who he is. The day he asked me to pass on a message to Regina will stick with me forever because the love he projected will be seared on my heart for eternity. Furthermore, if he hadn't requested Regina to step down from her investigation, I doubt Ryan would have left the interrogation room at Ravenshoe PD without cuffs on his wrists. Tobias saved our hides that day, so I'll never forget him.

"Does Regina know you are here?" My words convey my shock.

Before their run-in nine months ago, Regina hadn't seen Tobias in nearly three years. That's why she reacted as she did when I passed on her message. Even knowing seeing him again would add to her anguish, she hated the missed opportunity.

Tobias finalizes the last four steps before shaking his head. "This is out of Regina's jurisdiction."

I stare at him with shock on my face. We may be on the outskirts of Ravenshoe, but my home is in Regina's purview. She doesn't have the official title, but she will always be the head of law enforcement in my eyes.

"When Regina discovers you're responsible for breaking the restraining order she instigated, you'll be in trouble."

Smiling a grin that reveals he's looking forward to his penance, Tobias gathers my hands and then guides me to a wooden bench built into the curve of the stairwell. It is a smooth move on his behalf. This is a favorite spot of mine. It is where I spend my days reading during summer, so it instantly appeases my hostility.

Tobias is smarter than I first perceived. He not only has gentle eyes, but he gains trust quickly. Out of the three people surrounding me, he'd be my first pick if I were forced to choose who to trust the most. How fucked up is that? He's a stranger, yet I'd choose him over an ex-boyfriend and my mom. No wonder why I have trust issues—*issues I've kept very well hidden from my boyfriend.*

After filling half the bench with his backside, Tobias locks his eyes with mine. I tighten my core, anticipating a painful knock.

The prompts of my body are odd but spot on when he asks, "Do you recall the time your father came home with a bloody nose? He had veered to miss a deer and lost control of his car, resulting in him hitting his head on the steering wheel?"

I nod, not trusting my voice not to squeak. I remember his accident very well. I thought it was lucky his car didn't sustain any damage. Only now am I realizing I have everyone fooled. I'm not intelligent—not in the slightest.

"He didn't hit a deer, did he?" Disappointment rings in my tone. I'm not disappointed in my dad; I'm disappointed in myself. My intuition knew something was amiss that night, but believing my dad had already overcome his darkest days, I ignored it.

"No," Tobias answers with a shake of his head. "With Axel aiding in our investigations the past six months, we discovered your father was assaulted by members of the Petretti crew that night."

I vault out of my chair like my ass is on fire.

"It wasn't me," Axel swears, recognizing I'm five seconds from smacking him into next week. "I had nothing to do with it..."

His words stop when my open palm connects with his left cheek.

"You may not have done it, but you knew it happened. The entire time we were together, you hid this from me. If that doesn't make you scum, I don't know what does." My hand burns when I slap him for the second time.

Before I've disbursed one-tenth of my anger, Tobias wraps his arms around my waist and drags me toward the stairwell. Fury floods me when I spot my mom's shocked expression. She's disgusted by my unladylike behavior. I shouldn't be surprised. She went from cutting hearts into my sandwiches to handing me twenty dollar bills when my dad's wealth went from a peasant to a king.

Within months, she transformed from a loving, caring mother and wife to a greedy, narcissistic bitch. If I hadn't adored who she was before money sparkled in her eyes, her betrayal wouldn't have hurt as much. But since I loved her just as much as my father, it stung—it stung bad.

"That is how you protect someone you love," I snarl at my mother, ignoring the crocodile tears in her eyes.

This is just a game for people like Axel and my mom. One sick, fucked-up hoax.

When we reach the den at the bottom of the stairs, Tobias releases me from his grasp. I pace the polished marble like a mad woman—because that is precisely what I am. I'm too shocked to absorb the facts. I'm too stunned to do anything.

I freeze like a statue when Tobias says, "I'm not saying Thorn's assault aided in his diagnosis—"

"But there's research that indicates traumatic brain injuries can increase the risk of developing dementia," I interrupt, my words nearly a sob.

I've read every bit of information I could get my hands on about dementia and Alzheimer's. The chances of my father's assault being the catalyst of his condition are low, but it is still possible. He was a brilliant man, who, just like me, didn't have the APOE-e4 risk gene. There has to be more to his disease than just bad luck.

I argued with specialists for weeks that there was something iffy with my dad's diagnosis, but since I was unable to present a plausible reason, my worries were brushed off as an overbearing daughter. God, I wish my shock hadn't swallowed my stubbornness.

My lungs inhale their first breath in what feels like minutes when Tobias discloses, "For the past twelve months, we've been deep in operations to have the men responsible for your father's assault brought to justice. But when you shake feathers, some are bound to come loose. That is why I am here, Savannah. I want to lessen the ripple effect about to impact you and your father."

I stare, breathing but not speaking.

What does he mean? What ripple effect?

Tobias knocks the wind straight out of my lungs when he advises, "I want to put your family in witness protection."

My head shakes so uncontrollably that I look like I'm having a seizure.

Acting like he hasn't spotted my blatant refusal, Tobias says, "Let me do what I should have done years ago. Let me protect *all* of you."

I stare at him in shock, certain he didn't admit what I just heard.

The hits keep coming when he mutters, "I thought your mother's *connections* with associates in your industry meant she was the only one in danger. I was wrong." How he mumbles "connections" leaves no doubt about what he means. Ryan's father wasn't the only man she was sleeping with.

Ignoring the bile racing to the back of my throat, I ask, "You helped her leave?"

I don't know why I'm asking a question when the answer is staring me straight in the face. Tobias has one of the most honest eyes I've ever seen. Only two men can compete with their candor: Ryan and my dad.

"Why would you do that, Tobias? Why would you help her abandon her family?" I grit my teeth, loathing the anger in my voice. Tobias isn't culpable for my family's demise. That blame lies solely on my mother's shoulders.

Tobias takes a step closer to me before smacking me with straight-up honesty. "Because I underestimated your father. I thought he'd handle her decision to leave like a normal man."

"By treating her like she treated him?" I ask, my tone lowering to match his. "My father is a good man, Tobias. He doesn't believe in tit for tat."

Tobias nods, agreeing with me without words. "He

blindsided me. Even with your mother spelling out every horrible thing she had done, he still searched for her."

"My father loved her. He probably still does. He'd never hurt her just for revenge. He isn't that kind of man."

Tobias smiles, but his mouth remains tightlipped.

I calm my skyrocketing heart rate before asking, "I still don't understand what this has to do with me and my dad. We aren't in danger..."

My words trail off when Tobias shakes his head. It is only brief but quick enough for me to notice.

"Despite what Axel told you, my mom didn't steal Col's money."

"I know," he agrees, smiling softly. "I'm not here about Col's missing millions. I'm here because of this."

My hand rattles when I accept the folded paper from his grasp. "What the fuck?" I murmur under my breath when I read my name typed on the arrest warrant. I'm not usually a fan of profanity, but there isn't a more adequate reply than the one I just gave. "I'm not a criminal."

I snap my eyes to Tobias when he says, "Did you hand a financial ledger to the Ravenshoe Police Department nine months ago?"

Unable to speak through the lump in my throat, I nod.

Tobias arches a brow. "Did it have your handwriting in it?"

I should be shutting down this interrogation and demanding to speak to a lawyer, but I'm so interested in where our conversation is heading I can't do anything, much less speak.

Spotting my brief nod, Tobias discloses, "So you weren't just seen in numerous FBI surveillance images attending functions of notoriously well-known members of the underworld..."

"I attended as Axel's girlfriend. I wasn't there in a business manner..."

Tobias continues speaking as if I never interrupted him, "You also handed evidence of the money laundering activities you engaged in a minimum once per week for over a year to a woman who is obligated by law to share what she received."

My heart falls into my shoes. "I didn't launder money." I want to say more, but I start at the most concerning part of his confession.

"I didn't," I continue to defend myself when Tobias remains quiet. "I used the cash that arrived with the ledger to pay for invoices amassed throughout the week. I didn't launder anyone's money."

My last five words are nowhere near as confident as my first sentence when the routine I followed every Sunday morning smacks into me. I paid for purchases from businesses every week without bothering to check what was brought. I didn't care what was in the gym bags they handed me because anything Axel or his family purchased wasn't interesting to me.

Jesus Christ—could I have been more stupid?

I move to the stairwell to sit on the first step. If I don't sit, I'll fall.

"Am I going to jail?" I ask, my words shaky.

A four-by-four cell isn't scaring me. It is the prospect of leaving Ryan and my dad. That is worse than any sentence I could be handed.

The sturdy stairs squeak when Tobias takes the vacant spot next to me. "No, not if you agree to my terms."

I stop cradling my pounding head to peer at him. "What terms?"

He holds my gaze while asking, "Do you remember the businesses you collected the purchases from?"

I smirk. It isn't a joyful smirk. "How could I forget them? I visited them a minimum once a week for over a year." I aim for my reply to be playful, but my attempts are pathetic. I sound as stupid as I feel.

Tobias bumps me with his shoulder, attempting to quell the panic swallowing me whole. I appreciate his effort, but I don't think anything could take away my unease.

"There's the get out of jail free card you're looking for."

"That might be a get-out-of-jail-free card, but it is also a death sentence. If those men are associated with Col, and I go against them, I'm placing a target on my back." You can hear the turmoil in my voice.

Concerns for my father's well-being may have forced me to turn a blind eye to things that should be obvious, but I'm not foolish enough to miss the warning alarms bellowing in my ears now. Col Petretti is a horrible man. Axel and I barely escaped his wrath when we arrived at one of his events thirty minutes late.

Our tardy arrival wasn't even close to what Axel voiced to Ryan months ago. We weren't doing *anything* that resembled sexual activities. We merely trusted the directions of a gas station attendant. It was a foolish mistake—one of many I made that year.

Tobias's deep sigh returns my focus to him. "If you give me *everything* I need, Savannah, I *guarantee* to keep you and your father safe."

Even with his tone matching the promise in his eyes, it doesn't stop me from saying, "By hiding us? Pretending we don't exist—"

"By returning your life to what it would have been if your *parents* hadn't made the decision they did years ago."

He overemphasizes "parents," ensuring I know the brunt of our setback doesn't solely reside on my mother's shoulders. My father is somewhat to blame as well. He was so desperate to keep his family living in luxury he sided with an evil man. He made a mistake. I can forgive him for that.

"You will have a good life, Savannah. A good, *honest* life."

I wish Tobias's guarantee filled me with gratitude. It doesn't. I can't do this. My dad refuses to leave his room, and I refuse to leave Ryan. He has had me under a spell since I was four, but the few weeks we had while Axel was at football camp turned the spell into a full-blown trance. I honestly felt like I couldn't breathe the months following Justine's eighteenth. I wouldn't survive leaving him again.

Furthermore, I'd rather face the consequences of my actions than hurt him more than I already have. He's been through enough. He doesn't deserve more heartache.

"I can't," I mutter, my two words barely audible since they were forced through the fear clutching my throat. "I can't leave Ryan. I can't give him up."

Like I can be any more stupid, I up the ante. I'm racing for the front door of my house before Tobias even registers my legs are moving. I hear him shout my name, but nothing can stop my steps. It has been weeks since I've seen Ryan's smile in the flesh. I'm not giving that up for anything.

Not even a bullet.

CHAPTER 3

Savannah

"I'll be back." Although my pledge is worthless, I still issue it, praying it will keep me from getting shot. Mercifully, it does.

Tobias doesn't even draw his gun. He just watches me dive into the driver's seat of my car and kick over the ignition with an amused expression brightening his face. If I didn't know any better, I'd swear he was encouraging my evasion.

I have no clue what I plan to do when I reach Ryan, but it feels right to run toward him during a crisis instead of away from him like I usually do. He's the glue that kept my shattered remains together for the past five years. If it weren't for his touch, affection, and words over the past nine months, I wouldn't be half the woman I am right now. He didn't just fix my cracks. He repaired them so flawlessly that no one can see them. Even I have trouble spotting them. He made me whole again. He made me—me.

With blurry eyes and a heart in coronary failure territory, I somehow arrive at Ryan's residence in one piece. I don't recall which route I took or how many traffic lights I stopped at. But I am here—where I belong—finally.

If I am arrested and charged, it will be as bad as it can get. Not just for me but also for Ryan. He's a rookie police officer at Ravenshoe PD. This won't look good to his colleagues, no matter how brightly he shines a light on it. I know Ryan will support me. He will stand by my side no matter what happens. I just hope I don't drag him too far down. He's remarkable, but even the strongest men can only take so many knocks before they eventually crack.

I don't want to break him any more than I don't want him to break me.

After clearing the sweat from my hands, I grip the trestle I've climbed many times in my childhood before raising my head. I stare at Ryan's window without thought. My mind is so overworked I don't remember exiting my car, much less walking through the side gate.

I often suggested that he spray some fish oil on the hinges to stop its annoying squeak, but he never did. He likes having his own personal doorbell. The instant he hears the gate creak, he knows I am close, as I am the only person who uses it.

I've barely scaled two rungs of the ivy-coated wood when I hear my name being called by a voice a million years won't erase from my mind. I take a moment to clear the anguish from my face before cranking my neck to Ryan. I don't want him to see my turmoil—not yet—not until I've seen his smiling face first.

The air I've only just sucked in rushes out in a hurry when I spot Ryan standing next to me. With only a towel wrapped around his hips, his panty-wetting body is on display for the world to see. His hair is wet as if he has recently showered, and his heaving chest shows signs of exertion.

"What are you doing outside ...?" Shock resonates in my tone. Tonight isn't as cold as the weather in New York, but it certainly isn't warm enough to wander outside half-naked. "Why are you only wearing a towel? Aren't you cold?"

Ryan's lips twitch, but before a word can spill from his mouth, a weird moan sounds from the back of his house.

I jump down from the trestle, taking a dozen ivy leaves with me. "Is that your mom? Is she okay?" I ask, my tone half-worried, half-suspicious.

The sound was unlike anything I've ever heard. It wasn't quite a moan, but it wasn't a groan either. It was somewhat of a feminine roar. Or perhaps even muffled laughter?

"It's not my mom. It's nothing."

A dash of insecurity smacks into me when Ryan seizes my elbow in a firm grab. His eyes show hesitation at his unusual manhandling, but his aura screams desperation.

I want to pretend they are the only signs I'm reading from him. Unfortunately, they aren't. I can also sense betrayal.

What. The. Hell?

"If it's not your mom, who is it?" I strive to keep suspicion out of my tone. My attempts are below par.

My distrust is surfacing faster than I can contain. I genuinely feel like I am five seconds from losing my cool. I know my anger doesn't belong on Ryan's shoulders, but with my mind on the fritz, his eagerness to evade my question isn't helping matters. Unless he has something to hide, why won't he answer me? It is a simple question. I'm not asking for a cure for cancer.

"Is it the person responsible for occupying so much of your time today that you couldn't answer my calls or texts?"

I try to shut down my anger. I tell myself on repeat that Ryan is *nothing* like my mother, and my distrust is due to the trying day I've had, but when Ryan answers my question with a simple, "It's nothing," all my hard work comes undone.

"Who is it, Ryan? Why are you hiding them from me?" I ask, fighting to get out of his grip.

He firms his hold before he continues dragging me out his side gate. His wish to remove me from his backyard hurts more than anything. This is *our* spot. It is *our* stomping ground. It doesn't belong to anyone but us!

"Are *they* the reason you're wearing a towel?"

I can't say she. I won't say she.

"Why were you so desperate to stop me, you couldn't put on a pair of pants?"

My stomach heaves when my eyes lock in on a truth my brain refuses to acknowledge. "Is that lipstick?" I stop talking to settle the bile racing up my throat before continuing, "Oh my god. That's lipstick, isn't it?"

Moisture burns my eyes as an incalculable number of horrible thoughts blitzes me. This can't be happening. This is Ryan—*my Ryan*. He doesn't cheat. He doesn't break promises. He issues them with as much heart as I do. He trusts. He loves. He honors. This isn't him. This isn't the man I love.

With my heart determined to prove my brain wrong, I thrust out of Ryan's hold and charge toward the area where the moan/ripple/laugh came from.

I've barely stepped foot on the back patio of Ryan's family home when Ryan curls his arm around my waist and yanks me back. His sudden movements stir up the weird fragrance I smelled on him earlier. It isn't fresh like someone who just showered. It is sticky and sweet, like a man who has done a lot of sweating.

Oh god.

"Let me go, Ryan. Let me go! I want to see who it is," I scream, my words as raw as my heart feels.

I couldn't handle this on my best day, let alone my worst.

"I don't want you to see that, Savannah," Ryan mutters into my ear, breaking my heart even more. "It's not something I *ever* want you to see."

The honesty in his tone devastates me. He knows the image I'm desperately trying to see will shatter my heart. He also knows only one visual could do that: him with another woman.

"You promised you'd never hurt me, Ryan. You promised." My last two words are barely audible.

When he continues his silent stance, I yank out of his grasp for the second time. I have no intention of tracking down the person responsible for the pain tearing my heart in two. I just need some distance between us. I can't have him close to me and work through my anguish. It is impossible to be angry when all you're feeling is familiarity.

While swiping at the tears cascading down my face, I beg for my mouth not to fail me. *Now is not the time for stupidity.*

My pleas fall on deaf ears when I blubber, "Are you... Did you..."

The expression crossing Ryan's face hurts me more than his betrayal. All I want to do is shelter him from the pain, even when he's the one causing it.

"The distance became too much, Savannah. I got sick of waiting for you to come home," he mutters, his voice tormented.

I take a step back, shocked. "It's just your new job playing with your emotions, Ryan. It will settle down soon. If it doesn't, I'll request a transfer. I'll take a gap year. We'll make it work."

I sound desperate, and rightfully so. I am desperate— desperate to save him from the distress stealing the life from his eyes. I've only worked through half the damage his parents' volatile relationship caused, and I'm not willing to pass the baton to someone else. I was born for this job. I was born to protect him as devotedly as he has protected me most of our lives. I was born to love him.

It feels like a knife is stabbed into my chest when Ryan shakes his head. "It's too late for that. I've found someone else."

"What?" I ask, certain I heard him wrong. My pulse is thudding in my ears, so I'm confident my hearing is affected. "You're not like him, Ryan. You wouldn't do this to me. You wouldn't do this to *us*."

I know you.

You didn't do this.

Please tell me you didn't destroy us.

When he approaches me, I swipe my hands in front of my body, demanding that he stop. I need to see his eyes when he answers my next question, as that is the only way I will know if he's lying.

"Tell the truth, Ryan. Tell me why you want me to leave, and I will go. I'll walk away and never look back." *I will accept Tobias's offer and save you the shame of admitting you're associated with me.*

Ryan's Adam's apple bobs up and down before he mutters, "I don't want this life any more. It's time to move on."

I bite my bottom lip, praying the pain of my vicious bite will stop my tears from falling. My efforts are pointless. The honesty in his eyes is more than I can bear. This hurts more than anything. This utterly destroys me.

"If you wanted to move on, you could have just said so. You didn't have to cheat on me."

I swear my blood is boiling so furiously I'm moments away from an artery bursting. I've never been so angry and devastated in my life.

"I trusted you, Ryan. I believed every promise you spoke because I truly believe you are *nothing* like your father."

My cheeks redden when I lower them down Ryan's form, praying my hazy mind is making me mistake Carter genes. The man I love is standing in front of me, breaking my heart with every denial he fails to give.

"Clearly, I was wrong. But you don't use your fists to cause harm. You use your charm."

The viciousness of my reply shocks me, but with my heart last seen somewhere in Ryan's backyard, I'm hitting him in the spot I know will hurt him more than anything. I'm comparing him to his father. It is a mean and demoralizing thing to do, but the flicker of candlelight I've spotted in Ryan's window has me overcome with stupidity—*like I could be any more stupid.*

I want to run away. I want to never see him and his devastatingly beautiful blue irises again, but before I can do that, I must say goodbye. Even though he has torn my heart into shreds, I refuse to be my mother. I will not leave the man I love without saying goodbye to him in person.

"Goodbye, Ryan," I force out via a sob. "I hope she makes you happier than I ever could."

I turn my eyes to his window, hating the woman who stole him away from me but also admiring her determination. Ryan is a catch—that is why I panicked when I saw him with Amelia last year. I didn't want him to be miserable, but I didn't want to lose him either. I should have just left him alone. Then neither of us would be suffering this horrible heartache. He would have never seen the ledger, and I wouldn't owe him anything for saving my life. We would have existed—miserable, but still alive nonetheless.

Now I get to be miserable by myself.

I return my eyes to Ryan, my heartache so strong it is the fight of my life to issue my next sentence. "I'm not sorry I trusted you. I'm just sorry I fell for the same mistake twice."

Stealing his chance to reply, I pivot on my heels and race to my car. He doesn't follow after me.

That hurts more than anything.

"Does she have to come with us?" I ask, glaring at my mom.

She tried to speak to me when I returned from Ryan's house over two hours ago, but I've been giving her the cold shoulder. She knows the stains on my cheeks aren't red from being bombarded with unwanted attention. No matter how often I swore their coloring was from the lewd proposition two young movers made while securing the last of our boxes, she knew I was lying. But since the last person I want to speak to about philandering partners is a philanthropist of the club, I've kept my mouth shut.

"Once we have everything settled, we'll work on the rest," Tobias assures, stepping into the path of the death stare I'm issuing my mother. "Are you sure this is what you want?" His tone is as high as the one he used when I returned to my family estate within twenty minutes of fleeing it.

Tobias was so certain I was running he set the wheels in motion to move my dad to a safe location without my assistance. I was stunned. With how many police sirens I heard during my short trek from Ryan's house to my car, I thought he placed a bounty on my head. Just like nearly every day of my life, I was wrong.

The fact Tobias was going to let me fly free made my decision even easier. There's nothing here for me anymore, so no harm was done when I agreed to his offer. I just hope my face will quell my father's anxiety while we travel across state lines. I am more familiar to him than his surroundings, so as long as we are kept in close contact, the transition should be smooth. *I hope.*

"I'm sure," I mutter, understanding a man as communitive as Tobias won't accept a half-hearted nod as an answer. "I'll be there in a minute. I'm nearly done here."

He crouches down in front of me, the crinkles in the corners of his eyes more apparent in the bare bones of my bedroom. "You don't have to do this. It was just a suggestion to ease the congestion in your mind. Our brains don't shut down when our mouths choose not to speak."

He isn't referring to the agreement we made. He's referring to the letter I am in the process of writing. It is my final goodbye to Ryan, the words I couldn't speak hours ago. It is neither pretty nor spiteful. It is just straight-up honest.

"I want to do this as well," I assure Tobias, my voice more confident than my facial expression. "The people in it may never see it, but I feel better knowing I've written it."

Tobias smiles in a way that makes it seem like I've known him for years. The FBI chose well when they made him their leading man. He builds trust faster than I can snap my fingers, but not in an I'll-say-anything-to-get-the-job-done way. He speaks the truth—sometimes brutally.

He told me why he brought Axel here this evening. He knew Axel was lying when he said everything I had done for his family was of my own free will. My reaction to seeing Axel again proved what Tobias suspected. You can't trust any man with Petretti blood running through their veins.

Only after guaranteeing neither Axel nor anyone in his family would know our location did I agree to his offer of witness protection. I'm not just spilling secrets about Axel and his scheming ways; I'm sharing information that will have Col Petretti's second-in-charge walking the planks. I maintained his financial records for over a year; I know way more than anyone realizes. Stuff that will not only financially ruin Col but will take down many of his competitors as well.

Tobias was smart when he agreed with my demands. It is just a pity he scratched out my suggestion of adding my mom's name alongside Axel's. He's adamant I'll change my mind about her resurrection once the dust settles. I doubt it.

She cheated.

Ryan cheated.

The whole fucking world cheated.

I only turned nineteen last month, and I'm already done with society. I'll be one of those old, sad cat ladies. Except I won't be old. I'll just be miserable.

I'm drawn away from my negative thoughts when Tobias squeezes my shoulder. After mustering a fake reassuring grin, he says, "Take as much time as you need, Savannah. We'll wait for you outside."

Spotting my half-hearted nod, he exits my room, taking my displeased mother with him.

"She needs time," I hear him say as he guides her down the blank hallway.

I wait for their footsteps to stop booming into my room

41

before glancing down at the letter I've been writing the past hour. It is done, one page of handwritten print. It is only missing one final thing: my signature.

After a long and tedious deliberation, I settle on the obvious.

Anna Banana

CHAPTER 4

Ryan

Four Years Later...

Chris stumbles into his living room, his steps as wobbly as the snarl on my face. It is barely 11 AM, and he's already well on the way to being drunk. I'd like to say his inebriated state is because today is the fourth anniversary of his little brother's death, but I know that isn't the case. He isn't guzzling down beer because he wants to forget. He is guzzling it because he has become his father. He's an alcoholic.

The past four years have been tough on Chris. *No. Correction.* The past four years have been tough on us all. Chris's recovery is just longer than the rest of us. Brax and I have stood by his side the entire time, but nothing we say or do has helped his grief. He isn't just angry he lost his brother; he's mad as hell.

I can understand his anger. Michael was only four years old. He had barely lived before his life was cruelly stripped away. But shouldn't Michael's death encourage Chris to be a better man? Shouldn't it stop him from following the muddy footprints our fathers left behind? Shouldn't he appreciate the life Michael never got to live?

I want to say yes to all my questions, but I've never been fond of lying. Chris isn't living his best life; he's living his worst. He doesn't respect himself, much less those around him. He doesn't even bother hiding his drug paraphernalia from me anymore. He knows the field I work in, but he also knows I care about him too much to watch him waste the prime years of his life in jail alongside his father.

God—what a fucking soft cock I've become. Like I did my entire childhood, I am again keeping silent.

This has to stop.

I need it to end.

"Do you really need another, Chris?" I ask, noticing he isn't just clasping two beers. He has three. "Today is supposed to be about remembering Michael." *Not drinking yourself into a coma.*

Chris shoots me a disapproving glare before slumping into the springless sofa shoved against the far wall of his living room. Unlike me, Chris moved out of home within weeks of us finishing school. He is a mechanic at a local wrecking yard and has been dating a local girl for the past few months. The moving out part is like honey and milk, a perfect combination. My other two statements are more like oil and water.

The wrecking yard Chris works at is owned by a notorious man in our community. His name isn't on the title, and he hasn't stepped foot on the premises since the day it opened two years ago, but everyone knows it is one of Col's many last-ditch attempts to return his wealth to its former glory.

A little under three years ago, Col faced federal charges. The list of accusations was immense: racketeering, kidnapping, money laundering, attempted murder—you name it, it was addressed during his arraignment. The prosecution was sure they had a slam dunk case.

They didn't.

All but one remained after a yearlong trial: Col Petretti.

I followed the case with interest, not just because I am a member of the law enforcement community but because names mentioned during the trial piqued my interest. I had associated, hated, and fought against the men cited in the charges. I even knew some of them on a more personal level.

I was also hoping to see a familiar face.

I never did. Well, not the one I was hoping for.

Although Isaac was never summoned to testify in Col's trial, the prosecutors mentioned his name numerous times. I don't know if they were using him to aid in their case or discredit it. But at the end of the day, Col walked free.

His associates weren't as lucky. It wasn't just their assets stripped from their possession. They also lost their freedom.

Col inevitably resurfaced after keeping his location on the down-low for nearly a year. Unfortunately, his roots were too embedded in the Ravenshoe area to officially cut ties. At first, his dealings appeared above board, but as the months rolled on, rumors circulated.

Even though I don't have proof, I'm certain Col is back to his old tricks. You can strip a man of every possession he owns, and he will still see himself as a king. You can even remove his heart, and he will continue functioning without it. *I'm living proof of that.*

"Jesus Christ, Chris," I babble under my breath when he spills a year's worth of cigarette butts into my lap as he grabs for the remote control. "Watch what you're fucking doing."

While I stand from the stained couch, Chris snarks, "Do you really need another? How can you pay the electric bill if you spend all your money at the track? Why don't you tell me I look pretty anymore? My god—you nag more than Molly does. Blah, blah, fucking blah. No wonder Damon hit her. An old geezer who popped three blue pills only an hour ago would have difficulties keeping it hard with her voice yipping in his ear. I'm tempted to smack her just for a minute of peace."

I glare at him, too shocked to form words. The snarky smirk on his face shows he's trying to be playful, but it doesn't lessen my anger in the slightest.

"I swear to God, Chris, I will turn a blind eye to your obvious obsession with a bong, and god knows what else you're hiding with a couple of well-placed magazines, but if you *ever*— I mean even once—lay your hands on a woman, I will arrest you, I will haul your sorry ass to jail, and I'll tell Bruno to ride it until you're screaming your momma's name for help. Do you understand me? This shit isn't funny. Beating women isn't funny."

"Whoa, whoa, whoa." Chris stabs his half-smoked cigarette directly onto the coffee table. "One, I was joking. Two, I was fucking joking. And three, don't go acting like the stick shoved up your ass has *anything* to do with me. You're not here to 'help see me through my grief' or even mourn the death of your father. You're here because you don't want to think about *her*."

The tic in my jaw turns manic. I'm not fuming at the mention of my father. I am peeved at how he said his last word. Just like my dad, Chris hasn't said Savannah's name since the day she left. Not once. I thought he was doing that to save me the anguish. Only now am I realizing my assumptions are wrong. My dad's death was a godsend; Savannah's disappearance wasn't. She didn't just hurt me when she left; she hurt Chris and Brax as well.

"My brother died, Ryan. He's fucking dead." The pain in Chris's voice cuts me like a knife. "*She* left of her own choice. That isn't even close to the same thing."

I work my jaw side to side, reminding myself that I'm not interacting with a lifelong friend and brother. I'm talking to an addict—a person who can't see sense even when it is staring him in the face.

"This isn't about Savannah, Chris—"

"It isn't?" he interrupts, his short reply incapable of hiding the slur of his words. "Because this sure as fuck seems to be about her. Everything you do, every word you speak, is done with her entering your mind first. You preach for me to move on, yet you sit in denial, waiting for her. You're wasting your life as much as I'm squandering mine." He grins a nasty smirk. "But at least I'm giving it a decent shot."

47

My chest puffs when I huff out a laugh. "A decent shot? This isn't living, Chris. Drinking yourself into an early grave isn't living."

He stands from his chair, swaying like a leaf in a hot summer breeze. "How many times did you read her letter today, Ry?" he asks, not even attempting to deny my accusation. "How many times have you read it in the past week, month, fucking year?"

I feign ignorance, pretending I don't know what he's talking about. My acting skills are as hopeless as Chris's promise to quit drinking last month. We're both shit. I read Savannah's letter at least once a day, as it is the only reminder I have that she existed.

I have access to the best tracking equipment in the country, and I still haven't located a single reference on a Savannah Fontane. Her age and description haven't been located in the past four years. I even searched for her father, confident his extensive medical bills would leave a trail of crumbs for me to follow. They didn't. It is as if they never existed. They vanished without a trace.

I don't know if I've spent the last four years in grief or denial. It is probably a bit of both. I am also angry. Not just at Savannah but myself as well. I shouldn't have lied. Her disappearance is my punishment for breaking a promise I swore I'd never break. I took her choices away from her. In my eyes, that makes me as bad as Axel.

I'm pulled from my thoughts when I spot Chris prowling toward me like he always does when he plans to use his height to his advantage.

"Chris... don't!" I warn, my voice one I generally reserve for when I'm on the clock.

Chris is a few inches taller than me and a couple of inches wider, but with my mood the worst it's ever been, I'm not in the right mind frame to wrestle a drunken idiot who thinks we're still in high school.

"Not today, Chris. I can't handle your shit today."

Today isn't just the anniversary of Chris's brother's death; it is also four years to the day my brother killed my father, meaning in only a few hours, it will also be four years to the day I last saw Savannah. Four years ago, I broke her heart into a million pieces. And four years to the day, she returned the heartache with a letter I've read a million times since.

She never said she was coming back, but she never said she'd stay away forever, either. One day she will come home. One day soon. *I hope.*

Chris saw my lips move, but he didn't hear a word I spoke. His focus is locked on his target, and he won't stop until he gets it.

"It's not your letter; it's mine," I snarl, praying he will stand down before our words are replaced with fists.

Chris has always had a playful edge, but it has become more aggressive since Michael's death. "Bullshit," he shouts, his voice rumbling through the shambles he calls home. "Savannah was part of our group *long* before she was yours. That means her goodbye letter doesn't just belong to you. It belongs to *all* of us."

Some of what he is saying is true. Savannah didn't address her parting letter, but the signature reveals her intended recipient: me.

"Let me read it, Ryan. I want to see what it says," Chris asks, holding out his hand palm up.

I shake my head. It's all I have left of her. I'm not going to risk handing it to a drunk. The paper has thinned significantly in the past four years; imagine how much worse it will be with additional grubby mitts on it.

"I told you what it says; you don't need to read it." My voice is lower than Chris's and less arrogant as well.

"I want to read it myself. I want to read what she wrote about *me* with my own two eyes." I swear, he sounds like a twelve-year-old boy having a tantrum because the ice creamery ran out of sprinkles.

When he charges for me, I push him away, accidentally shoving him onto the coffee table. Numerous empty bottles of bourbon join his ashtray on the floor when he lands on his backside with a thud. Even without a heart, my intuition remains spot on. He isn't just hiding an addiction to marijuana from me; his drug usage goes way beyond an occasional joint.

"Fuck, Chris. What the fuck are you doing with your life?" I ask, stepping closer to him as I absorb the numerous baggies filled with white powder, a burnt spoon, and a crack pipe.

I'm so torn. I feel bad for shoving him, but I'm so angry he is throwing his life away like this, I want to push him for the second time. Chris has always been a mischief-maker. If there was trouble to be found, you could be sure he was first on the scene. But this extends beyond recreational drug usage to forget a shit week. This isn't an addiction. It is a life sentence to a miserably bleak existence. I know this all too well, as it is the exact path my brother is traveling.

"Why are you doing this, Chris? I know you lost your brother. I know you're hurting, but this shit won't solve anything. You can't bring Michael back. He is gone. He's dead. He can't come back from that. But you can, Chris. You can live a life worthy for you both."

The anger in Chris's eyes switches to panic when I grab the bags of powder from his coffee table and storm into his bathroom.

"No, Ryan. No!" he screams, following after me. His cries remind me of the ones he howled when I told him Michael had died.

"I won't let you follow in your dad's footsteps, Chris. You deserve more than the life of an addict."

Using his thick, long arms, Chris wraps me up in a bear hug. "You don't know what you're talking about." He isn't holding me for comfort. He's using his body weight to stop me from flushing his drugs down the toilet. "My dad is a brilliant man. He had a great life."

"Was a brilliant man, Chris. *Was.* Until alcohol took everything away from him. He killed your brother. *He* did that. Not your brother who asked for a ride. Not the van driver, who was found not to be at fault. *He* did it! Your father killed Michael."

"No! No!" Chris shrieks on repeat.

I don't know if his screams are because he doesn't want to hear the truth or because I've just flushed over six ounces of drugs down the toilet.

I realize it is the latter when he snarls, "Why the fuck would you do that, Ryan? What the hell is wrong with you? Do you have any idea how much that shit costs?"

He drops to his knees bowl-side, seeking any evidence of drugs in the circling water. The manic pulse of the vein in his neck grows when the cistern stops flushing, revealing not a single particle of white dust.

"That was my freedom! My way out! I don't want to live like you, miserable and fucked up over a woman who left your sorry ass."

Before I can stammer that being a drug addict isn't living, Chris continues his obnoxious rant, "Savannah fucking left you, Ryan. *She* left *you*. How about you go deal with those facts before fucking with other people's lives?"

"I'm fucking with your life?" I bang my fist on my chest, increasing the wild thump of my heart. "I saved your life! *Me*. I did that. Not that pathetic man sitting in jail for getting behind the wheel intoxicated with his four-year-old son in the back seat. Me!"

Chris rises from his crouched position and fists the scruff of my shirt before I complete an entire blink. His stability is so off-balance we crash into the wall in the far right corner. My body doesn't register the discomfort of the towel rack digging into my back; my brain is too busy processing the agony in his eyes to register something as weak as pain.

"Take it back," Chris roars, his alcohol-laced breath hitting my face. "Take back every word you just said about my dad, or I'll smash your teeth into next week."

"No," I reply, shaking my head. "I'm sick of you defending people who don't deserve your sympathy. I get it. I do. I understand why you want to protect them, but there comes a point in your life where you have to realize some people aren't worth saving. Your dad isn't worth it, Chris, and neither is your mother. She's an abusive, manipulating, two-headed bitch who treats your brother like scum. And your father... your father... he's not even your fucking father."

The instant the words leave my mouth, I want to ram them back in there. I didn't mean to say my last sentence. I was angry and upset and saying things I should never say. God, I hope Chris didn't hear my last sentence. Please let this be one of the many times his addiction has him mistaking my words. I don't want him to find out like this. He doesn't deserve to find out like this. Not today. Not on the anniversary of his brother's death.

My silent pleas go unanswered.

"Chris..." I barely whisper when he releases my collar from his fists.

"Chris," I repeat when he turns on his heels and stalks to the other side of his living room.

"Chris?" I question in confusion when he snatches his keys from an entranceway table covered with empty beer cans and over-stacked ashtrays.

"Chris!" I shout when he charges out of his home like he has a missile strapped to his back.

When the loud growl of his engine rumbles through my heaving chest, I push off my feet. I make it into the passenger seat of his car by the skin of my teeth. His anger is so white hot that I doubt he knows I am sitting next to him. His focus remains on one thing and one thing only—seeking clarification to the secret I just exposed.

We travel across Ravenshoe at a record-setting pace. Remarkedly, Chris's intoxication doesn't hinder his driving ability. His skills are as hair-raising as ever.

Dust billows around us when he takes the dirt track of his parents' property at the same speed he did the gravel road. We stop mere inches from a side entrance hidden by large hedges. Chris's perfect parking is compliments of him yanking on the parking brake at the same time he spun the steering wheel.

"I didn't mean what I said. I was talking smack."

Chris ignores my pledge like he did the half dozen I issued during our five-minute trip. He knows me well enough to know I am lying. It is what makes us brothers as much as it makes us friends. I should have told him what the coroner's report said years ago. I wanted to, but ethically, I couldn't. His father pled guilty, so the dispute in paternity was never made public. Neither Chris nor Michael are Trevor's sons. They bear his last name, but only Noah carries his bloodline.

Usually, paternity doesn't rise in cases involving family, but something Regina heard in the seconds leading to me fleeing the hospital four years ago altered the perspective. The DA wondered if the accident was indeed an accident or if Trevor was seeking revenge for the lies his wife had told.

One look into Trevor's devasted eyes answered the DA's questions without a word spilling from Regina's lips. He didn't kill Michael for revenge. He didn't even know he wasn't his son until Regina visited him the week after the accident. He was as blindsided by our findings as Chris is now.

My heart races at the same frantic pace Chris is charging through his childhood home, shouting his mother's name on repeat. My eyes go wild as I chase after him. This is the first time I've been in his home. I wish it were under better circumstances.

I stop taking in the raked ceiling and polished marble floor when we enter a kitchen bigger than the lower level of my home. I thought Chris's family was as poor as mine. I had no clue he lived in such opulence. This house isn't as large as Savannah's family mansion, but it has a regal feel that makes it seem more like a castle than a residence.

"Is it true?" Chris asks, storming to his mother.

I linger to the side when I notice his mother's face doesn't hold the same disdain it did when she greeted Noah years ago. She has love in her eyes, not hate.

My gaze snaps up from the floor when Chris yells, "Are you abusing Noah?"

His mother startles, as shocked as me. I thought he was coming here to seek answers about his paternity. I had no clue he was here for Noah.

"You promised it was the only time! You said it was part of your grief!" Chris yells when she fails to answer his question promptly. "How many times do I have to tell you Noah isn't to blame for what happened to Michael, Mom. He was just a kid. He is *still* a kid."

"He's *his* son—"

"He's your son too!" Chris interrupts, his anger growing. "You're the one who had him when Grumpies raised suspicion on my birthright. You wanted to sink your hooks into Trevor's inheritance. Noah gave you a hook." He waves his hands around the state-of-the-art kitchen. "Noah gave you this. If Dad didn't have a *true* heir, you would have never inherited Grumpies' house."

"He took my son! He killed him," Chris's mother argues with tears streaming down her face.

"No, he didn't," Chris denies, shaking his head. "*Your* husband did that. *Your* ticket to Easy Street killed Michael. Noah didn't do anything wrong." He stares down at his mother, his head shaking as much as his body. "I'm telling Noah the truth. He deserves to know the truth."

"No," Chris's mom fights back, grabbing his arm when he pivots away from her. "You said you'd take your secret to the grave. You promised to keep my secret—"

"I promised to protect a woman who lost her son. I didn't agree to watch my brother suffer. This is wrong, Mom. What you are doing to Noah is wrong."

Chris's trek through his family home is faster than his first. The room he wants is only a few feet from the kitchen, the smallest room in the house. It appears to be an old maid's sleeping quarters.

The color heating Chris's cheeks drains to the sole of his shoes when he walks into the barren space. Other than a dirty mattress sitting in one corner, the room is completely bare.

His mother blubbers out a string of incoherent words, no doubt a lengthy plea about the reason her teenage son's room resembles one you'd expect to see in a crack house despite the rest of the home being furnished with priceless antiques and modern appliances. Nothing she's saying makes any sense, but Chris doesn't need to hear her words for the truth to smack him in the face.

"Chris!" I shout when his open hand connects harshly with his mother's right cheek.

Anger reddens Chris's face as he tries to articulate the million thoughts running through his eyes, but not a word seeps from his lips.

"You're a liar and a cheat, and I'm ashamed to call you my mother," he eventually settles on.

When he exits Noah's bedroom, it takes me a few seconds to follow him. I'm too stunned to force my legs to move. He hit a woman right in front of me, but instead of arresting him as I had warned, I nearly cheer him on.

Fuck. Am I becoming my father?

CHAPTER 5

Ryan

"He's not here," I assure Chris when his manic search of his family home fails to find Noah. "He rarely stays here anymore."

Chris's chest reveals his exhaustion, rising and falling at double the rate of mine. I want to pretend his fatigue is merely from scanning every room in his massive home, but the width of his pupils reveals that isn't the case. He's gasping in breaths, hoping it will ease the guilt on his chest.

How do I know this?

He has the same look on his face I did when I searched Savannah's family mansion four years ago. First, he was panicked. Then, he was angry. Now, he's confused. I tackled every emotion you could imagine the day Savannah left. I was

THE WAY WE WERE

so confident foul play was involved I called Regina the instant I entered Thorn's empty room.

It was only when Regina stumbled upon Savannah's letter tucked into a copy of the first romance book she read did reality dawn. For the first time in my life, my acting skills were above par. Savannah believed every lie I spoke. She thought I had moved on.

She had left me.

Shaking my head to rid it of disturbing thoughts, I return my focus to Chris. Today isn't about Savannah. It is about Chris.

"Noah lives with his friend Jacob." I keep my tone low, hoping my confession that I've been keeping an eye on his brother doesn't re-spark his agitation.

I'm not watching Noah from afar because of my job. I watch him because the slap I witnessed him endure four years ago wasn't the only one I've seen. Noah's mom is a female version of my dad; she just abuses her teenage son instead of her partner. In a way, that makes her worse than my father. Children are innocent, no matter what.

"He's with Jacob?" Chris asks, his voice unlike any I've heard. He sounds lost, void of a soul.

Unable to speak, I nod.

"How long?"

I lick my dry lips before replying, "Permanently, a few months. But he's been back and forth for years."

"Good," Chris huffs out in a groan, his eyes fixated on someone behind my shoulder. "He's better off there."

Snubbing his mom's request to sit down and talk, he exits

his family estate with as much gusto as he entered it. After dipping my chin in farewell to his mother, I follow after him. It is times like today I wish I were a vindictive person. She doesn't deserve my courtesy, but I can't stop myself from issuing it.

Our drive back to Chris's desolate house in the middle of Ravenshoe is made in silence. I have a million questions I want to ask and another million to answer, but easing his anguish is more important than settling my curiosity, so I keep my mouth shut.

From the stories Chris shared over the years, I know that the man he mentioned when confronting his mother is his grandfather. Chris said although his infamous nickname was given in jest, the title suited him well. He was grumpy, but in a way, Chris couldn't help but admire and emulate him. Even without having a drop of the same blood, Chris's personality mirrors his father's old man.

I stare at my hands, wondering how long Chris has known Trevor isn't his father. Was it something he's always been aware of but never shared? Or was it only just unearthed? Is it the cause of his addiction? Or another piece of shit added to the pile he's been accumulating the past few years?

A couple of years ago, I would have only needed to look into Chris's eyes to seek answers to my questions. Today, I am stumped. Chris has never been family-oriented, but up until four years ago, that didn't extend to Brax and me. Things changed when Michael died. The stronger Chris's grief became, the more he pulled away from us. He's still the same mischievous man he's always been, just a watered-down, heartbroken version—kind of like me.

I drift my eyes from my hands to Chris when he says, "That house you saw—that big ugly pile of bricks and mortar my mom puts above anyone—she doesn't even own it." He chuckles. It is a painful, tormented laugh.

"My mom kissed Grumpies' ass for years, and what did she get for it? Nothing. Not a single fucking thing."

He turns his pained eyes to me. "I'm not even his grandson, yet he still left me one-third of his estate. An even share. Everything he owned was divided between Michael, Noah, and me."

He shakes his head while looking at the clapboard home he is pulling his rusty, beat-up sedan in front of. "I live in this shithole while my name is on the deed of a property with a greater land value than I'll earn in a decade."

"Then do something about it. Have her evicted," I encourage. No parent should suffer the loss of a child, but Chris's mom is milking it for all it's worth. She didn't grieve her youngest son; she plotted how she could benefit from his death.

Chris purses his lips. "I considered it when I saw her strike Noah after Michael's funeral. I even contacted a lawyer about it. But she had just lost her son... She was grieving. I couldn't kick her out. She had nowhere to go."

His eyes reveal his hesitation. "She also promised it was the first and last time she'd ever strike Noah." I hear the rattle of his heart when he asks, "It wasn't, was it?"

I want to save him the pain, but I also don't want to lie, so I shake my head. Chris's face scrunches up as he struggles to compose himself. He does a good job. If it weren't for the pained moan simpering from his lips, I'd be none the wiser to the anguish swallowing him whole.

"You can fix this, Chris," I assure him.

"How?" he asks, his short reply incapable of hiding his torment.

"We'll... Brax and I...you'll..." *Come on, brain, now is not the time to fuck up.* "We'll always be here for you, Chris. Brax and I will always have your back."

He barely swallows a sob. "And what about Noah? Who has his back?"

"You do." When the absolute agony in his eyes doubles, I stumble out, "And me. He'll have me as well. You're my brother, Chris. That means Noah is as well."

He wipes the contents from his nose onto his long-sleeve shirt before muttering, "You'll look after Noah? Treat him like your brother?"

I nod. "Yes. Always."

"Okay," he replies, copying my half-hearted nod. "Alright. Good."

I eye him with caution when he undoes his belt and clambers out of his car. Although we've been at odds most of the day, now it feels ten times stranger. I want to say his lukewarm response to my pledge is normal, but there's a weird feeling twisting my stomach, warning me to remain cautious.

I stop shadowing Chris up the cracked sidewalk when the rumble of a motorbike sounds through my ears. Air whizzes from my parted lips when I spot Brax's Harley gliding down the street. My response is one a man hiding from insurgents would give when spotting a Boeing XE-15 bomber in the sky. I am relieved beyond belief.

The cavalry has arrived, but instead of being strapped with AK47s and nuclear bombs, his saddlebags are loaded with Chris's favorite whiskey and spicy buffalo wings.

"Has he been like this all day?" Brax asks, dumping a dozen empty bottles of beer into the trash can at the side of Chris's house.

I follow the direction of his gaze. "Yeah. Other than an unexpected trip to visit his mother's house, he's been sitting on that couch all day," I reply, peering at Chris through the torn lace curtain of his living room.

Feeling our inconspicuous gawk, Chris lifts and locks his eyes with us. The accuracy of his stare is shocking. He didn't even scan his surroundings. I want to say the past ten hours have cleared the angst from his eyes, but unfortunately, that isn't the case. They appear as lost now than they were earlier today. If only I could read him as well as I can Brax, then I'd have an idea what is going on in that head of his. He keeps his emotions as tightly locked as a bank vault. He is impossible to crack.

Incapable of returning Chris's haunted stare for a moment longer, I return my eyes to Brax. "Did he tell you what happened this morning?"

Brax scrubs his hand over the stubble on his chin. "Somewhat? He didn't make any sense. He mentioned something about a house belonging to Noah. And that he's got a plan to make things right." You can see the confusion on his face. "Other than that, he slurred the rest of his words." His tongue delves out to replenish his dry lips while he contemplates how to ask, "Is he only intoxicated?"

I freeze for barely a second, but it is long enough for him to see the truth in my eyes. He can read me as well as I can him.

"*Fuck...* What's he on?"

I shrug. "I didn't get a good look at it before I flushed it down the toilet."

Air puffs from Brax's nostrils. "You flushed his stash down the toilet?"

I glare at him, stunned by the humor in his voice. *Now is not the time for laughing.*

"Come on, Ryan, don't give me that face. I know what today is. I know what he's been through, but it's also been four years. His grief should be easing, not getting worse," Brax says, his voice more mature than his twenty-two years. "You've gone through just as much shit, but you're not walking the same path Chris is."

"This is different—"

"How?" he asks with raised brows. "His dad is an alcoholic. Your dad was an alcoholic. His mother is fucked in the head. Your mother is fucked in the head. He lost his brother. You pretty much lost yours. You are two men dealing with the same shit, but you got up and dusted off your shoulders. Chris hasn't even attempted to move past the first stage of grief."

"We can't force him to move on—"

"Why?" Brax interrupts again, his voice not malicious or rude. He's genuinely confused.

"Because that's not how grief works. Just because you're told you shouldn't miss someone doesn't mean you don't. There's no suitable timeframe to overcome the loss of a loved one. For some, it can take months. For others, it is years." *For fools like me, it could be an eternity.*

I grow uneasy that I said my last sentence out loud when the worry on his face doubles. Only when I notice his focus is on something behind my shoulder do I take another breath.

"What is it...?"

My words trail off when I notice the sofa Chris has been occupying the past ten hours is void of his backside. I'm not going to lie; I am surprised he can walk. My dad's veins pumped more alcohol than they did blood, and even he would have had a hard time functioning after the copious amount of scotch Chris consumed this evening.

"He's probably just hitting the can," Brax surmises. "I'd rather him use the bathroom than make the mess he did last year. I swear I can still smell his piss in my carpet."

"Yeah, probably," I reply, struggling to ignore the knot in my stomach.

"Ryan..." Brax warns in a low growl when I push off my feet and head back into Chris's house. "If he thinks you're babying him..."

He stops talking when he hears flowing water.

"He's taking a shower?" Nothing but shock resonates in his tone. One of the first things Chris abandoned when Michael died was his showering regime.

65

"Chris? You alright?" I ask, racking my knuckles on the bathroom door.

When he fails to answer me, I rattle the doorknob. It's locked.

"Chris!" Brax shouts, ensuring his deep timbre is heard over the heavy flow of water. "Did you pass out again? I told you not to have that last shot. You're such a soft cock."

My heart thumps against my ribs when Chris fails to respond to Brax's rile. That isn't like him at all. It doesn't matter if he's as drunk as a sailor on shore leave, if Brax is stirring the pot, Chris adds more spice. Brax knows this, which is why he uses it as a tactic to coerce him out of the bathroom.

"Go grab the crowbar out of my patrol car," I advise Brax before pushing my ear against the door to seek any signs of life.

If Chris has passed out, I hope he is on his side. I don't want him choking on his vomit like he nearly did on his twenty-first almost a year ago.

"What do you want with a crowbar?" Brax asks, half-chuckling, half-confused. "Gonna knock some sense into him?"

"Just go get the fucking crowbar," I snarl, my voice void of the humor Brax's has.

Can't he feel the tension in the air? It is so thick it's nearly suffocating me.

While Brax races to my patrol car parked half a block down, I continue coercing Chris out of the bathroom. "You know Molly will be pissed if you use all the hot water again."

I rattle the doorknob for the second time, praying the lock will give out to the force of my spin. Unfortunately, it is one of those industrial-sized locks that barely wobbles when a size thirteen boot kicks it.

"Come on, Chris. It's been a long ass day, and I'm not up for more antics. We're all tired. How about we call it a night?" If he thinks I'm a nag, he's about to be taught a hard lesson.

"Brax is into your private magazine stash. He's gonna color in all the centerfolds again..."

My words trail off when a coolness hits my feet. It is wet and sloshy.

Bile surges to the back of my throat when I drop my gaze. Water is seeping under the bathroom door, soaking the shaggy green carpet under my bare feet.

"Chris!" I scream, banging my fists furiously on the door.

When he fails to answer me, I take a step back. Pain rockets up my leg when I slam my foot into the strip of titanium separating us, but I continue kicking down the door, only stopping once the solid paneled wood fragments at my feet.

My panic surges to an all-time high when my eyes lock in on the cause of the overflowing water. Chris is slumped in the bathtub. A needle is stuck in a vein in his arm.

"No, Chris. No. No. No. No," I mutter on repeat, racing into the room.

Hooking my arm around his torso, I drag him out of the bathtub. The water seeping into his clothes makes him triple the weight he usually is.

"R-ry..." he barely whispers when I lay him on the slippery floor.

"I'm right here. Just stay with me, okay?" I answer while tugging the needle out of his arm and loosening the plastic hose wrapped around his bicep. "What did you take, Chris? Was it heroin? Cocaine? How much did you take?"

"N-N-Noah."

He's not stammering from the whiskey he's been guzzling down all day but from the big shakes hampering his body. The water in the bath was freezing, nearly as low as his body temperature.

"P-p-promise me, Ry. Promise me you'll look after him."

I shake my head. I'm not promising him that. If I promise him that, he won't fight. He'll give up like everyone has given up on him the past four years. I won't do it. I'm not giving up on him.

"Noah needs *you*, Chris. He doesn't want me helping him. He wants you," I reply while grabbing every towel in the vicinity to wrap around his body. If I don't get his body temp up, he could go into hypothermic shock. "I need to know what you took and how much. Was it heroin? Did you take heroin?"

I slap his cheek with the back of my hand, returning his focus to me when his glassy eyes stare into space. "Tell me what you took, Chris. Tell me, then I'll promise."

Chris locks his light brown eyes with mine. I can see the hope in them. "H-h-he—"

"You took heroin?" I fill in, my voice as shaky as my hands.

When he nods, I ask, "How much? How much did you shoot up?"

Chris has a decent build, but if his drug of choice for the past few months has been heroin, there's no guarantee how his body will react. Long-term drug users are more at risk of

THE WAY WE WERE

overdosing than first-time users, as their bodies are already weak from prolonged use.

"P-p-promise me, Ry," Chris begs with tears in his eyes.

I shake my head once more. "No. Then you'll give up. I'm not letting you give up! If you want to help Noah, you have to stay with me. You have to fight."

"P-promise. Y-you said you'd promise." I swear I can see the life in his eyes fade with every syllable he utters.

I curl my shuddering hands around his blue-tinged jaw. "Don't make me do this, Chris. Please don't make me do this."

I don't bother clearing the tears filling my eyes. Maybe if he sees how devasted I am, he'll fight harder.

"P-p-promise," he begs, his words garbling in his exhausted state. "P-please, Ry. *Please.*" His last word is barely a whisper.

It takes me three attempts to force two minor words out of my mouth, and even then, a sob strangles them. "I promise."

I stop watching a tear careening down Chris's bluish cheek when the scuffling of feet booms into my ears. I'm shocked I can hear anything, much less the stomp of Brax's bare feet. My pulse is roaring through my body so hard I feel like I'm submerged in three thousand feet of water.

"Jesus Christ. I thought you flushed his drugs?" Brax mutters, freezing halfway into the bathroom. He has a crowbar in one hand and his riding boots in another. Apparently, he was planning to kick down the door if the crowbar was ineffective.

"I did. Well, I thought I did. He must have had a hidden stash," I reply, my tone partially frustrated but mostly devastated.

My panic grows when Chris's body convulses against the

drugs in his system. His eyes roll into the back of his head as his hands clamp into fists.

"Call an ambulance. He's overdosing."

My request has only just left my lips when Brax charges out of the bathroom.

"My cell is on the kitchen counter," I shout when I hear him rummaging through the hundreds of car magazines covering Chris's coffee table.

While he stomps to the kitchen, I grind my knuckles over Chris's sternum, striving to get a response from him. "Come on, Chris," I beg when he fails to respond.

My breathing comes out in ragged pants when I lower my ear to count his exhalations—they are far and few between.

"God, Chris, don't do this to me. Not today."

After removing the towel I placed under his head, I tilt his head, plug his nose, and seal my lips over his. I breathe into his mouth two times, supplementing the air his fritzing brain can't command his body to take.

I drop my eyes to his chest, waiting for it to rise and fall.

It doesn't.

"No, Chris. Come on."

I return my ear to his mouth. He's no longer breathing.

"Brax!" I scream, alerting him to my worry. "Advise first responders he's going into coronary failure. He's not breathing, and he doesn't have a pulse."

As I rip off the towels I just placed on Chris to keep him warm, Brax relays an update to the emergency responders on the other end of the line.

"One... Two... Three... Four..." I compress his chest in the same rhythm I did to Savannah years ago while striving to ignore the horrible memories resurfacing. "Five... Six... Seven... Eight... Come on, Chris." I increase the pressure of my pumps, finally recognizing that hurting someone to save them is okay. "Don't do this to us, Chris. We can't be the three musketeers without a third man."

After announcing the paramedics are on their way, Brax falls to his knees next to me. "What do I do? I don't know what to do." His voice is as panicked as mine was when I pulled Savannah from her watery grave.

"When I reach thirty, blow air into his mouth two times."

My words are as foggy as my brain. I feel like I'm watching the entire charade from above as if I'm dreaming. This doesn't feel real. It can't be real. Life can't be so cruel that I have the lives of two of my best friends in my hands within years of each other.

"Twenty-nine... Thirty."

Brax does precisely as instructed. Chris's chest rises and falls in rhythm to Brax's breaths, but his pulse remains flatlined.

"What now?" Brax asks, his voice riddled with so much panic he sounds like a pubescent teen.

"We keep going until the paramedics arrive. We don't stop. We never stop. He will pull through. He won't do this to us." *He won't do this to me.*

Anguish clouds Brax's eyes before he faintly nods.

"One... Two... Three..."

I don't know how long it takes the first responders to arrive. It is long enough for my worry to switch to anger but not enough for me to give up on Chris. I don't know who I am angrier at. Chris for placing me in this predicament, or myself for leaving him unattended for even a minute today. I didn't visit him from sunup to sundown on this exact day every year for the past four years for no reason.

Chris will never admit it, but he has suffered from depression for the majority of his life. I only realized his diagnosis during my six months at the academy. The psychological training was as intense as the physical. Chris's depression is the reason he always takes risks or causes trouble. He doesn't feel as if he is living unless surrounded by havoc or chasing his next hit.

For years, I thought his drug of choice was adrenaline. Now I realize I was way off the mark. But he'll be okay. He'll pull through this. Just like Savannah, I kept his heart pumping. When the first responders shock him with the defibrillator, he'll be right as rain—*right?*

Right.

Then why is this horrible feeling twisting my stomach?

"Charge again," the male paramedic advises the female medic kneeling next to the defibrillator, which just shocked Chris for the third time.

Nodding, she does as instructed.

Four sets of eyes stare at the graph, waiting for the

inevitable dip and fall that should follow Chris's heart being zapped with electricity for the fourth time.

It doesn't come. It remains in one straight line.

"Do it again," I demand when they eye each other with reservation. "Shock him again."

The male paramedic shakes his head. "We can't. He's been shocked too many times. I'm sorry, but your friend is gone."

"No!" I argue, shaking my head like I'm psychotic. "Do it again. He's just tired; he needs an extra boost."

When they ignore my request, I scoot across the tiled floor, not the least concerned the tub's water is seeping into my clothes. "Shock him again."

I stab the charge button of the device, preparing to zap Chris myself if they deny my request again.

The female paramedic yanks the defibrillator out of my grasp. "We've done everything we can do. We administered naloxone twice; we've worked on him for over forty minutes. He's gone."

"No," I deny, not wanting to acknowledge the honesty in her words.

Acting like I can't feel three sets of eyes staring at me with sympathy, I restart my compressions on Chris's chest. "Come on, Chris. Come on. You've got this. You're just playing. You're always playing."

When I reach fifteen compressions, I lift my eyes to the female paramedic, requesting she squeeze the bag of air sealed over Chris's mouth.

"Please," I beg. "He just needs a little longer. Don't you,

Chris? You're always the difficult one, rocking up late and causing havoc."

I scrub my knuckles over his sternum again, praying he will move, moan, or yell at me for nagging.

He does nothing.

Not a single thing.

I gave him my word, and he gave up.

This is all my fault.

CHAPTER 6

Ryan

"They're about to start. Are you coming in?"

I stop scanning the street for a familiar face before I drift my eyes to Brax. He's standing in the entranceway of a little white church in the middle of Ravenshoe. His favorite jeans and Henley shirt have been replaced with fitted black trousers and a light blue long-sleeve dress shirt. His face is void of the scruff it usually has, and his hair has been contained in a low ponytail. If it weren't for the massive set of bags under his eyes, you'd think he was here to attend a wedding, not the funeral of our best mate.

Chris died three days ago—exactly three days before his twenty-second birthday. Instead of letting us have this day to grieve, his mother decided to lay him to rest.

How fucked up is that? She had her choice of days, yet she

picked today. If I didn't already believe she was the spawn of Satan, I now have no doubt.

After scanning the street one last time, seeking a hair color I'll never forget, I nod. Brax doesn't utter a syllable. He doesn't need to speak for me to hear the words he wants to say. *"She isn't coming, Ryan."*

I spend the first half of Chris's service peering over my shoulder, absorbing the hundreds of faces surrounding me—some new, many old. With Chris being born and raised in Ravenshoe, the number of people crammed into the tiny church is staggering. I wish he could have seen how many people cared for him, then maybe he would have fought a little harder.

Chris thought he was alone in the world. Today proves he wasn't. He was loved—more than he'll ever know.

"What?" I ask, returning my eyes to the front when an elbow lands in my ribs.

"It's our turn," Brax nudges his head to the podium Noah just left. "You ready?"

No. No, I'm fucking not.

Instead of saying what I want to say, I nod again.

Even while reading the eulogy I wrote at 1 a.m. this morning, I continually scan the many entrances of the church. She should be here. Even if she believes I deceived her, Savannah should be here for Chris. He was her friend as much as he was mine, so why isn't she here? The service is almost over, and she still hasn't shown up.

THE WAY WE WERE

The longer Chris's funeral progresses, the angrier I become. What Chris said the day of his death is true: Savannah was part of our crew *long* before she was my girl, so why isn't she here? Why hasn't she come to say a final goodbye to the boy who crushed on her as hard as I did during middle school? Did Chris's friendship mean so little to her that she couldn't set aside her anger for one day?

If so, that's fucked. Chris doesn't deserve to be disrespected like this. He was always there for Savannah—*always.* Even when Brax told me to move on after Justine's eighteenth birthday, Chris kept his opinions to himself, as he'd rather stay quiet than disrespect her. He even drove her to school, for fuck's sake. How could she forget all the times he's been there for her?

If this doesn't already make me mad, the fact my concentration is centered on her instead of giving my best friend the send-off he deserves frustrates me even more. I'm so fucking angry; if I hadn't promised Chris I'd keep an eye on Noah, I'd be out of this town first thing tomorrow morning. I stayed for her, yet she's the one who gets to live her life without anguish.

That's bullshit.

"You heading out?" Brax asks, stopping my steps midstride.

I drift my eyes around Chris's monstrous family house to ensure we don't have any onlookers before replying, "Yeah,

Noah left with Jacob around an hour ago, so I'm going to hit the sack for a few hours before my shift tomorrow."

Brax flicks his half-smoked cigarette out the back door before spinning around to face me.

"I thought you quit?"

He bows a dark brow. "I thought you were taking a few weeks off work?"

I grimace. "Guess we're both shit at quitting stuff that's bad for us."

I don't need to say whom I'm referencing. Brax knows my comment has nothing to do with my job and everything to do with a green-eyed, honey-haired girl I once knew.

After a quick swallow to clear my throat of nerves, I say, "I want to put a few hours into Justine's case."

Brax nods, understanding my objective. Savannah's best friend was mauled by a dog three weeks ago. Details are sketchy, but Regina is certain mafia fingerprints are all over the case.

I guess that should have been my first sign that Savannah was never coming back. Justine will survive her injuries, but it is the scars we can't see that will take years to heal. *If they ever heal.* If Savannah isn't here to support Justine through this, why would she come back for me?

"Have you seen Justine yet?" I follow Brax to my truck, the hammering of my heart hiding the anger in my voice.

Brax clears a drop of ash from his bottom lip before shaking his head. "I called her last week. She said she wasn't up for visitors. Maybe next week?"

I squeeze his shoulder. "Maybe."

I never got an update on what happened with Brax and Justine years ago. The last I heard about their "non-date" was the night Chris and Brax spiked my Coke with vodka. He never mentioned her since that day. But with the worry in his eyes doubling when I asked about her, they've kept in contact.

I want to say I've maintained an amicable friendship with Justine as well, but unfortunately, that isn't the case. When I grilled her on Savannah's location, the pain in her eyes told me she didn't know where she was. I was just too stubborn to acknowledge it. She answered every call I made for the first six months. Then they dwindled to two or three a week until she eventually stopped responding to them altogether. It wasn't that she had forgotten Savannah; she just couldn't tolerate my confusion or anger anymore. I can't say I blame her. Misery is always best handled solo.

God—everyone in this town must think I'm a fool.

Not anymore. I'm done. I've spent more time searching for Savannah than I've known her. I should have realized years ago that you can't force someone to see sense. I couldn't drum it into my mom's head, and I can't force it on Savannah.

When she's ready, she'll come home.

I just won't be waiting for her.

CHAPTER 7

Savannah

Now...

"*L*ose the shirt."

The already scorching day gets ten times hotter when I raise my eyes from the retro CD player I'm struggling to connect to my outdated iPod. The owner of the club I am auditioning at is glaring at me, as shocked by my attire of choice as I was when I noticed his waitress's state of undress. They're not wearing shirts. They're not even wearing bras.

"My shirt?" I ask, acting daft.

He smiles a slick grin. It is lucky his looks override his greasy demeanor. "Yes, sweetheart, your shirt. I need to see what I'm working with."

"If you give me a minute, I have a whole audition prepared." I return my focus to the CD player, praying it will magically play the song I've rehearsed for the past two weeks.

"Please," I beg the CD player. "I don't want to take off my shirt."

I jump out of my skin when a roared, "Next!" ages my hearing by a decade.

"Oh no, please, I only need a minute," I shout when a blonde close to my age sashays onto the stage. The gold tassels on her boobs reflect on her knee-high boots.

"I'm not done yet." I gently clutch her elbow to direct her back off the stage. "But you look great. I'm sure you have this gig in the bag," I add when she glowers at me.

"Look..." The club owner stops talking to glance down at the clipboard. "Abby." The way he pronounces it sounds as foreign as it does when I say it. "I'm not looking for dancers. I'm looking for *dancers.*" His dark eyes stray to the scantily clad women waiting to audition. "Unless you can give me what they can, you're not going to give me what I need. Capiche?"

I stare at him, more confused than ever. *Is he speaking English?*

Spotting my bewilderment, he simplifies his reply, "Unless you remove your shirt, you're not what I'm looking for..."

His words trail off when I whip my shirt over my head. Although the bra I'm wearing should *never* be seen in public, I'm so desperate I'll wear it like it is made out of the most expensive silk in the world.

"Better." The club owner scans my frame in a slow,

dedicated sweep. "Much, *much* better." He licks his lips before demanding, "Now your bra."

My hands dart up to cover my heaving chest. "You said I only had to remove my shirt."

His lips purse. "True. But I wasn't anticipating ...*this.*" He waves his hand across my hideous grandma bra. "Is that a nursing bra?"

"No!" I deny, shaking my head. "I don't think it is?" Since I'm unwilling to remove my hands to test his theory, I stick with my first reply.

"You asked me to remove my shirt. I did as you asked. Now can I perform my routine?" You can hear the plea in my voice.

I should be ashamed I'm begging for the chance to sashay my ass on stage in front of a man who lacks morals, but I'm not. When backed into a corner, you either come out swinging or lose. Since this is a fight I have no plans of losing, I come out swinging.

"If you'd just give me a chance, I'll prove that naked breasts aren't the only sexually satisfying visual you can get from the female anatomy."

The dark-haired man takes a moment to contemplate.

I swear it is the longest thirty seconds of my life.

For the second time in my life, it also ends nothing like I had anticipated.

"I'm sorry. The men who visit my club want naked breasts. They want ass shaking. They want..." He scans his practically isolated club before finishing his sentence. "*Anything* you are willing to give them. Are you willing to do that? Give them *anything* they want?"

"Anything?" I double-check, certain the circumstances of my day have me mistaking the dip in his tone.

"*Anything,*" he clarifies.

Disappointment forms in his eyes when I shake my head. I may be desperate, but I'd rather live in a shelter than do... *that* for money.

"I'm sorry, sweetheart, you're not what I'm looking for."

I beg for the tears pricking my eyes not to fall. I will not cry like a defenseless, idiotic woman who needs a man to rush in and save her. I will dust off the shit and move on to the next stage of my life. I. Will. Not. Cry.

I'm crying. Not enough for anyone around me to notice, but enough to dent my ego even more. I need this job. With my last two years of university spent as my dad's in-house caregiver, I have no education to fall back on. Then, a few years after my father's death, Tobias passed away, leaving the operation he had personally handled the past six years in limbo. No one knew of my existence, not even the local US Marshalls. I was merely referred to as Witness #11734.

I thought once Col Petretti's case had been brought before the courts, I'd be free from witness protection. I was wrong—very, *very* wrong. Tobias's efforts to keep me safe tripled when Col walked away from court without a conviction. He knew someone had tattled and was doing everything he could to discover who it was. In the year prior to Tobias's death, I moved more times than I did the five years earlier. We were forever on the move, ensuring no breadcrumbs were left behind.

The only reason I am free now is because Col was killed in a joint police/FBI sting over a year ago. Although that stage of my life is now over, I'll never live without fear of repercussion. I'll always look over my shoulder, waiting for my past to catch up with me.

After brushing away a tear that settled in the groove of my cheek, I gather my iPod from the floor and shove it into my tattered gym bag. The lady with the gold tassels on her nipples is strutting across the stage. Her dance routine is as hideous as her fake boobs that are on display for the world to see.

The club owner's approving nod of her provocative grind on the stripper pole reveals what I've always known: men are idiots. I could add a few more words, but that one is the most appropriate, so I'll stick with it.

"Perfect. Beautiful. Wonderful. You're hired."

I gag more at his last praise than his first three. Nothing about her routine was entrancing. It was hideous. If I could get down my satin ribbons bolted to the ceiling without the help of the club's maintenance man, I'd be long gone from this strip club on the outskirts of town. But since I haven't grown a smidge since I turned fifteen, I keep my feet planted on the ground.

Another four girls perform before the lackey is given the green light to assist me. Every girl was hired—even the one who had underarm hair longer than the hair on her head.

"Didn't give you the time of day?" The young man I'd guess to be mid to late twenties asks, peering at me through lowered lashes.

I shake my head. "No. I wanted to keep my shirt."

He huffs. "Pity. We could sure use some lookers like you in

this place. When you've seen one set of silicone tits, you've seen them all."

The playful gag at the end of his sentence makes me laugh. "How can you be so sure my boobs aren't silicone? You've only seen them through a baggy tee."

His Adam's apple bobs up and down. "I was out back when you whipped off your shirt." The guilt in his eyes triples when he discloses, "They have cameras of the main stage area in the dressing room."

"Oh."

I want to say more, but I can't form a reply. Removing my shirt in front of one man was hard enough. I wouldn't have done it if I knew I had an audience.

"The image was grainy, but I'm fairly certain your tits aren't from Silicon Valley," the dirty blond with a devasting grin mutters.

I smile. Don't ask me why. I am as stunned by my body's reaction as you are.

Bobbing down to gather my ribbon strands in his hands, he asks, "Are they?"

I glower at him.

He doesn't really want me to answer him, does he?

"No. They're all mine," I mumble a short time later when he arches his brow, waiting for a reply.

His grin enlarges. "I knew it." He jerks his chin to the satin ribbons bolted to the ceiling. "So what's the deal? Do you use these in your routine?"

Shocked by the shift in our conversation, I nod.

"Show me." He's not suggesting. He is demanding.

I swear, I'm going to get whiplash at this rate.

Our conversation is worse than a one-sided tennis match. All serve and no return.

Deciding to play along, I ask, "Show you what?"

His lips tug high. I really wish he'd stop smiling. He has a gorgeous grin that has me thinking recklessly. *It has me thinking of him.*

The stranger runs his sweaty hand down his denim jeans before standing from his crouched position. "Your routine. I want to see what you've got."

He thrust the satin ribbons toward me. "Come on, what have you got to lose? I've already seen your tits. I know they're not fake. We're practically best friends."

I smile for the second time in the past five minutes.

This guy is a ball of mischief but in a playful, non-threatening way.

"You won't get in trouble?"

"Nah," he overemphasizes, waving his hand like he's shooing a fly. "He *thinks* he runs the show, but nothing happens here without my approval."

I follow his gaze. The man who dismissed me over an hour ago is standing at the main bar, talking into his cell phone.

"Show him he's an idiot," the blond encourages, moving to the side of the stage. "If nothing comes of it, you saved yourself a trip to the gym."

For a man who appears to know nothing about gymnastics, he's got knowledge by the bucket loads. Just ten minutes of aerial ribboning equals an hour of cardio.

"Music?" I ask, nerves rattling in my tone.

He shoves a cherry-flavored lollipop into his mouth. "Who needs music? Your heart has its own beat. Work with it."

My lips crimp. "Okay... I can do this." My words don't have an ounce of confidence in them.

After a quick stretch to ensure I don't risk injury, I curl the satin ribbon around my arm before racing to the end of the stage. The satin catches me midair, winding around my body as I have trained it to do for years.

Within seconds, my love for aerial acrobatics overtakes the nerves fluttering in my stomach. I complete my routine with the precise accuracy awarded by years of study. I tumble, twist, and glide down the silk as if it is an extension of my body. I've always felt free dancing, but this is an entirely different experience. It is like I am soaring, flying freely in the air. I finally feel at peace when I'm floating amongst silk.

I plan to end my routine as practiced, with a daring death roll. I can only hope the quick calculations I made on arrival are accurate, or I'm two seconds away from landing with a smack on the hard wooden floor.

I land with half an inch to spare, my touchdown perfect. It looks risqué and on edge, yet graceful at the same time.

Smiling like a loon, I unwrap the satin from my thigh and stand to bow. I'm not bowing expecting an uproar of applause. I'm showing my thanks to the arts and bowing in gratitude.

"Woohoo!" shouts a deep voice from the side. An ear-piercing wolf whistle complements the lackey's praise. "Holy shit. That was hot as fuck."

An unexpected giggle graces my smile. "Thank you," I reply, curtseying as if I've just performed for royalty.

After bolstering his praise with a bump of our hips, the unnamed man wraps his half-consumed lollipop into a crinkled package, stuffs it into his jeans pocket, and then pulls down my ribbons.

He's barely yanked on the pully twice when a husky voice to our side says, "Wait."

The club owner throws his cell onto the glistening countertop before strutting our way. Yes, I said strut. He just needs to fan out some feathers, and his rooster walk will be as perfectly executed as my routine.

"That... *thing* you just did..."

"Aerial ribboning," I fill in, still giddy.

He nods. "Yes... *that*. Can you do it with less of... *this*?" He waves his hand at my plain white tee and faded black shorts.

"Do you mean naked?" I double-check, confident in my intuition.

My clothes may be outdated, but they leave nothing to the imagination. Even with my tee a little baggy, my shorts are so tight-fitting I couldn't look any more naked unless I *were* naked.

The dark-haired man's lips twitch as he struggles to hold back his smile. "Would you be open to the possibility of doing it nak—"

"No," I interrupt him, not the least bit worried about my bitchy attitude.

Like it always does, my ten-minute acrobatic routine stripped the anguish from my mind, freeing me of turmoil. I was unsuccessful in securing a job today, but that doesn't mean I will be unsuccessful tomorrow. *I hope.*

I shift my eyes to the lackey watching our exchange with

amusement slashed across his features. When I capture his attention, I nudge my head to the hoist, requesting he continue to lower my ribbons.

When he does as requested, I pad to my gym bag left dumped on the floor.

The club owner shadows me. "Topless?"

"No," I answer, shaking my head.

He follows me off the stage, his desperation interesting me more than his suggestions. "What about a glittery little number with a few well-placed tassels..."

The rest of his sentence rams into his throat when I shoot him a vicious sideways glare. "I'm only here because your ad said you were looking for dancers. If it had mentioned the word stripper, I wouldn't have auditioned."

"Huh," he huffs out with a chuckle. "Did you not see the big 'Gentleman's Club' in bright red letters in *numerous* spots outside the club doors? You're here, sweetheart..." He doesn't emphasize his term of endearment as pleasantly as he did the first few times. "...because you are like every other girl who walked through those doors today. Desperate."

Having no plausible defense, I remain quiet. I saw the signs he mentioned. They flashed into my eyes like big ass warnings, yet I still walked through the doors because I am exactly what he said I am: *Desperate.*

"So, what is it? Are you paying a hefty tuition fee, running, or are you an addict?" His eyes scan my body. I wouldn't say it is an overly sleazy gawk, but it isn't friendly either. "Considering you're a little too old to be saddled with school fees, I'll say it is one of the latter."

I roll my eyes, not looking any more mature than my nearly twenty-nine years. "I'm not doing any of those things. Maybe I'm just a poor, lonely housewife who wants to stick it to her old man by shaking her moneymaker for paying clients instead of his lazy ass."

I startle to within an inch of my life when he seizes my wrist and yanks me toward him. I'm five seconds from showing him aerial ribboning isn't the only way I've kept fit for the past ten years. I also practice martial arts.

He's saved from discovering my love of boxing when his lackey says, "Come on, Pete, let her go."

Pete ignores his request. "No track marks on your arms. Where do you shoot up? Between your toes?" His eyes drop to my bare feet.

I yank my arm out of his grip. "I'm not a drug addict."

"So you're running?" he surmises, reading between the lines.

"I didn't say that," I snarl, snatching my ribbon from where it landed on stage.

I need to leave, and I need to leave now.

I raise my eyes to the man observing me with worry. He's no longer sucking on a lollipop like someone much younger. His squinted gaze is bouncing between Pete and me.

When the late-hanging sun reflects in his glistening eyes, it dawns on me why I felt immediately comfortable around him. He has wise, old eyes like my dad had.

God, I miss him.

Every. Single. Day.

There's only one person I've missed nearly as much. He's the same man who restored my faith in humanity before destroying it beyond repair. The one man I'll always love even when I hate him. *Ryan.*

I thought our five-year separation when we were teens was torture, but it was nothing compared to the past ten years. Ryan deceived me, yet the man who creeps into my dreams isn't a liar or a cheat. He's the boy I fell madly in love with when I was six. The man who chased away my demons while making me feel whole. He's a knight in shining armor, but instead of riding in on a white horse, he had a dark blue bike with recently removed training wheels.

I dared Ryan to step out of his comfort zone that day, and he challenged me to step into mine. If it weren't for his words of wisdom whispered in my ear every night, I would never have the courage to do what I am doing right now. To an outsider, it looks like I've hit rock bottom. To me, I'm striving for better— one day at a time.

After stuffing my ribbons and bolts into my gym bag, I return my eyes to the stranger, who is once again sucking on his beloved lollipop.

"Thank you," I mouth, my worry about being homeless incapable of excusing my manners.

He grins around his treat before dipping his chin. "Until next time."

Smiling at his assumption there will be a next time, I pivot on my heels and stalk to the main entrance, tugging on my hoodie on my way. Nothing against this club, but I'd rather not be seen entering and exiting it.

My quick strides across the highly buffed floors slow when an Italian accent shouts, "I'll pay you fifty dollars a night to do your routine." They come to a complete stop when he continues, "I'll even let you keep your clothes on."

Although tempted by his offer, I'd never survive on three hundred and fifty dollars a week, so I negotiate, "Fifty dollars a routine."

Pete laughs, amused by my negotiation skills. "That's fifty dollars for ten, twenty minutes max. No fucking chance," he scoffs. "I could have my dick sucked for less than that."

"Fifty dollars for thirty seconds of work? Your odds don't stack up, Pete," pipes up a husky voice from the side.

"Shut up, Jet," Pete snarls, glaring at his right-hand man. After returning his slit eyes to mine, he says, "Fifty dollars a night. Take it or leave it."

"Okay," I reply, shrugging my shoulders like it's no big deal. "It was nice meeting you." My praise isn't for him. It is for Jet.

I wait for Jet to dip his chin again, acknowledging my comment before I continue for the door, praying I didn't misread the desperation in Pete's voice. I really need this job. I thought my mom left my dad and me high and dry the first time she vanished. It was nothing compared to the second fleecing she issued me months after his death. That old saying about not having two nickels to rub together—that's been the story of my life for the past four years. Except now, I'm not just broke. I'm homeless as well.

I stop halfway through the main entrance door when Pete shouts, "One hundred dollars a night, and you keep your tips." The last half of his sentence is forced, as if it pained him to say.

I crank my neck back to the stage. "How much will that be?"

Once again, my question isn't directed at Pete. It is for the dirty blond with a devastating grin. Jet—my stranger/ally.

Jet purses his lips. "Normal girls... Fifty, maybe a hundred a night. You..." His smile forces my knees together. "An easy two hundred."

"A night?" I clarify, wanting to make sure we are on the same wavelength.

Jet's smile reveals he didn't miss the shock in my tone. "Easy," he guarantees in a rumble.

I bounce my eyes between Pete and him while contemplating a reply. That's more per night than any job I've been offered, but can I do this? Can I take something I love and sex it up to entice dirty old men out of their hard-earned money?

Yes. Yes, I can.

For her, I'll do anything.

"I can wear my clothes?" This time, my question is for Pete.

He points to my rundown getup. "Do you have anything more enticing than that?"

It shames me, but I shake my head.

"Give her a wardrobe budget—"

"Shut up, Jet!" Pete demands again, the veins in his neck bulging like he's about to have a coronary.

Pete runs his eyes down my body enough times to creep me out before he pushes off his feet and heads my way. If Jet weren't eyeing him with as much caution as me, I'd be fleeing. Mercifully, his reassuring glance keeps my feet planted on the ground. He has my back, even though we were only strangers minutes ago.

"Although I'd rather you wear one of the outfits we have out back, you're not going to do that, are you?" Pete asks, smiling a slick grin.

I shake my head.

Huffing, his hand slips into his trouser pocket to dig out a bundle of bills. "Keep your receipt. I plan to claim anything you buy on my taxes."

His command shocks me. I didn't think businesses like this kept records anymore. I assumed when Col went down, all legitimate business dealings for establishments like this went right along with him.

Realizing his business dealings have no impact on me, I accept the three hundred dollar bills Pete is thrusting at me before nodding.

"We open at 9 p.m. Make sure you are here no later than 8."

Not waiting for me to reply, he spins on his heels and stalks back to the stage Jet stands on, giving me the thumbs up. Pretending I can't feel my stomach swirling at the base of my throat, I return his gesture.

CHAPTER 8

Savannah

"Ten minutes, Abby."

"Yeah, I know. I'm coming," I assure Jet, glaring at my reflection in the mirror.

My father would be rolling in his grave if he could see me now. Not only am I wearing a bathing suit as if it is an outfit, but my makeup is also done in a palette that can only be described with one word: trashy. The red lipstick is classic old Hollywood, but my dark shadowed eyes and contoured cheeks make me look years younger than I am and much more risqué than my celibate lifestyle entails.

After adding a few more pins to the rich chocolate brown wig I've been wearing for the past three weeks, I stand to make sure the girly parts of my body are covered.

Well, as hidden as they can be in a two-piece someone my age shouldn't be wearing.

I fan my sweaty cheeks with my hand when I take my position in the wings of the stage, waiting for my introduction. The crowd has grown the past few weeks and is graciously missing the vicious chants and unmissable boos my first routine was welcomed with.

The clients at Vipers were as unimpressed with my dressed form as Pete was the first time he saw it. Fortunately, the topless waitresses' mingling around the club kept their interest at bay long enough for me to perform my routine without incident.

When I finished, pin-drop silence spread across the club. I was sure I was seconds away from being pummeled with rotten tomatoes.

Something was hammered that night.

Mercifully, it wasn't my body with rotting fruit.

It was my eardrums.

The crowd of approximately thirty men responded in the same manner Jet did the first time he saw my routine. They cheered. They clapped. Then they threw money at my feet.

I was so damn excited I bobbed down to gather the bills like the novice I was. After ushering me off stage, Jet explained it was his job to collect the tips at the end of each performance, and he would have them waiting at my dressing table by the end of the night. Although trust has become a significant issue for me in the past ten-plus years, I held Jet to his word.

He didn't disappoint.

I made one hundred and eighty-three dollars and fifteen

cents in tips my first night. Although it was a little short of the figure Jet had assured earlier that day, it was pretty damn close, and I didn't remove an article of clothing.

The first week, my money went toward the deposit for a two-bedroom apartment. In my second week, I used my earnings to connect the gas and electricity. This week, I'm aiming high. I need a car. I don't care what condition it is in. I just need it to get me from Point A to B. The four-mile walk from Vipers to my apartment is growing old fast. After twisting myself around two slips of silk for three hours in four-inch heels, I'm exhausted. A car will be a godsend.

The lights dim two times, announcing it is time for my performance to begin. I move to the X marked on the middle of the stage. Wanting to give his clients the same dramatic edge he got, Pete requested I start my routine as I did the first time he saw it: by leaping off the stage.

A smile touches my lips. You won't believe how many clients hold out their hands, preparing to catch me. Doing my routine without any safety measures enhances the clients' *thrill level*, which, in turn, increases my bank balance. It's a win-win, really.

Once I have the silk positioned around my right arm, I twist my neck to Jet standing at the side of the stage. Although he's barely seen in the dim lighting, the white stick of his favorite cherry lollipop makes him identifiable.

Within seconds of me dipping my chin, advising I am ready, soft, sensual music filters around the club. I breathe out two times before sprinting to the end of the stage. Just as they do every time I perform, the regular clients of Vipers hold out their arms to catch me, and the newbies gasp in shock.

I love this. Even taking something I adore and ramping it up to entice larger tips can't change my love of acrobatics. I get so immersed in my routine that within seconds, I forget I am performing. I am simply free—floating amongst silk.

By the time my performance reaches the end of my playlist, I am sweating profusely and smiling without shame. The crowd is even more robust than usual. My love of aerial ribboning is as contagious as the flu; they can't help but smile.

With it being Friday night, I climb to the very top of the silk rungs, wanting to achieve the most drastic death roll possible. I'm halfway through twisting the ribbon around my midsection when I lower my eyes to calculate my risk.

The satin slips from my sweaty grip when my eyes lock on a man at the edge of the stage. Usually, the stage lights hide the clients from my view, but since I'm positioned higher than the lighting, I have no trouble recognizing the blazing brown eyes and shoulder-length hair of a man I once knew.

"What the hell are you doing here, Brax?" I mutter to myself, my furious heart rate resonating in my tone.

I applied for positions on the outskirts of Ravenshoe, knowing my old crew would never be caught dead in this part of town. Clearly, the years haven't made me any wiser.

While I finish twisting the ribbon around my waist, I scan the club, praying Brax's appreciation for skimpily dressed women isn't shared by his friends—most notably, a man with ravishing blue eyes and cut facial features.

Failing to find any signs of Ryan in the club, I exhale three times before rolling down the silk. Though I'd like to say my eagerness to end my routine is compliments of the large bundle of money I see sitting mid-stage, that isn't true.

I need to leave, and I need to leave now.

With my mind fritzed from seeing a familiar face, my calculations aren't as precise as usual. My worry about being spotted working at a strip club switches to panic when my tumble toward the wooden stage occurs at a faster rate than I usually descend.

Moments away from impact, my thoughts drift. I want to pretend only one person is occupying my thoughts. Unfortunately, there isn't. He enters the equation no matter how angry I am. Ryan—my first and only love.

My heart lurches into my throat when my freefall stops just inches from the stage. I suck in ragged breaths as I scramble to my feet. I was so certain I was about to plunge to my death that I'm both stunned and relieved.

After ungracefully stumbling out of my ribbons, I curtsy to the wolf-whistling crowd before darting off the stage. I don't know where I am going or what I plan to do when I arrive, but I shove the cosmetics scattered around my station into my handbag like a madman within two seconds of hitting backstage.

"Abby?" Jet questions, his one word as breathless as my panicked composure. "Did you nearly fall...? That was cutting it close. I don't think you should do that again. You scared the shit out of me..." His words trail off when he notices me packing. "Where are you going, doll face? You have another two performances."

"I... I'm... This..."

I can't get my words past the panic curled around my throat. I don't know what is more distressing, wondering if my cover has been blown or my near-death experience. Considering I'd rather be dead than caught, I'd say it is my first worry.

"Abby..." Jet follows me into the dressing room, darting between a dozen topless dancers on his way.

I flick on the outdated bulb before moving to the section reserved for my clothes. Although Pete's first three hundred dollars went toward two outfits, the remaining eight spread sparingly on three feet of hanging space belong to me. I paid for them out of my profits, hoping a change-up in outfits would keep the regulars entertained until I devised more daring routines.

"Stop and think about this, Abby. You need the money." Jet isn't prompting me about my dire financial state because he's concerned about Pete's profits. He is reminding me because he has become more of a friend than a coworker in the past three weeks.

I stop shoving my clothing into my gym bag when he adds, "Running won't get you anywhere fast. It hasn't in the past. It won't now. It's time to face your past, Savannah."

I clamber backward, shocked and void of a reply.

I never told him my real name—not once.

"Oh... come on. Don't be scared. It's me. Lollipop Jet." He digs a cherry cola pop out of his pocket before shoving it into his grinning mouth. "Look in my eyes, Savannah. Tell me what you see. It isn't a man who will hurt you."

He steps back, placing an unthreatening distance between us before raising his eyes to mine. It feels like I've been kicked in the stomach for the second time tonight when the reason behind his familiar eyes comes to light.

How did I not see this earlier?

Have I been walking around with blinders on?

"Jeffrey...?" My words are as unconfident as my facial expression. "Jeffrey Moat?"

I see Jet's tongue curling around his lollipop from the broad grin he's giving me.

"But you moved to Cali years ago. Your dad is a lawyer." I scan our location. Although Vipers glistens like my skin after a dusting of body glow, it is still a strip club. No amount of sparkle can alter that fact. "You *shouldn't* be working at a strip club."

"Why not?" He chuckles under his breath.

"Because... because..."

I'm stumped. I work here, so how can I give a valid point without degrading myself?

"You've lost a *lot* of weight." I roll my eyes. *That's the best you could come up with?* Anyone would swear I was meeting with the ladies who used to run our primary school PTA, not a boy I went to school with until grade seven.

"And you've gained a few pounds... in a good way." Jet's last sentence comes out in a hurry, unfazed by my snarled growl.

I groan for the second time when his eyes fail to deviate from my chest.

"Sorry. Old habits die hard." If he weren't smiling, I might have believed him. "You were always a looker back in the day, Savannah. I'm glad to see nothing's changed."

His compliment removes some of my worry. "When did you move back to Ravenshoe?"

I can't believe how different he looks. When we were young, Jet was *very* overweight. He wore thick-rimmed glasses, and his left shoe was padded because one of his legs was longer than the other. He didn't look like *this*... hot enough to fight off three to four eager women every night. The Viper's female clientele don't arrive at precisely six every night for cheap drinks. They come for Jet.

"A couple of months ago," Jet answers, reminding me that I asked a question. "I ran into some trouble in Cali. Decided to start afresh. You?"

He asks his question without any stipulation. If I don't want to answer, I don't have to.

"Same."

He nods, not deterred by my short reply. "So you inevitably knew tonight would happen, right? You can't come home and not expect to see old faces. It would be nice but very unlikely."

Sweat slicks my skin. "You saw Brax too?"

He nods again. "Hasn't changed, has he? I swear he's been rocking that hairstyle since kindergarten."

I laugh. "It suits him."

"Yeah, it does," Jet replies with a shrug, unconvinced. "But you need to shake things up a bit, dust off the cobwebs, so to speak."

I immaturely roll my eyes. "Are you sure your family moved to Cali? Or did you just don a skirt and hang out with the seniors at Ravenshoe High?"

My voice is snarky from memories of Amelia saying

something similar to Ryan years ago. What I said to Ryan over a decade ago was true, Amelia was a nice girl, but neither of them saw the bitchy looks her friends gave me when she said her comment loud enough for me to hear. Although peeved, since I had a long way to go to repay the money I believed I owed Axel, I was happy Ryan was moving on.

Somewhat.

Maybe.

That's a lie.

I was devastated.

He deserved to be happy, but I'd always hoped we'd find that happiness together.

God—how wrong was I? I just wanted him to wait a few more months...

Ten years later, I still haven't gotten my shit together. At least this time, I'm not solely to blame for our separation. Ryan instigated it. I'm merely sustaining it.

"Brax... really? I never saw that one coming."

I glance at Jet, confused by the shock in his tone.

"That worried look on your face. That's from Brax?" His facial expression doesn't reveal if he's asking a question or stating a fact.

"Nothing happened between Brax and me."

He breathes out dramatically. "Good, because he always looked at you like a little sister, so that would have been weird—"

"Ryan, on the other hand," I interrupt, praying he doesn't say he also saw me as a sibling, as that wouldn't just be weird. It would destroy every fantasy I've ever had.

Jet smiles a blistering grin. "Ah… so you two finally sorted your shit out?"

A grin cracks my mouth. "Somewhat. We kind of dated for a few years… Then things went sour. Then we dated again…" A grimace finishes a truth I don't want to acknowledge.

"Then things went sour again?" Jet fills in.

I nod. "As sour as you can get."

He shoves my half-packed gym bag onto the counter we're standing next to before nudging his head for me to sit. When I do, he crouches in front of me like a coach about to give a pep talk to his star quarterback.

"What happened?" His tone is not intrusive or rude.

I take a moment to consider how to reply maturely.

I shouldn't have bothered.

"Ryan cheated," I blurt out.

Jet falls onto his backside, making me giggle. "Ryan-Take-a-Chance-on-Me-Carter cheated? No fucking way."

I take a mental note to book an appointment with an optometrist when I roll my eyes for the third time in under five minutes.

"You must have misread what you saw… Smoked crack… Knocked your fucking head because there's no way Ryan Carter would cheat. The guy wouldn't even let me glance at his paper when we took a third-grade spelling test. Cheating isn't in his vocabulary."

After blowing air out of my mouth so fast my lips wobble, I stand and return to the wardrobe. "I would have believed you if he hadn't revealed his philandering ways himself."

Jet stares at me, blinking and mute. "Are you sure that's what he confessed to?" He hands me a wrapped lollipop like sugar is the answer for everything.

I twist off the plastic and pop it into my mouth before nodding. "He said he got sick of waiting, so he moved on."

"He couldn't have waited to tell you he wanted to move on before moving on? That's whacked."

"Whacked? We are too old to say 'whacked,'" I giggle, my words extra throaty from the sugary spit my lollipop is creating. I can understand Jet's fascination. They are delicious.

"Speak for yourself. I lived under my dad's command for twenty-five years. I've got years of youthful misdemeanors to make up for."

"Ah. Now the strip club job makes sense." I barge him with my barely covered hip.

He grins while waggling his brows, confirming my suspicion. "You sure you want to do this?" He nudges his head to the two original outfits I started with. "This is the first time I've seen anyone I know here. Maybe Brax's visit was a one-off. He was standing with Keke. I've heard rumors they're more than friends."

I take a deep breath. "I can't risk it. Ten years of silence will already make things awkward, let alone if it happens here."

Jet glances into my eyes for two heart-thrashing seconds before dropping them to my midsection. I don't need to peer down to know what he's looking at. I've felt its significance long after the burn wore off.

"It's not what you're thinking—"

"I didn't say it was," Jet interrupts, returning his eyes to mine. "But it's got to mean something, and I'm fairly sure it is the reason you sashayed into this club three weeks ago with your head held high even though you'd hit rock bottom."

Sick of lying, I nod.

The ink on my hip is precisely why I am here.

Pretending he can't hear Pete shouting his name, Jet runs his hand down my goosebump-mottled skin. "Then take a step back and breathe. You're earning a living. Nothing more. Nothing less. If you decide this isn't what you want, hand in your notice. But if it is what you *need*, there's no shame in admitting that." His wisdom matches his wise eyes. When I nod, he takes a step backward. "I'll tell Pete you've got woman issues." The cheeky glint in his eyes doubles when he drops them to my teeny tiny white pants.

"Even Pete won't have any issues understanding why you can't perform your last two shows."

I nearly correct him that there are feminine products that stop that from being an issue, but when his glance lingers on my bare thighs longer than what could be deemed acceptable, I realize he isn't worried I'll represent the club in a negative light —he's perving.

"The loss of an eye will be worth the sacrifice." He chuckles when I grab one of the stilettos resting near my knee and peg it at his head.

His dash out of the dressing room slows to a snail's pace when I call his name. I wait for him to spin around and face me before asking, "Why Jet?"

I know why I picked the alias I did. It is the same reason my name changed at least five times in the past ten years—my safety. But what purpose does Jet have for a name change?

"Do you want the honest answer? Or a watered-down version?"

My arched brow answers his question on my behalf.

He pulls his lollipop out of his mouth before licking his lips, adding to their glossy appearance. "Because I make women come faster than a rocket."

I pop my eyes open.

That was not the answer I was anticipating.

My shock doubles when he adds, "If you ever want to test my skills, give me a holler." A bold wink seals his cocky offer.

Stealing my chance to reply, he disappears into a sea of half-naked women who don't bat an eyelid at his boastfulness. It is business as usual, making me suspect everything he said was true.

Even the parts including his sexual abilities.

CHAPTER 9

Ryan

"Are you sure this is the address Damon gave?" I question down my cell, glancing at a crumpled piece of paper my mom handed me earlier this evening. "It's not what I was expecting."

After my mom assures me I have the correct address for the third time, I lift my eyes to the flashing sign in front of me. It's been years since I've been to Vipers, so the address didn't register when I saw it.

I shouldn't be surprised Damon selected this location. He rocks up out of the blue for the first time in years and requests me to meet him at our dad's favorite strip joint.

Brother of the Year material right here, ladies and gentlemen.

After glancing down at my dark blue trousers, white button-up shirt, and jacket, I head to the main entrance. The last time I walked through these doors was the evening of Justine's eighteenth birthday.

Who would have been able to predict the obstacles I'd go on to face?

If you had told me I'd be walking in these doors ten years later as a detective at Ravenshoe PD, I would have laughed. I never saw my life taking the path it has—not in a million years.

Keeping my chin braced on my chest, I pay the high entrance fee before slipping into the main floor area of the club. My face isn't famously known around these parts like Isaac's, but it is known enough I have the possibility of being spotted.

Most likely by criminals, but detected nonetheless.

I guess that's why Damon chose this location. Corrupt men are less likely to confront their own in their territory. If it weren't for the pull I've amassed over the past six years, Damon's extensive list of criminal activities would be higher than it currently sits. He took my word of protecting him from my father's murder and twisted it in a completely fucked up way. He didn't just expect me to take the fall for our father's demise. He anticipated I'd handle every misguided thing he does.

I have news for him. Just like my search for a pretty blonde with green eyes ended years ago, so did my offer of the safety net I've been using to catch him for the past ten years.

I swore to protect him on the promise he wouldn't become our father. He lied, so I no longer need to continue my side of our agreement. I've done everything I can: extensive rehab and drug counseling; I even set him up with an apartment in town when he rocked up eight years ago. What did I get for my efforts? Lies, lies, and more lies.

Damon has gone so far down the rabbit hole I honestly don't know if he can still lie straight in bed. With every request for money came a dishonest pledge. I caught on to his games years ago.

Mom is still learning.

You'd think she'd be more clued into the games abusers play after handling my father's antics for twenty years, but she's none the wiser. Instead of her life improving when my dad passed away, the baton of burden shifted to Damon. She will go without groceries for a week to ensure Damon's drug habit is maintained.

It is a vicious, demoralizing cycle that has no end in sight.

I love my brother, but I hate the man he has become.

Spotting Damon and Brax in a far corner booth, I increase my pace. Although I appreciate the many flirty smiles I get from the staff at Vipers, I'm not so desperate for female company. I'm willing to part with my hard-earned money to achieve it. My detective salary certainly is a step up from the rookie income I lived off when I joined the force a decade ago, but it will never be high enough for me to drop coins on something I can get for free.

I'm open to the prospect as long as she doesn't have honey hair, green eyes, and a lack of self-respect. But if there's any requirement involving money, I'm not interested. Not in the slightest. It's never going to happen. Nada.

When I reach my brother, I hold my hand out in offering. "Damon."

He accepts my offer, although hesitantly.

"It's been eight years, man, time to let bygones be bygones," Brax mutters into my ear, greeting me in a friendlier nature than the one I issued my brother.

I wasn't shocked when Brax called to say he received an invitation from Damon. Damon might be a liar and a cheat, but he's also smart. He knew Brax was the perfect buffer. He's the equivalent of our brother without the blood or the official title.

Brax did everything he could to get Damon on the straight and narrow ten years ago. He went out on a limb for him, but because he was only working with half-truths, he didn't fully comprehend the mammoth task he was undertaking.

As far as anyone in this town is concerned, my mother killed my father—even Brax believes this. When my mother returned from the rehabilitation home where she resided for nearly two years, she wasn't shamed, ridiculed, or spoken down to. She was seen as a matriarch of the domestic violence community, which is distressing considering her current predicament.

My mom has grown a lot in the past ten years, but she still isn't half the woman she could be. She will always find a shadow no matter how much light I shine on her. It is who she is. Nothing can change this.

Brax slaps my back three times, drawing my focus to the present.

"You know why he picked here to meet, don't you?" I ask, pulling back from his man hug.

Brax quirks a brow. "Yeah, I know. But there's nothing wrong with an off-duty detective spending his weekend looking at some fine ladies."

He gestures for me to slide into the booth before him, understanding my objective to remain inconspicuous. If anyone here remembers my dad, I'll be pinned as corrupt in less than a nanosecond. I worked my ass off for years to have the mud removed from my family name. I won't let anything taint it.

Forty minutes pass in silence, adding to my agitation. Damon has had two lap dances since I arrived, but I've failed to see him remove his wallet. I'm not a regular at these establishments, but don't businesses demand payment prior to service? You don't watch a movie before paying for the ticket, so how can you secure a stripper without proving you have the means to pay the tab?

I chuckle under my breath. *Is Damon the problem or me?* Perhaps I've disconnected so far from society that I don't see things as they are anymore. I do work—*tirelessly.* Maybe I'm out of the loop?

I can't remember the last time I went out. I'm reasonably sure it was a year ago when I succumbed to Regina's suggestion of letting her set me up with someone she knew.

After seeing Izzy for the first time, I wish I had surrendered to Regina's nagging years earlier. Without hesitation, I can testify that Izzy is gorgeous. Big chocolate eyes, dark temperamental locks, and the personality of a girl who should be a whole lot uglier. For the first time in years, my interests were piqued.

It is a pity she's Isaac's girl.

Izzy did a stellar job pretending she was unaffected by Isaac's domineering personality, but within minutes of watching them interact, her ruse came undone. I wouldn't necessarily say Izzy was under a spell, but Isaac's prompts reminded me of a guy I once knew: my young, stupid self.

For the years following Ophelia's death, Isaac was a ghost. I hadn't heard or seen him in years. When Ravenshoe boomed, his presence became more known. Within months, the shadow swamping him vanished, and our mutual interest in a pretty brunette at one of his clubs resurrected our natural competitive nature.

That is why I kissed Izzy.

I shouldn't have, but the competitive edge Isaac always instigates from me was rearing its ugly head that night. I wanted to show him the expense of a suit has nothing on the man wearing it. Did I go in strong? Yeah, I did. Did he react how I expected him to? Yeah, he did. Do I regret it? No, not at all. Why? Because the words he spoke when he returned to pick up his date have stayed with me since then.

"I once asked if you could fight. You said, 'You don't need talent to fight. Anyone can take a hit; it is how you accept it that proves your worth.' I never understood what that meant... until now. I'll accept your hit like a man, Ryan, but you must accept mine in return."

He stepped closer, bringing his gray eyes level with my baby blues. "Love is about guts. If you have it, you fight the world to keep it. If you don't, you fight no one but yourself. This isn't your fight. It's mine."

He didn't realize he admitted to loving Isabelle that night, but Cormack and I heard it clearly. In that instant, we realized Isaac was no longer in the game we had been playing for years. I threw him a curveball. He hit it out of the park. Game over.

I crank my neck to the side when Brax's elbow lands in my ribs. "What's the deal? Why is he back?" He gestures his head to Damon.

I toss back a nip of whiskey before replying, "I don't know. A few days ago, he sent Ma a message saying he might head back this way in a few months. He turns up on her doorstep the very next day."

"You think he's running from something?" Brax questions, hearing the underlying message in my reply.

"Something or someone." I take another generous swig of my whiskey, hoping to force the bile racing up my esophagus back into my stomach.

Brax huffs while scrubbing his hand over the stubble on his chin.

Wanting to shift the focus off me and my fucked-up family, I ask, "So what's the deal with you? I've seen you turn down three girls since I arrived. That's not the Brax I know." Thankfully, my tone comes out playful despite feeling anything but.

The whiskey I've only just swallowed threatens to resurface when he mutters, "I think my cock is broken."

"What?" I gasp, my one word breathless since I'm nearly choking to death.

Brax tracks a blonde sauntering past our booth. Since her hair is more platinum blonde than golden, I take a moment to appreciate her generous curves.

"Beautiful ass, a sinful body, and a rack I'd love to bury my face in."

I nod, agreeing with his assessment. This blonde is a knockout. *If only her hair were a little darker.*

"Nothing. Nada. It is fucking broken," Brax mutters, glancing at his crotch.

I shouldn't laugh—*I'm an ass for laughing*—but the more I try to hold back my laughter, the louder I laugh.

My chuckles are nipped in the bud when I spot the genuine worry in Brax's eyes. He truly thinks his cock is broken.

"Maybe things have just gotten too easy for you?" I suggest, my tone sincere.

He's never had his heart ripped out and stomped on, but that doesn't mean he's undeserving of my sympathy. For a man as sexually promiscuous as Brax, a broken cock is the same thing.

"You need to mess up that pretty face of yours. Make it more of a challenge. Your dick has gotten bored with the ease of the game."

I wait for him to nod, agreeing with the shit dribbling from my mouth. He does no such thing. He knows me well enough to know I have no clue what I'm talking about. Game? What fucking game? I'm so far out in left field that I can't see the batter anymore.

When Brax whacks me in the arm, I rub the spot his knuckles landed while turning my eyes to the crowd. It's not an ideal location to put out feelers for a mate, but a weird excitement thickens my blood, encouraging my defiance. My rebelliousness has nothing to do with the two dozen half-naked women mingling around our booth. It is a peculiar feeling that is hard to explain. It is familiar yet odd. If that makes any sense?

Shutting down my bizarre behavior due to a tiring week, I return my eyes to Brax. "You still buying into Inked?"

Inked is the tattoo parlor Brax began working at when we were in high school. He thought the probation his grandmother arranged would tie up a few weeks of his time. He had no clue it would open doors he never knew he wanted to walk through.

When we were teens, Brax avoided work like the plague. Now, I don't think he's had a vacation day in years.

I can't talk. The three days between Chris's death and his funeral were the longest I've been away from Ravenshoe PD. I wouldn't say I'm a workaholic...

Nah. Fuck that. I hate liars.

I'm a workaholic, but if it saves me sitting at home, twiddling my thumbs while thinking about a girl I have no right to think about, I'll wear the title with pride. I'd rather be a workaholic than a miserable, lonely old man who acts like he's ninety when he's only twenty-eight.

Denial isn't lying, right?

Right.

Then why do I feel like a fraud every time I say it?

CHAPTER 10

Savannah

"Don't say anything."

Jet pulls a lollipop out of his mouth with a sassy pop. "I didn't say anything."

I stop restacking my cosmetics before spinning to face him. I don't need to peer into his eyes to know he's lying. I heard it in his undertone.

"What?" He chuckles while shadowing me to my dressing nook. "An hour ago, you were packing like a mad woman. Now..." He scans our location to ensure we have no unwanted listeners. "Now, you're going to work at a brothel."

"I'm not *working* at a brothel." I cringe when my reply comes out louder than anticipated. "I'm *performing* at one. That is completely different." My voice is as low as my heart rate. "Besides, it isn't a brothel. It's a bordello."

SHANDI BOYES

Jet's blond brows shoot up into his hairline. "If I wrap a piece of shit in a candy wrapper, do I get to call it candy?"

"No," I reply, faking a gag.

"Exactly!" he shouts, holding his hands in the air. "Just because you give a brothel a fancy title doesn't alter the facts. Maison's is a brothel. Their 'house representatives' are *paid* for their *services*."

The way he says "services" leaves no doubt about what he's implying.

"Maison's clients aren't like Viper's clientele. Our guys are happy to pretend the little strip of material you use to cover your gorgeous tits from their view isn't there. Maison's clients won't just demand the strip be removed. They'll want to feel what is under the strip, taste it, then spill their nasty cum all over it."

I gag for real at his last sentence. "That won't happen. I have it in writing that I'm solely performing my routine for thirty of their dearest clients."

Jet snatches the paper I'm referring to out of my hand. "You mean the dirty old geezers who pay for sex clients. Nothing about them is 'dear,' *dear*."

I zip up my gym bag while mumbling, "For a man who works at a strip club, you're very Negative Nancy about the sex industry."

He stops reading the handwritten contract Keke, the manager at Maison's, drew up when she cornered me backstage fifteen minutes ago to glower at me.

When Keke first handed me her card, I wadded it up and threw it in the trash.

118

I underestimated her negotiation skills.

Within minutes, she had me eating out of the palm of her hand. She doesn't just have the gift of the gab; she's a shrewd businesswoman. If I didn't know better, I'd say it is more than just a managerial role informing her business acumen. She is as invested in Maison's as her clientele, who pay top dollar to use her services.

"Showing your assets is one thing, Savannah, but letting people feel them up is a different kettle of fish."

"No one is feeling anything. I'm just performing." Guilt riddles me when my tone comes out bitchier than intended. I'm not angry at Jet; I'm just peeved I am in this predicament to begin with. "People pay thousands for ballet tickets, so who's to say they won't spend a hundred dollars to see me? It's three thousand dollars, Jet. I can't turn down that amount of money. I need that money... *badly.*"

When I slump into the wooden chair across from my dressing area, Jet sits next to me. I want to ramble about how unfair life has been to me over the past ten years and that if I could just catch a break, I'd never whine again, but if there's one thing I've learned the past five years, complaints get you nowhere fast. If you want to change something, you have to do it yourself. Relying on anyone only guarantees failure. I've been taught that lesson numerous times in my past nearly twenty-nine years.

"I'm smart, Jet. I won't get caught in the net Keke is setting." I wish my tone was this confident when I told Ryan I didn't regret trusting him.

Although I'll never regret loving Ryan, I regret trusting him.

Trust issues have been my biggest downfall in the past decade. It doesn't matter if it is signing a slip of paper presented by a US Marshall or accepting a drink from a stranger at a bar, not being able to trust people's motives is my biggest personality flaw.

How can you expect someone to give you their trust if you are not willing to do the same?

You can't. That not only makes you untrustworthy, but it also makes you a hypocrite.

"Let me come with you—"

"No," I interrupt, shaking my head.

If I want to walk down a dark, unlit path, that's my choice. But I'm sure as hell not taking anyone down with me. I laid in a bed I shouldn't have. Now, I'm trying to smooth out the wrinkles.

"No, Jet," I reply more forcefully, ramming his rebuttal into the back of his throat. "Even if you hadn't revealed your true self earlier tonight, my answer would still be no. I need a friend, not a superior."

He shoves his lollipop back into his mouth, swishing it around as if he's ridding the horrible taste my words left. "Alright, but if you get an itty bitty touch you don't want—"

"You'll be the first man I'll tell," I fill in, smiling.

I don't need his protectiveness, but it is nice to have.

"Nah. That wasn't what I was going to say." He stands, extending to his full height. "I was going to say, hit them with your stilettos. Those fuckers hurt." He rubs his arm I aimed for earlier, feigning injury.

I laugh, loving the one-eighty our conversation just took. It has been like this every day for the past three weeks. We bicker like we're vying for a spot on the national debate team before laughing like teens who huffed down a sneaky joint between final periods. Although Jet's bouncing personality is confusing at times, it is also refreshing.

After tapping his knee against mine, Jet gestures his head to the back door of Vipers. "Go on, get out of here. Pete accepted your womanly excuse. Just make sure you hunch over on your way out. I told him your cramps were so bad you looked like the Hunchback of Notre Dame."

A smile raises my cheeks. "Are you sure you won't get in trouble?"

He cocks a brow, not needing to speak to relay his words.

Pete isn't running this show. Jet is.

"Alright. Thank you." I almost kiss his cheek before remembering that it isn't something I do anymore. Keeping everyone at arm's length is a safe, respectable distance.

I pull back with only a moment to spare, making my near slip evident to Jet *and* everyone surrounding us.

"Awkward," Jet murmurs under his breath, loving the snarled glances directed my way. "I might have to take two home tonight just to save your head from the cutting block."

"Haha. Don't blame me for your promiscuity," I reply, half peeved, half relieved.

After grabbing my handbag from my dressing station and securing a hoodie over my golden locks, I bump Jet with my hip and head for the back entrance. Anyone would swear the place is on fire for how fast my steps are. I haven't been home before 4 a.m. for three weeks, so my eagerness can't be contained.

I push through the heavily weighted door with force, adoring the nip of freshness in the air. I've always loved Florida in the fall. It's warm during the day but perfect snuggling weather at night. Ideal!

Well, it would be if I had a significant other to cuddle with.

Hearing my name being called from inside, I twist my torso. Jet is racing for the back door that is rapidly closing. His face is washed with concern. I try to stop the doors from closing, mindful of the alarmed locks Pete had installed late last month. Once the doors shut, they can't open for another five minutes without inputting a safety code. The boost in security was implemented after two dancers snuck clientele in via the back entrance, pocketing their entrance fees as tips instead of handing them over to their rightful owner.

They didn't just lose their jobs. They nearly lost all the honest dancers their wages as well. Pete was pissed, so much so that he doubled the cover charge. That would have been bad news for the entertainers, as the more money patrons hand over to enter, the less they have to share amongst the dancers. Considering one-third of the dancers at Vipers aren't paid a wage, they need those tips. Thankfully, Pete's anger dulled when he was lavished with his employees' attention. Instead of opting for tighter security measures, he kept the entrance fee at the agreed amount.

My endeavor to stop the door from closing is hindered by my shoe getting snagged in a grate. It slams shut, leaving Jet and his incoherent blubbering on the other side.

"I'll come around," I advise Jet when the thick door swallows his words. All I can hear is his muffled voice. Nothing he's saying makes any sense.

"His... out...front... wait ...Savannah." His clear words are separated by ones I can't make out.

"Give me a minute. I'll be right around," I say with a groan, shocked by his eagerness to talk to me. I don't know what is so urgent it can't wait until tomorrow, but considering he went out on a limb for me tonight, I can't pretend I didn't hear him.

I keep my chin close to my chest when I round the main entrance of Vipers. Although I wear a wig while performing, I've been caught out three times the past week doing the most mundane tasks. Once, I was questioned at the laundromat. I was blinded by the client's eagerness to speak to me, even more so since he was standing next to his wife.

Deny. Deny. Deny. Then flee. That's the motto I've lived by for the past three weeks.

My brisk pace down the cracked sidewalk slows when a familiar voice jingles into my ears—a voice I'll never forget. A voice that sweetens my dreams as much as it blackens them. *Ryan.*

"I told you last month, Ma. He isn't using the money to pay his rent... No, you don't understand. Giving him a way out won't teach him anything... You're not hurting him by denying him, Ma. You're helping him..."

I can't see him, but I'm certain he has sensed my presence, as his voice didn't lower because his mother interrupted him. It dipped like it always did when I tried to catch him unaware.

"Ma, I'll call you back." I hear a familiar beep, closely followed by a throat clearing.

Pretending I can't feel the world falling from beneath my feet, I glance around my location, seeking a quick exit. My choices are the packed parking lot on my right or returning down the dark, scarcely lit alleyway on my left. Neither option is appealing, but it can't be any worse than my predicament.

Deciding to wait for the alarm to unlock the back door is my best option, I spin on my heels and dash toward the alleyway.

My steps are stopped when a deep, gritty voice says, "Savannah?"

A million replies stream through my head, but not one seeps from my lips. I can't command my legs to move, much less speak. So, instead, I keep my eyes planted on my shoes, pretending I'm not who he thinks I am.

My pulse rages through my body when Ryan noisily huffs. It isn't the huff of a man in shock. It is the moan of an angry, tormented man.

I don't know what he has to be angry about. I'm not the one who tore his heart to shreds. He did that to me, not the other way around.

After clearing the anguish from my eyes, I raise my chin sky-high. "Ryan, hi," I greet him, my voice as over the top as the grin on my face.

I saunter toward him like I have the world at my feet while chanting the same mantra on repeat: *He didn't break my heart. He didn't break my heart. He didn't break my heart.*

"What are you doing here? I didn't think these types of establishments were your thing?" I question, leaning in to place a kiss on his cheek.

What? Old Savannah would have done that. I'm not relishing his unique, manly scent or getting a better look at his soul-stealing eyes. I'm being polite. That is all.

Yeah, right.

Ryan is wearing a suit. Not just a shabby old suit you see on a hundred men, but a suit that showcases every spectacular cut of his body. His hair is a little shorter than I'm used to, and the scruff on his chin is a little thicker, but his panty-wetting face, mind-numbing eyes, and lips as soft as a cloud haven't changed in the past ten years. This shames me to admit, but he's as reckless to my composure as he has always been.

Now I'm even more annoyed. A cheater doesn't deserve to have this hold over someone. He broke my heart. Not partly. Not just a smidge. Wholly. He destroyed me. *He destroyed us.*

"It was lovely seeing you again, but I really must go." I bite the inside of my cheek, loathing that my voice is croaky as if I'm seconds away from crying. I don't cry—not for this man. I shed enough tears a decade ago to last a minimum of three. I will not cry another tear for this man.

I barely get two steps away from Ryan when he asks, "What are you doing here, Savannah?"

He says my name so bizarrely like he hasn't mentioned it in years.

Perhaps he hasn't? Maybe she *doesn't like him talking about me?*

"Uh... I was just... umm." Spotting a flyer flapping in the cool breeze, I settle on, "A mix-up in dates. I thought it was ladies' night. My mistake."

Ryan nods as if accepting my excuse.

It is a pity his eyes don't hold the same confidence.

"Your ride?" He nudges his head to a gleaming gold Mercedes pulled to the curb at the front of the club.

After soundlessly thanking my blessings, I stammer out, "Yes! I better get a wiggle on. He hates waiting."

I hope the past ten years have been more detrimental to Ryan's hearing than his looks, as my voice is doused with so much deceit even a stranger would detect it.

"*He?* You brought a *guy* to ladies' night?" Ryan interrupts, his tone rife with suspicion.

"Uh-huh," I reply, annoyed by his uncalled-for interrogation. "Come on, Ry. We're in the twenty-first century. Lots of relationships step outside the box these days."

He glares at me. "Ryan. No one calls me Ry anymore."

Ouch. *Hello ego, here, have a bruise.*

"Sorry... *Ryan.*" I peer over my shoulder, certain my mother has joined the party. The way I sneered his name was low— nearly as low as my heart now sits. "I wasn't aware the shortening of your name was damaging to your sanity. I'll be sure not to make the same mistake next time." I stop pacing to the stranger's Mercedes to add a final nail into the coffin of our conversation. "*If* there's a next time."

My dash to the Mercedes is fast, but not fast enough to miss Ryan's quick exhalation of air. He isn't the only one fuming. How dare he be so rude. I'm not a piece of gum his shoe picked up on the sidewalk. I was his first love—*his first lover!* I should always hold a special place in his heart.

Blinded by anger and confusion, I throw open the Mercedes' passenger side door and slide into the warm leather seats without a second thought. The driver startles, as shocked by my arrival as I am by my eagerness to evade Ryan. Am I so desperate to get away from him I'm willing to put my life at risk?

I realize my answer is yes when I blubber out, "I will pay you any amount you request if you drive out of this parking lot right now."

The man I'd guess to be in his late forties advises his caller that he'll call back later before housing his cell in his suit. The longer his glassy eyes scan my features, the tighter his brows knit.

"Abby?" he queries, his slight intoxication not affecting his ability to remember my name. "They said you won't do private dances."

I lose the chance to confirm his suspicions when I spot Ryan in the passenger side mirror, striding closer to the Mercedes. The curiosity on his face matches that of the man whose car I've hijacked.

"I don't... *usually*. But if that's something you're interested in, I'm sure I can arrange something." My voice is full of shame.

The stranger's face lights up, answering my offer without words.

"Okay, great, but I need you to drive first. Now. *Please*."

He peers at Ryan approaching his vehicle with caution before dragging his eyes down the street as if expecting undercover officers to jump out of the bushes and arrest him for prostitution.

I understand his apprehension. Even with Ryan out of uniform, he still looks like a cop. He has the swagger of an officer, never mind the fact his hand is braced on his waist where his gun usually sits—if it isn't still positioned there.

Ryan has the same cutthroat determination Regina has. I doubt he ever clocks out.

"Please," I beg the stranger when Ryan spots my inconspicuous gawk in the side mirror, not only speeding up my heart but his steps as well. "I'm doing an exclusive show at Maison's Bordello next month. I'll get you an invitation."

"Really?" His tone is way too sleazy for a man of his age.

I swallow my dinner for the second time tonight before nodding. "Yep. Definitely."

I don't care if his cover charge costs me every penny I've earned this week. I'll pay any amount to stop the pain throwing my heart back to the point it was ten years ago. I'll even lower my dignity to that of a whore because no amount could shred my ego any more than my exchange with Ryan just did.

Our reunion was brutal, ten times worse than I imagined. He looked at me like he hated me, like I was the one who broke his heart.

That hurts even more than his reflection fading in the side mirror as I drive away from him in tears for the third time in my life.

CHAPTER 11

Ryan

I stand on the sidewalk of Vipers, watching the taillights of a gold-flecked Mercedes, shocked and speechless.

I just saw Savannah Fontane for the first time in ten years.

Savannah Fontane.

The only girl I've ever lied to.

The only girl I let break my heart.

The only girl I've ever loved.

And what did I say? *"Ryan. No one calls me Ry anymore."*

Wow. The douchebags of Ravenshoe have a new leader.

The past ten years have been testing, but I still expected a better response than anger. Anger is a quick, futile reaction a lesser man gives when they can't work through their emotions.

I'm not a lesser man. I've grown a lot since I last saw

Savannah. I attended counseling to work through the issues my parents' volatile relationship caused. I speak at domestic violence support groups a minimum of once a month. I even donated my share of my father's inheritance to a domestic violence shelter in Hopeton.

I'm not a lesser man.

There's just something about Savannah that causes my composure to slip.

Time has been kind to Savannah—*very* kind. Her dimples are more defined since her cheeks are a little rounder. The dowdy, oversized hoodie she was wearing couldn't hide the generous swell of her breasts, and even the low hang of her head couldn't conceal her alluring green irises from my avid stare.

She's more gorgeous now than she's ever been —*unfortunately.*

Don't get me wrong. I'd never wish an ugly, debilitating disease on anyone, but maybe, just maybe, her absence wouldn't sting as much if one glance at her beautiful face didn't have my cock pressing against my trouser seam.

Ten years she's been gone, yet my body still reacts as if she owns it.

Ten, long miserable years, yet I want to forget why I'm angry at her.

Maybe I'm not mad at her?

Perhaps I'm angry at myself?

If ten years can't work her out of my system, how many more do I have left to suffer? Murderers serve less time than I have.

Grumbling at the fucked-up world I live in, I make my way to my patrol car parked at the back of the dimly lit parking lot. I'm so stunned by the events of my night my steps are slow and sluggish. The beginning of my night played out exactly as I expected: Damon wants money. The last part... fuck, I never saw that coming.

Savannah is back.

Finally.

Out of all the places I anticipated seeing her again, I never thought it would occur at a strip club. Don't get me wrong, Vipers has had a dramatic facelift since the days my dad disgraced it with his presence, but it is still way below the standards of a woman with qualities like Savannah's.

Perhaps that is why I was shocked into rudeness. Savannah was only a girl the last time I saw her. Now, she's a woman—*one hundred percent.* My cock is still throbbing from recalling her scent. Although it was a little muskier than usual, her familiar rose aroma was in abundance.

Shaking my head at my body's ludicrous response to her closeness, I open the driver's side door and slide inside the warm cab. Just like Savannah is no longer a girl, I'm not a teen either. My body should *not* have responded the way it did. I'm a grown man, for fuck's sake. I don't get raging boners at stripper establishments. I'm a well-respected and dedicated member of law enforcement. I am not a teen praying to have his dick sucked. I don't care how pillowy her lips looked with her vibrant red lipstick. I'm not interested in having Savannah Fontane suck my cock.

I sure as hell hope that sounded confident to you, as it was nothing but a string of lies to my ears.

Peeved, I jab my key into the ignition. I tell myself on repeat that Savannah and anyone associated with her are not my business.

She's not my girl.

She is not my worry.

She's not even my friend.

Does my brain listen? No, it doesn't.

I'm punching the Mercedes' license plate into the dashboard of my patrol vehicle without a second thought. I'm not planning to track Savannah down. I just want to know where she's been hiding the last few years.

The new equipment Isaac donated to the force six months ago brings up a match nearly instantaneously. The Mercedes' owner has no prior convictions, and his registration and insurance are up to date—*unfortunately*. The address on his record is for a new estate on the south side of Ravenshoe—the pretty, more affluent side of town.

A hiss of air parts my nostrils. Now I know why I haven't spotted Savannah. It's not often I get called to those parts of town.

With my heart thudding against my chest, I hover my index finger over the address highlighted in blue. One hit, and I can see firsthand where Savannah has been slumming it.

It's not stalking. It is my moral obligation to the public. If the Mercedes' owner is a take-your-woman-to-a-strip-club type of guy, who's to say he isn't a menace to society? I'll be doing the public a favor by taking a closer look at him.

THE WAY WE WERE

Right?

Right.

Then why the fuck does this feel so wrong?

Shutting down my inner monologue for a more appropriate time, I leave the scarcely lit parking lot, scanning up and down the street. Traffic isn't an issue. Since I'm on the outskirts of town, the usually densely packed roads are quiet. I'm just struggling to choose which road to take. The high one? Or the low one?

"Ah, fuck it," I grumble to myself, taking a left.

I'm taking the high road. I don't care that Savannah is back in town. It doesn't bother me in the slightest. She has her life, and I have mine—no misconception whatsoever. My body reacted like every man's body does when confronted by an old mate. Men are naturally promiscuous. We tend to think with our lower head before using the more controlled, smart one on our shoulders. My reaction was completely normal and wholly anticipated. If my cock hadn't responded the way it did, I would be worried.

I'm normal.

I'm a grown man.

I'm not thinking about Savannah Fontane's plump lips wrapped around my cock.

Growling at the number of lies I'm pumping out tonight, I guide my car into the underground garage of my apartment building faster than usual. The grinding of the metal frame is barely heard over my tires skimming across the concrete from me slamming on the brakes.

While clambering out of my vehicle, I wonder how many hoon calls the department will receive after my effort.

Needing to rid myself of the adrenaline pumping through my veins, I open the emergency exit stairwell next to the slick new elevator to begin my fifty-eight-story ascent. I've got nowhere to be and no one to impress, so arriving at my apartment covered in sweat won't affect anyone but me and my hot water bill.

By the time I walk into my recently purchased apartment, my muscles are aching, and I'm sweating profusely. With my brain working overtime to command my lungs to breathe, you'd think it would be clear of thoughts. Unfortunately, that isn't the case.

Even without much air in my lungs, there's enough for me to huff in annoyance. *She* doesn't deserve my thoughts. *She* left of her own choice, then married some twat-waffle who thinks gold paintwork makes his already overpriced ride look more expensive.

She isn't my problem.

I doubt I've entered Savannah's mind in the past ten years, so why the fuck am I killing myself to wipe her from mine?

Grumbling, I walk through my dark apartment, shredding my clothes on the way. One of the many good things about living alone is that no one nags me when I leave my smelly socks on the kitchen counter. Not that I've done that. But I could if I want to.

While waiting for the shower water to reach scalding, I toe off my shoes and then tackle my belt. My heavy breaths switch to frustrated grunts when I slide my trousers down my aching thighs. I'm still hard enough to bounce a nickel off. If I weren't conscious of keeping my drinks in my line of sight, I'd be suspicious Brax slipped Viagra into my whiskey. It wouldn't be the first time he's done that. He is the reason I rarely drink in public anymore.

I spent the entire night of New Year's Eve last year sitting in a booth at the Dungeon Nightclub like a noob. It wasn't that I didn't want to accept the numerous offers to dance. I just didn't want to explain why my pants were pitching a tent. If I had my gun, I would have shot Brax that night. I'd never been more humiliated in my life.

Well, except once.

But since I'm not thinking about her, I'll leave that little nugget on the back burner.

Steam billows around me when I step into my upright shower. The hot water is a godsend to my overworked muscles. I've just finished my seventeenth shift in a row. I'm beyond exhausted. I had planned to spend my five-day weekend watching baseball in my sweats while consuming my weight in sugar. I never intended to exhaust my muscles to the point of Jell-O. I'm shocked I can stand with how much my thighs are shaking.

The painful situation between my legs becomes more apparent when I run a suds-loaded shower puff down my body. I stare down at my erect cock, impressed by its determination but pissed by its lack of morals.

"She didn't just walk out on me. She left you high and dry too, bud."

After scrubbing my thighs clean, I return the shower puff to my midsection. My scrubs are a little harder than necessary, but so the fuck is my cock. It is extended well past the bumps in my midsection, announcing that this *situation* won't take care of itself...

Fuck it. I'm a man. I can take care of business if needed. I don't need anyone or anything. I've got everything I need right here.

After curling my hand around my rock-hard shaft, I glance over my shoulder. I don't know who I'm looking for. I've lived alone for the past five years. But since it's been even longer since I've fondled my cock, I want to ensure there are no witnesses.

Confident I'm alone, I glide my hand down my shaft. A pleasing zap shoots through the vein feeding my throbbing cock. This should feel wrong on so many levels, but it doesn't. It's too relieving to resemble anything less than pleasure.

I'm not stroking my cock because I can't get Savannah out of my mind. I'm doing it to ease my confusion. Until I tackle the reason for the lack of blood to my brain, I'll have no chance of working through my turmoil. This isn't about pleasure; it is about wit.

Yeah, right.

While increasing the speed of my pumps, I close my eyes and part my lips. The suds from the shower gel have eased the friction, leaving nothing but a smooth, silky glide. My heavy pants add to the steamy conditions when I scan my memory bank, seeking inspiration for my relief. I have plenty to work with. Not only were the women at Vipers barely clothed, they were beautiful. Exotic. Intoxicating.

Blonde with entrancing green eyes.

I grip my cock harder, punishing it for my mind's drift in focus.

I will not think about her and her puffy lips, cock-thickening eyes, and body that could bring mere mortals to their knees.

She's not the cause for the rock sliding between my slippery hand.

She isn't the reason I'm pumping my shaft at a rate faster than I've ever fucked.

She isn't the trigger for my breathless state, tightening balls, and the glistening of pre-cum on the crest of my shaft.

I'm not thinking about her.

I will not think about her.

She. Will. Not. Make. Me. Cum.

"Argh," I grunt when a stream of hot, thick cum rockets out of my cock.

The crystal clear memory of Savannah smiling in the seconds leading to her sucking down on my crown makes my climax one of the longest and most brutal I've ever had. I come like I've never come before, a climax that has my knees buckling more than my grueling late-night workout.

While resting my free hand on the tiles above my head, I slow the speed of my pumps. My breaths are even more ragged than they were when I climbed the stairwell of my apartment building, and my body is covered with sweat.

That was intense—*wrong*—but oh-so-fucking-good.

Although pissed Savannah's face was the first and last one to enter my mind during my pursuit for release, I'm not surprised.

It didn't matter how many times she sucked my cock when we were teens, she awarded me the same smile every single time. I used to think it was because she loved the effect she had on my body. Only now do I realize it wasn't about that—not in the slightest. She wasn't worshipping my cock because she loved the taste of my cum; she did it because she loved me.

I rarely had a moment of peace my entire life... except when Savannah's lips were wrapped around my cock. That is the one time the focus was solely on me and my pleasure. I didn't have to impress anyone or place anyone's needs above my own. It was all about me.

She sucked my dick because she loved me. Then she broke my heart because I told her she wasn't good enough.

I was a fucking idiot.

For years, I've blamed Savannah for every bad thing in my life. Not all the blame belongs on her shoulders. What I did was dumb and naïve, but the steps Savannah took afterward were just as stupid.

I can forgive her for ignoring me; I can forgive her for breaking my heart. But I can't forgive her for what she did to Chris.

She should have been there for him. She should have been there for me—but she wasn't.

She has no excuse, either. I used money I didn't have to place notices of Chris's funeral in every newspaper in the country. It was plastered over social media and shared by the mutual friends we had amassed over the years. I didn't do that because I wanted to see Savannah again. I did it so Chris would know he was loved.

He died thinking he was unloved. He killed himself because he couldn't see what was directly in front of him. I wanted to prove him wrong. I wanted him to know that he was loved—*is loved*. I wanted to ease the heavy burden on my shoulders since that day.

My best friend killed himself because I exposed secrets I never should have shared. I did that because I was hurting. I shifted my anger onto Chris to save myself the agony.

I killed my best friend because Savannah broke my heart.

I'm a fucking idiot.

CHAPTER 12

Savannah

"What the hell do you think you're doing?"

I stop twisting a daisy stem between my thumb and index finger to crank my neck to the owner of the angry voice. Although the late afternoon sun shadows his face from my view, I know who's accosting me in a cemetery without needing to see his features. He hasn't left my thoughts since I ran into him last month. *Ryan.*

While rising from my seated position, my hands sweep at the wetness on my cheeks. "Sorry, I didn't realize time had gone by so fast. Brax said you don't usually arrive until five."

"You're talking to Brax now?" Ryan replies, stepping out of the shadows.

The anger in his voice matches his snarl. His beautiful

features are hardened with anger, and lowered lids hide his blue irises.

I dust my dew-stained hands on my backside. "Ah... Yeah. Long story."

I wish I could offer a more confident reply, but I'm so unaccustomed to this side of Ryan that I'm void of a better response. I've never seen him so aggressive. I didn't think he knew how to snarl, much less direct it at a woman. I guess it isn't solely my personality that's done a one-eighty the past ten years. Ryan's has been overhauled as well.

"I'm sorry I broke your tradition. I just wanted him to know he's in my thoughts." I drift my eyes to Chris's headstone during my last sentence.

Just seeing his name engraved in stone causes a fresh upwelling of tears. He was too young to die—*way* too young.

Ryan adjusts the six-pack of beers resting on his hip while muttering, "You didn't show up to say a final goodbye, so why bother now?"

"I beg your pardon?" I ask, certain I heard him wrong.

I didn't. He straightens his spine, locks his squinted gaze with mine, then repeats his sneered comment without remorse.

I glower at him, feeling my anger wind up from my stomach to my throat. My cheeks heat, and my fists ball. I've never been more angry, but since my respect for Chris is higher than my desire to tackle the significant chip Ryan's shoulder has grown the past few years, I harness the urge—barely.

After snatching my hoodie from the ground, I kiss Chris's headstone then make a beeline for the cemetery's only exit.

I'm not even three steps away from Ryan when he snarls out, "That's it, Savannah. Run away like you always do."

I spin on my heels so fast my hair smacks my flaming cheeks. "I'm not running. I am leaving before you make a fool out of yourself."

He laughs, apparently amused. "Well, I guess that's different. Why didn't you just say that?" He places his beer on the blades of grass my sweater flattened before dropping his eyes to Chris's headstone. "Can you believe this shit? She made me look like an idiot for years, but now she's worried about me stepping up to the plate to wield the bat she's been swinging for years."

"Don't bring Chris into this," I say, my words hissing from my mouth like venom.

"Why not?" Ryan shrugs. "You're just as much to blame for his death as I am."

I take a step back, stunned. "Chris committed suicide. *No one* is to blame for his death. Not even himself."

I don't know what's more distressing: Ryan placing the blame for Chris's death on me or the fact he thinks he is also to blame. He may be a liar and a cheat, but what happened to Chris isn't his fault. I hate that Chris couldn't see through the darkness, but pointing fingers does more harm than good. I know that better than anyone.

"What happened isn't anyone's fault. Chris just wasn't himself—"

"How do you know that, Savannah? You weren't here for him. You didn't know what he was going through! He couldn't

142

THE WAY WE WERE

get out of bed without guzzling a can of beer first. He blamed himself for things that were out of his control. You couldn't even show up to his funeral, for fuck's sake, yet you feel you have the right to say what he was thinking! You don't know shit."

His words sting, but they don't stop me from saying, "I might not have been here, but I know *nothing* said or done would have changed the outcome. Chris didn't just take his life on a whim. He had been planning it for some time. That day just gave him an excuse to end the pain."

"No, it didn't because his pain didn't lessen. It got worse!"

The agony in his voice cuts me raw. This isn't about Chris. This is about Ryan.

Chris is at peace.

Only Ryan is left battling his demons.

Ryan steps closer to me, shadowing me with his frame that has nearly doubled in width from when he was a teen. "Why weren't you there for him? Why didn't you come home when he needed you?"

Tears stream down my cheeks when I see the sentences his mouth failed to produce.

"Why didn't you come back for me?"

"I wanted to be here. God, Ryan. When I found out what happened... what he had done, I immediately started packing. I didn't care about the risk, I wanted to go home. Chris wasn't just my friend, he was a brother I never had."

My hands sweep at my cheeks as I contemplate what to say next.

My pause is pointless when I stammer out, "They wouldn't

143

let me go. I begged them to let me attend the church service, but they said it wasn't safe."

I still recall the day I read about Chris's death in a national newspaper. My heart shredded into a million pieces when I was informed of his cause of death. He had always been the goofball, but those closest to him knew the man behind the shield. He had a huge heart—one too big for this world. That's why he lived his life so recklessly because he knew it would be short.

"You know Chris never intended to grow old, Ryan. He didn't want gray hairs or wrinkles. He said the picture on his headstone would be the hottest one in the graveyard." I drift my eyes to the smiling photo in the top right hand corner of his headstone. "He got his wish. Nothing said or done would have stopped him from achieving that."

After inhaling and exhaling three times to loosen the weight on my chest, I return my eyes to Ryan. The anger on his face has slipped away for confusion. He heard what I said but still doesn't understand what I mean, so I simplify it for him.

"I'm sorry I wasn't here for you, but don't mistake that as me not wanting to be here. I did everything I could to come home, but sometimes, no matter how hard you wish for something, it doesn't come true." I dance my watering eyes between his while saying, "We're living proof of that."

CHAPTER 13

Ryan

I watch Savannah race away from me with my heart in my throat, and my mind shut down. If I didn't know her as well as I do, I'd say her heart-tugging speech was a ruse to shift the topic away from us, but I know that isn't the case. Savannah speaks from her heart. She doesn't sugarcoat her replies or dress them up to be socially acceptable. Even if she knows what she's going to say will hurt you, she'll still say it, as she would rather tell the truth than lie.

Chris always joked that he would be the stud of the afterlife. I was so accustomed to his sick humor that I took it in stride. I never thought he meant it. Brax has often said the same thing Savannah just did, that nothing would have changed the outcome of that night, but I struggle to believe it.

What I did that morning hurt Chris. Was it enough for him

to take his own life? I don't know, but only one person can answer that question. He's resting in the ground I'm standing next to.

That has been the hardest issue for me to work through the past six years. I'll never know if I'm to blame for Chris's decision. I can only assume I am.

Upon hearing leaves crunching under boots, I peer over my shoulder. As anticipated, Brax is heading my way with a six-pack of beer and a bucket of wings.

We do the same thing every year.

We share beers with our brother.

"Was that Savannah?" Brax's tone is low, wary of how I will react.

"You didn't tell me you'd been speaking with her," I reply, answering his question with an accusation.

He smirks hesitantly. "You knew she was back. I didn't realize I had to update you on every conversation we have." He skirts past me before racking his knuckles on Chris's headstone. "Can't believe you left me to handle these two by myself. Talk about leaving a brother hanging."

I nearly have a go at him for using Chris as a decoy, but with memories of me doing the same thing to Savannah mere minutes ago filtering through my mind, I keep my mouth shut.

"Why were you talking to Savannah, Brax?" I stammer out before I can stop myself.

I snag a beer out of the six-pack I brought with me, mindful I'll need alcohol in my veins before hearing what he has to say. I can't remember the last time I spoke about Savannah without being intoxicated. I even chugged down four shots of scotch before I called Brax last month to advise him of her resurrection. He thought I was high, as usually he's the one who brings her up. Or my drunken self who doesn't know any better.

Brax waits for me to gulp down two mouthfuls of beer before saying, "She's renting my old apartment."

Malted liquid flies out of my mouth, spraying both Chris's headstone and Brax.

"You're supposed to share your beer with Chris, not my face," Brax mutters while using his shirt to clear the beer away.

"Savannah's renting your apartment? Since when?" You can hear the shock in my tone.

Brax shrugs like it's no big deal.

I don't understand his lukewarm response. This is a big deal —a *huge* fucking deal.

"I don't have a say about who moves into my old place. That shit isn't on my shoulders," Brax mutters, incapable of ignoring my glare for a second longer.

"Then how do you know she's renting your apartment?"

His nose scrunches. "She found some old photos my grandma had stashed in the back of the closet."

"So she just gathered they were yours?" I prompt, hurrying him along.

The suspense is fucking killing me. The address on the registration of the Mercedes that picked Savannah up last month is nowhere near Brax's apartment. Brax doesn't live on the poor side of Ravenshoe, but it's pretty fucking close. Going from Ravenshoe's equivalent of Bel-Air to the Bronx is a significant drop in residential status. Did that happen by Savannah's choice? Or did her well dry up?

I'm not saying the Mercedes' owner is Savannah's sugar daddy, but when the sky is dark and grumbling, I'll forecast a downpour. If he isn't her sugar daddy, their age gap is as nasty as the lukewarm beer I'm guzzling like soda.

After draining my beer in one chug, I dump it on the ground and then shift my eyes to Brax's amused gaze. "I swear to god, Brax, you have five seconds to tell me what you know before I introduce my fists to your teeth."

He throws his head back and laughs. "You two need to stop hanging out. I'm getting confused about who is who," he cackles, bouncing his slit eyes between Chris's headstone and me.

I punch him in the arm, inciting even more laughter.

Our friend is dead; he shouldn't be making jokes.

"Don't even go there, Ryan. That shit got old real quick six years ago," Brax warns, his voice void of his earlier humor. "If given a chance, Chris would rise from the dead just to kick your ass for all the shit you've been hanging yourself with since his death. Chris doesn't blame you for what happened. I don't blame you. Savannah doesn't blame you. So stop fucking blaming yourself. Chris made a choice. We have to live with it."

"This isn't about Chris. It's about *Savannah*," I whisper my last word, annoyed that I can't drop my inquiries for a few more hours. Today is the sixth anniversary of Chris's death. My focus shouldn't be on anyone but him.

Brax nudges his head to a section of grass across from him. "Make yourself comfortable, and we'll tell you everything we know." He speaks about Chris like he's still with us. Always has. Always will.

When I do as instructed, he keeps his word. "On my way out on a Friday night, I bumped into Savannah in the lobby of my building. She handed me the box of photos. I asked where she found them. She told me. End of story."

No, I'm not exaggerating. That's precisely what he says.

"Every time I've seen her since, she was as avoidant as you've been the past six years. She wouldn't even look me in the eye when speaking to me."

This shocks me more than finding out she isn't living in the fancy-schmancy house I may or may not have driven by multiple times the past month.

"Did you ask around town why she's back?" My tone is more inquisitive than friendly.

Brax takes a swig of his beer before nodding. "Yeah. I heard rumors, but none I'm willing to share."

"What does that mean?" The hammering of my heart echoes in my tone.

He stares me straight in the eyes. "That means I'm not doing the legwork for you, Ryan. If you want answers, ask the person who can give them to you."

I lick my suddenly dry lips. "Did you see her face on the way out? I don't think she's up for interrogation."

"Did *you* see her face on the way out? This interrogation is ten years in the making. It just isn't her head on the chopping block."

"And mine is?"

He shrugs for the second time, adding to my annoyance.

149

"She left, Brax. She walked out on *all* of us."

"You lied, Ryan. You walked out on her first."

I grit my teeth, struggling to hold in my retaliation. I did what needed to be done. Was it the right thing to do? At the time, yes. Do I regret what I did? Yes, every fucking day. But wading through the same shit time and time again isn't getting me anywhere fast. I can't change my past. I can only live with the consequences of my mistakes. Chris's death is a constant reminder of that.

Spotting the groove between my brows, Brax suggests, "Say what you want to say, Ryan. No one here will judge you. You judge yourself enough there isn't room for anyone else."

You might think he's being snarky, but I know better. He's pushing me to express myself as he has done for the past ten years. No. Scrap that—the past twenty-three years. Chris was the jokester. Brax is a realist. Just like Savannah, he calls it as he sees it.

"She's hiding something from me. I don't know what it is, but I know it's something major. You're not the only one she won't look in the eye. She pretended she didn't know me last month. If my huff didn't call her out as a liar, she would have fled. Who does that? Who acts like family isn't family?"

"A person who doesn't have any," Brax replies in an instant, his voice not angry or frustrated. He's just straight-up remorseful. "Where's her family, Ryan? Where are the people who have her back like I have yours, and you have mine? Have you looked into that? Or are you too busy analyzing every man she crosses paths with that you've missed what's really going on? Stop wondering who she is with and start wondering who is with her. If Chris's decision should teach us anything, it should be not to waste a moment. Regret doesn't end when you die, Ry. It follows you to the grave. Get rid of yours before it's the cause of your demise." Smirking at my slack-jaw response, he stands, then taps his knuckles on Chris's headstone. "I love you, brother. I'll see you soon."

After whacking my shoulder three times, he stalks in the direction Savannah fled only ten minutes ago. My gaped mouth doesn't close until the rumble of his Harley sounds like a mosquito buzzing away.

I'm frozen in both shock and awe. I always knew Brax would be a brilliant man, but he just floored me. Selfishness has never entered his vocabulary, but neither has compassion. He doesn't want an apology from Savannah. He doesn't need it. He has already forgiven her.

I wish I could do the same.

––––––––––

Another fifteen minutes pass before I say goodbye to Chris in the same manner Brax did. I would like to say our alone time was used wisely, but that would be way off the mark. I sat in silence, drinking beer and contemplating what Brax and Savannah said.

I've known about Savannah's return for a little over a month, but instead of investigating the reason for her sudden homecoming, I'm pretending she is still a missing person.

I guess old habits do die hard—even ones you'll do anything to ignore. Even anger couldn't stop my body from reacting to seeing Savannah again. Except this time, it wasn't just my cock getting excited—my heart went crazy as well. I've told myself every day for the past six years that I don't love Savannah. Not once has my heart believed my lies.

I'm disturbed from my thoughts when a shimmer of white secures my attention as I head back to my truck. Speaking of old habits... no matter how often I tried to sell my truck over the past decade, I never accepted a single offer. A collector of classic cars even offered me twenty thousand dollars above the asking price, yet I still couldn't let her go.

It isn't just the memories I have of Savannah in this truck that cemented her place in my life. It is the ones I have with my brothers. The years before things soured, Chris put more hours into her motor than I did. She belongs to him as much as she does me, so it isn't right for me to sell her.

After placing my empty beer bottles in the passenger seat of my truck, I snag the slip of paper tucked under the windshield wipers. "Abby Rowe," I mutter to myself, reading the name printed above a Florida state cell phone number.

I scan my truck's pristine paintwork, seeking any damage. Other than the scrape down the left-hand side I've never gotten around to buffing out, there doesn't appear to be any damage, so why was I left contact details?

Shrugging off the note as a woman too shy to approach me, I slide into the driver's seat and crank the ignition. She fires over with one turn. I don't know what Savannah did when she worked on my motor all those years ago, but she hasn't missed a beat since that day.

I find myself traveling the same route home as I have

numerous times in the past month. It isn't the direct route but the one that meanders by the Mercedes owner's address.

Even knowing Savannah doesn't live there hasn't stopped my curiosity. There's a connection I'm missing—I just know it.

As my truck glides down the pristine tree-lined estate, portions of Savannah's disclosure play through my mind like a movie. *"They wouldn't let me go. I begged them to let me attend the church service, but they said it wasn't safe."*

She said "them," not "him." Does that mean she didn't miss Chris's funeral because the old geezer she was shacked up with wouldn't let her go? She wanted to come, she just couldn't. But who would stop her from attending? And why would they think it wasn't safe?

I yank my truck off the side of the road when a disturbing thought smacks into me.

No... she wouldn't have.

I dial Regina's number on repeat. She retired over a year ago but is still the first person I call when seeking legal advice.

When she fails to answer my call for the fourth time, I dial the second person on my list.

It isn't who you'd expect.

"Izzy, do you have any contacts in the FBI?" I ask, not bothering to issue a greeting.

Izzy, my partner, giggles. "Hi, Ryan, nice to hear from you too."

I'm not surprised when a low growl follows her greeting. Isaac says he has no issues with me and Izzy working together, but he's full of shit. He has jealousy issues a mile long when it comes to Izzy.

I can't say I blame him. There's no way I'd let my girl work with a guy she kissed directly in front of me. He'd be locked up in a four-by-four cell, not her superior.

"Why do you need the FBI? I thought you hated them 'pissing on your turf.'"

Isaac's growl turns into a chuckle.

"Seriously, Izzy? You have me on speakerphone. What if I planned to whisper all those naughty thoughts into your ear like last week? We discussed this. Isaac can *never* know about us."

Isaac's laughter is nonexistent. "I swear to god, Ryan. I will kil—"

His words are drowned out by Izzy switching off the speaker. "Ryan! I can't believe you did that." She sounds breathless, like she's running. "You have no idea of the dangerous situation you've put me in. Now I have to calm the beast."

I'd be worried about her if she didn't sound so excited. I don't know why Isaac has trust issues with Izzy. She's as smitten by him as they come.

"You've got five minutes before Isaac breaks down the bathroom door. Get talking," Izzy warns.

She isn't joking. I can hear Isaac coercing her out of the bathroom. His tactics are not ones I'd use during a hostage situation. They make my stomach twist, and my dick shrink.

"Remember that girl I told you about on your first day at Ravenshoe PD...?"

"Savannah," Izzy fills in, impressing me with her memory.

I bite on my lip to hold my grin. "Yeah. She's back in town."

"Ah... so that's the house we've been 'monitoring' the past month." I can hear her smile in her words.

My eyes roll skywards. "Yeah, anyway, she said something today that didn't make sense... until you popped into my mind."

"Thinking about me on your days off? Maybe I should tell Isaac about the stories you've shared the past six months." She laughs, having no idea my days are being numbered for every second I steal her away from Isaac.

"I wasn't thinking about you, more your situation."

She sighs, faking disappointment.

I shake my head. No wonder why I was attracted to her. Her personality reminds me so much of Savannah.

"Do you still have access to the FBI database?" I ask, attempting to steer our conversation back on track.

This time, Izzy's sighs for real.

"Alex never saw me as a member of his team when I was an agent. There's no way I'd still have access to their servers," she replies, sounding annoyed. "Why? Do you think Savannah's disappearance has something to do with the FBI?"

Even though she can't see me, I shrug. "Probably not. I just don't want to leave any stone unturned."

She hums before suggesting, "You could call Alex and ask him?"

Now it's my turn to sigh.

"You worked together on Isaac's case. That means he sees you more as a friend than a foe." Her last two words are barely heard over the splintering of wood. "Isaac—"

"Goodbye, Ryan." Isaac disconnects my call, his farewell fast but not fast enough for me to miss the warning in his tone.

I'll pay for my tease. Maybe not this week. Maybe not next month. But it is coming.

I stare at my cell for several minutes, contemplating my next move. I've got nothing to lose reaching out to Alex, so why am I hesitating?

Because you don't want to face the truth. Savannah isn't hiding a secret from you, Ryan—she was just hiding from you.

Ignoring my inner monologue, I dial the number for the local FBI field office. Not even two seconds later, the operator directs my call to Alex's private cell.

"Alex Rogers," a deep, gruff voice greets.

"Hey, Alex, it's Ryan. Ryan Carter." I'm tempted to add on my credentials, but when he grunts, acknowledging he understands who I am, I don't bother.

"What can I do for you, Ryan-Ryan Carter?"

The mock in his tone shocks me. He's never been a jokey type of guy. I can't recall seeing him smile once when we worked together on Isabelle's kidnapping and attempted murder charges. I'm pretty certain only one thing will cause a smile to creep across his face: the arrest of Isaac Holt. Hate is a strong word, but I'm reasonably sure it is the right word to describe Alex's dislike of Isaac.

"I was hoping to get your help on a potential espionage case." It might be a stretch, but Alex won't give me any leeway if I don't make my investigation sound interesting.

"Espionage?" You can hear the eagerness in his voice.

"Yeah. I've only got a name, but if I get any more, I'll extend a branch to your team."

"What's the name?" he asks with curiosity in his tone.

156

I swallow the brick in my throat before replying, "Savannah Fontane."

Fingers tapping on a keyboard sound down the line before Alex grunts. "Nah. I've got nothing."

He's lying. A man as controlled—and, quite frankly, anal—as Alex doesn't use words like "Nah." He would also never admit to having nothing, even when he has sweet fuck all.

"You've got nothing?" I double-check, my tone advising I didn't miss his lie.

"Nope. Nothing."

I clench my jaw. I don't need to see him to know he's lying. I can hear it in his tone.

"Is there anything else I can help you with, Ryan-Ryan Carter?" he asks a short time later.

You not being such an asshole would be great.

Instead of saying what I really want to say, I reply, "What about any information on an Abby Rowe? Do you have anything you can share about her?"

I don't know what inspired me to ask. It could be a coincidence that Abby's name was placed under my wipers on the same day I ran into Savannah again, but I've never been a fan of flukes. It may not be full of roses, but only you influence your destiny. That way, you can't blame the outcome on anyone but yourself.

"Abby Rowe," Alex babbles, drawing my focus back to him.

My heart beats in an unnatural rhythm when he asks, "What do you want to know?"

CHAPTER 14

Savannah

"*D*id you park on the roadside again?" Jet chuckles to hide his suspicion.

I nod, preferring to lie without words.

"Do you want a ride to your car?" Hope echoes in his tone. He's offered me a lift every night for the past week. I always deny his request.

"I need to stretch out my muscles, or they'll seize up." Because I'm not lying, it comes out sounding as it should —honest.

Jet sighs heavily. "All right. I'll see you tomorrow?" Every night, without fail, his farewell is a question. I just don't know if he's questioning his dedication or mine.

"I'll be here," I reply, holding back the remainder of my reply. *Will you?*

Like he heard my unasked question, he replies, "I'll see you then."

After a hesitant wave, he guides his sedan out of the empty parking lot. I grimace when my eyes drop to my watch. It is a little past 4 a.m. My nights are getting later and later the past two weeks.

Since I don't want anyone to know I'm without transportation, I make sure I'm the last to leave each night. Pete sees it as dedication. Jet isn't as convinced. Thankfully, my walking days are numbered with my performance at Maison's scheduled for the end of next week.

Eight more nights—the countdown is on.

A short time later, tires rolling over gravel booms into my ears. I move to the far edge of the asphalt, protecting both myself and the driver. Rarely do any cars pass me at this time of night, but when they do, they're more startled by my presence than I am by theirs. I should probably get out in the sun more often. Then my bright white legs wouldn't be so glaring.

My heart rate breaks into a canter when the vehicle fails to pass in a reasonable amount of time. They slowly creep behind me, scaring me more than the prospect of an alligator having a late-night swim.

While washing down the bile burning the back of my throat with a swallow, I quicken my pace. I'm at least half a mile from the nearest residence, so screaming won't help, no matter how badly I wish it would.

It doesn't matter how many steps I take, the distance between me and the vehicle tailing me remains the same.

When my brisk strides break into a jog, the moisture

gleaming in my eyes nearly topples down my cheeks. I tell myself on repeat that I am safe and unknown, and no one will harm me, but my panic doesn't weaken in the slightest.

I got too comfortable.

Even if I believed I wasn't being followed, I should have changed my route more regularly.

God—how could I have been so stupid?

I'm practically panting, crying, and out of breath when the reason I'm being tailed is unearthed. Red, blue, and white flashing lights illuminate the nearly pitch-black sky, stopping both my sprint and my heart.

You'd think I'd be relieved a member of law enforcement is following me. I'm not. I don't trust anyone, much less those who *think* they have the power.

Besides, why are they following me? There's no law against walking on the roadside. If a sidewalk is unavailable, pedestrians are within their legal rights to use the edge of the road.

Believe me, I checked.

I secure my first full breath in nearly five minutes when a gritty voice streams through the passenger window of a dark blue sedan. "Car troubles?"

After clearing any evidence of panic from my eyes, I crank my neck to the voice a million years couldn't erase from my mind.

"Yeah, something like that," I breathe out heavily. Not having a car is technically a car problem, isn't it?

"Get in. I'll give you a ride home," Ryan offers, his speed as slow as my steps.

I smile, hoping it will soften my rejection before replying, "It's okay. I need the exercise."

My feet are killing me, but I'm not eager to amass more damage with my ego still nursing bruises from our exchange at Chris's gravesite last week.

"You're a mile out of town. Three from your apartment. No one needs that much exercise," Ryan interjects.

I feign shock at his admission. It's not my best acting job. I knew the instant I ran into Brax in the foyer of our building three weeks ago that my cover was blown. I was just grateful it occurred there and not at work.

"Savannah..." Ryan grumbles, sounding annoyed at my lack of response.

I stop walking so I can take in some deep breaths. I'm not tired. I am panicked. This could create an attachment I can't afford to make. This isn't just about me anymore. I'm not only risking my heart. I am risking hers as well.

Sensing my hesitation, Ryan pulls over and clambers out of the driver's seat. He doesn't approach me or utter a syllable. He just lets his eyes speak on his behalf.

You can trust me, Savannah.

I wish I could believe him. I'd give anything to pretend he never deceived me as he did. But ignoring one lie only opens the door for more.

I let him betray me once.

I won't fall for the same trick twice.

"Thank you for the offer, but I'm fine walking."

His lips tug as he struggles to hold in his sneer. "All right. Have it your way." He curls back into his vehicle before mumbling, "I'll just follow you the next three miles... with my lights on... maybe even my siren."

I swallow the brick suddenly lodged in my throat.

He's joking, right?

He wouldn't follow me through town like I'm a criminal.

Not only would that be highly embarrassing, but it would also gain attention—attention I don't want or need.

"Fine," I snarl, spotting the determination in his eyes. I mumble incoherently while sliding into his passenger seat and fastening my seat belt. "I can't pay you anything."

My eyes dart to Ryan when he says, "I wouldn't have any place to put the crumpled-up bills, anyway."

He keeps his eyes facing the road, acting like he didn't say what he just did. It is a pity the tic in his jaw undoes his Oscar-worthy performance.

"I'm not a ...I don't remove my clothes," I mumble, incapable of saying the word "stripper."

His teeth graze his bottom lip before he swings his eyes to me. "I know."

His blasé response knocks the wind from my lungs. He isn't confirming my admission because he believes me. He's stating a fact.

Has he seen me perform?

"How many times?" I blurt out before I can stop myself. When his eyes return to the road, I twist my torso to face him head-on. "How many times, Ryan?" Before he can answer me, the truth smacks into me. "You're the man in the suit the girls have been raving about all week."

I don't know why I sound peeved. Ryan isn't mine, so my

colleagues have every right to get giddy in his presence. I just preferred not knowing who they were gushing over. It didn't sting as much when I assumed it was a stranger.

Feigning disinterest, I stammer, "You're a fool for knocking back Melena's offer. Her lap dances start at two hundred dollars. I heard she offered you the *full* package for free."

When Ryan smirks, my back molars smack together. I return my slit eyes to the scenery whizzing by my window. I couldn't sound more jealous if I tried.

Although shocked by the excited rumblings through the dressing stations the past week, I didn't give two hoots who the gentleman in the suit was. Vipers attracts a range of men, so I just brushed it off as one of the many new clients amassed in the past two months. I had no clue it was the man who hasn't left my thoughts for a second the past decade.

While peering at Ryan's reflection in the window, another truth smacks into me. "Oh my god... that was you!" I rummage through the stash of notes in my purse like a madwoman, seeking the rare hundred-dollar bills I've already gained five times this week. "I knew Jet was full of shit. My tips didn't drastically increase because of my new routine. You sweetened the pot."

Ryan doesn't deny my claims.

He doesn't do anything.

That fuels my agitation even more.

I was blown away Monday night when my tips jumped from the low two hundreds to mid three hundreds. I had been mixing up my routine to keep things fresh for the regulars, but I was still anticipating a dip in tips, not an increase.

Now it makes sense.

"I'm glad you enjoyed my performance, but I'm not a charity case," I snarl, throwing three one hundred bills to Ryan's side of the cab.

I'm reasonably sure I owe him another two hundred dollars, but considering my comment about not being able to pay him for the ride wasn't a lie, the remaining bills must wait until later.

The money I was once ecstatic to earn floats through the air like feathers on a warm summer night. When they come to rest on Ryan's splayed thighs, he doesn't gather them in his hands or acknowledge their presence.

That pisses me off more than anything.

"You have nothing to say? *Nothing* at all?"

He scrubs his hand over the stubble on his chin, praying it will hide its manic tic.

It doesn't.

"Say what you want, Ryan. I'm a big girl. I can take it."

I clench my stomach, expecting his words to hit me square in the stomach.

I should have prepared an organ a few inches higher, as my heart is the only one sustaining a brutal blow when he snarls, "What would your dad say, Savannah? You work at a... *Club.* You're a..." He's as incapable of saying "stripper" as I am.

His words slice through me like a knife, but they don't stop my retaliation. "He'd be proud I'm putting one foot in front of the other and doing anything to keep my head above water—"

"By working at a strip club?" Ryan interrupts, shouting.

"Yes! If that is what it takes, that is what it takes!" I reply, my vocal cords hindered by tears begging to be released.

My body jerks to the side when Ryan abruptly yanks on the steering wheel, stopping his patrol car just before the 'Welcome to Ravenshoe' sign. "Then take my money. Use it for whatever the fuck you seem to think is more important than living with morals."

When he tosses the bills at my chest, I gather them, scrunch them up, and then return them to him as if they're trash. "Unlike *some* people, I do have morals." The way I sneer "some" leaves no doubt to whom I'm referring: him. "I don't lie, steal, or *cheat*. I'm earning a living. An *honest* living."

The fury blackening my veins doubles when my yank on the door handle fails to open it.

I scan along the doorframe, seeking the lock.

There isn't one.

Knowing self-locking doors are usually only installed in the back seat of patrol cars, I lean across Ryan's torso—ignoring his scrumptiously inviting scent—press the lock button, then throw open my door.

My ass hangs mid-air when a grumbled, "I didn't cheat on you," booms through my ears.

Believing the anger enveloping every inch of me is the cause of my poor hearing, I continue scrambling out of his car. My steps crunch on the asphalt, grinding the heels of my stilettos as severely as my teeth are gnawing together.

My dad would have never wished for me to live this life, but I still believe he is proud of me. The beliefs he raised me with have kept me fueled for the past five years. If I didn't have him guiding me, my life would be a hundred times worse. Ryan may think I've hit rock bottom, but he's not seeing the entire picture. My morals might not be as shiny as they once were, but my self-respect is high.

My dad's favorite quote will never leave me: "Work for a cause, not for applause. Live to express, not to impress." If I had other options, I would take them. But when you're required to work forty hours a week just to pay the exorbitant rent on a rundown apartment, you must look at alternatives. It may be unfair and unjust, but it isn't unreal. Many people in America are worse off than me, so who am I to complain?

When the sky opens up, adding to the moisture gliding down my cheeks, I lower my hoodie to shield my eyes. Although Ryan hasn't said anything, I know he is still following me. I can see his headlights, but they're not the reason I can sense his presence. I can feel it in my bones.

When the sprinkling of rain turns torrential, Ryan's patrol car glides to my side. "Get in the car, Savannah, or you'll catch pneumonia."

I continue walking, acting like I didn't hear a word he spoke.

"Savannah... for once, stop being so goddamn stubborn." His pause is worthless. He's angrier now than he was at the gravesite last week.

His remark rolls off my shoulders like water rolling off a duck's back.

If he thought I was stubborn when we were younger, he has no clue.

"Savannah..." He lines up the front quarter panel of his

patrol car to within an inch of my bare, quivering thigh. "Get. In." He's not asking. He's demanding.

My steps don't slow. I know he won't hurt me, so I have nothing to fear.

I sneak a glance out of my hoodie when a deep rumble booms through my ears. The source is evident when I spot a furious Ryan stomping my way.

Before I can demand he stop, he curls one arm around my waist while his other hand clamps my shrieking mouth.

I wail with so much force I lose a stiletto halfway to his patrol car.

When kicking his shins fails to loosen his grip, I shift my focus to his hand covering my mouth. I bite down without reservation, returning the pain his snarled comments inflicted to my heart.

"Jesus Christ," Ryan sneers when my teeth break through the skin on his hand. "You're not an animal. You don't bite people."

When his damaged hand falls from my face, I scream with all my might. I'm not in fear for my life. I am fearful of my body's response to his closeness. My nipples are budded, and the wetness between my legs can't be entirely blamed on the rain.

I'm angry, so I should *not* be horny.

My screams for help are muffled when Ryan throws me into the back seat of his patrol car. I really shouldn't say throw. He doesn't quite throw me, but he doesn't place me gently either. He kind of tosses me in there.

After sucking in a deep breath to clear the inane spark of lust in my eyes, I crawl to the door Ryan is in the process of slamming shut. My body's reactions are ludicrous but also anticipated. During my first three months of college, Ryan and I had many late-night discussions about what we planned to do in his patrol car's back seat. My memories are detailed—*very* detailed. They have kept my self-coping mechanisms well-stocked for the past ten years.

My endeavor to flee like a criminal is lost when the back passenger door comes to a stop within an inch of my nose.

Like I could act any more idiotic, I bang my fists on the window. "Let me out. I haven't done anything wrong."

My thumps wobble the glass, but they don't incite a reaction from Ryan. He merely collects my discarded shoe from the roadside before curling into the driver's seat.

Because his anger is so hot, steam billows around him when he cranks the heater.

"Let me out," I demand, speaking through the little circles in the plexiglass wedged between us. "This is illegal. You are an officer of the law. You can't kidnap people."

"I'm not kidnapping anyone," Ryan snarls while tugging on his belt. "I'm arresting you."

"For what?" Shock resonates in my tone.

He swings his squinted gaze to me, forcing me to swallow. I've never seen him so angry.

"You attacked an officer of the law. *That* is illegal, so I'm within my right to arrest you."

"I didn't attack you. I defended myself." I fold my arms over my chest, acting unaffected by his threat. "Go ahead, arrest me. Then, when my charges are thrown out of court, I'll sue you for every penny you have."

I see the pegs of his teeth in the rearview mirror when he flashes me an angry grin. "I already gave you every penny I have, Savannah." The divider blocks me from seeing what he nudges his head to, but I don't need to see the bills to know what he's referring to. "I ain't got any more to give."

"You *haven't* got any more to give," I correct. I'm not so annoyed that I'll miss an opportunity to correct his grammar as he had always done to me.

Ryan huffs but remains quiet. I mimic his stance. I'm not worried. He doesn't have a vindictive bone in his body. He'll drive me home, I'll leave without thanking him, and then he'll go back to avoiding me like he as the past few weeks.

No skin off my nose.

My calm, collected composure continues to crack the further we travel. Ryan didn't take a left on Rainer Circle. He turned right. We cannot reach my apartment building by traveling this route. It has only one entry and exit point. It is the reason I chose to rent it.

"You're not really arresting me, are you?" I scoot to the edge of my seat.

Ryan lifts his baby blues to the rearview mirror but remains as quiet as a mouse.

"Please," I beg, my tone revealing I'm not below getting down on my hands and knees.

After the tumultuous few years I've had, the last thing I need is my name on an arrest warrant. I don't care about facing charges. It is who may see my name that has my heart sitting in my throat.

I stop peering at Ryan in the rearview mirror when we stop

169

outside a large, mansion-like house on a pretty tree-lined street. Nothing against Ryan, but I'm reasonably confident this isn't his home. The clothes I've seen him in the three times we've run into each other indicate he's more financially stable than his parents ever were, but he wouldn't have the means to purchase a house like this.

Ravenshoe's real estate prices haven't just boomed in the years since I left; they have skyrocketed out of the universe. Even an average apartment costs more than a standard home in other states.

"Whose house is this?" I ask Ryan, confident I've never seen it before.

This area was nothing but dirt hills when I lived in Ravenshoe. Ryan, Chris, Brax, and I used to ride our bikes through the tree-studded landscape when we were kids.

Before Ryan can answer my question, a shiny gold Mercedes reversing out of the driveway solves my confusion.

Shit.

"You willingly entered the car of a man you didn't know," Ryan growls, his words as low as my heart rate. "What if he was a rapist? Or even worse, a murderer?"

"He wasn't—"

"But what if he was!" Ryan interrupts, yelling so loudly the veins in his neck bulge.

He glares at me in the rearview mirror, his chest rising and falling in rhythm with mine. "You were so desperate to get away from me you put your life at risk."

Once again, he isn't asking a question; he's stating a fact.

I return his stare, preparing to lie but unable to.

"Jesus Christ, Savannah," Ryan seethes when I nod, agreeing with him.

I was desperate to get away from him.

"That night hurt me," I mumble, my words barely a whisper. "You were so angry. You *are* so angry." I glance down at my hands, incapable of looking at him while admitting, "I don't understand why you hate me."

"I don't hate you!" He lightens his stern tone before saying for the second time, "I don't hate you. I'm just... confused. Angry. Annoyed."

Air puffs from my nose. "Take what you are feeling and multiply it by a hundred, then you'll experience half of what I felt when the man who promised he'd never let me down did."

The rawness of my words shocks me. It has been ten years, yet I still can't get past his betrayal. Losing my father broke me —but Ryan's betrayal utterly destroyed me.

I float my eyes up from my hands when Ryan says, "I didn't cheat on you, Savannah. I would *never* betray you like that."

"You—"

"Lied. I lied. That's all I did. I didn't cheat." He swivels his torso to face me head-on, ensuring I can see the honesty in his eyes. "I broke my promise. I deceived you. But I didn't cheat. There was *never* anyone else. *There has never been anyone else.*" His last sentence is so low I'm unsure if he meant to express it out loud.

"Why would you do that? Why pretend you had moved on?" I try to mask my shock. I fail. I'm so stunned, I am surprised I can speak.

Tears pool in my eyes when he replies, "I wanted you to leave me."

"Then why not just break up with me?"

His Adam's apple bobs up and down twice before he mutters, "I couldn't give you up. *I still can't.*" His low tone reveals I wasn't supposed to hear his last confession.

He tilts his torso back to the front, starts his patrol car, and then begins to drive again like he has no clue he's left my heart hanging by a thread.

I want to speak. A million thoughts stream through my brain, but not a syllable escapes my mouth. I'm not just shocked into silence. I am heartbroken. I gave up my entire existence because I thought he had betrayed me. That lie changed my life in more ways than Ryan could ever comprehend.

Some were good, but the majority were bad.

"Thank you," I force out when Ryan releases me from the confines of his vehicle at the front of my apartment building.

I lean in to kiss his mouth before stopping.

His confession didn't change anything.

He still deceived me.

It may not have been with another woman, but he still lied.

"Savannah," Ryan whispers when I pull back, leaving his cheek untouched.

"I just..." I sigh heavily. "I need time. *We* need time," I add when I see the strain on his face.

I'm not the only one who has had a difficult few weeks. He appears as exhausted as me. Dark circles ring his alluring blue eyes, and his usually clear skin is mottled. He's missed as much sleep in the last decade as I have.

"I'll... uh... see you around?" I don't know why that sounded like a question.

When Ryan nods, I spin on my heels and head to the foyer of my building.

I halt midstride when he asks, "Will you stop working at Vipers?"

I exhale a deep breath before pivoting to face him. "No," I reply, hitting him with the honesty I wish he had bestowed upon me ten years ago. "It may not be a reputable job, but it is still a job. It pays my bills."

A deep groove settles between his brows. "The people you work with—"

"Are my friends," I interrupt, stopping him before he says something he may regret.

"Jet is—"

"I know, Ryan. *I know*. But before you judge Jet or any of the women I work with, remember their family and friends are judging me in the same light. Anything you say about them, you are saying about me."

The torment on his face doubles. "You're not *them*."

Pretending we aren't talking like strangers in the middle of a downpour, I step closer to him. "I'm not like all of them, but I wish I were some of them." When his brows stitch in confusion, I add, "Syndi, the young brunette manning the main door..." I wait for him to nod, acknowledging he knows who I'm referring to. "She works at Vipers to pay her brother's college tuition. When he gets drafted, she plans to join him in his host city. Chastity, Rowena, and Nelly are only months from graduating. And Jet... he's clean and getting his life back on track. Some women strip for the wrong reasons, but there are just as many who do it for the right reasons. But even then, it isn't our job to judge them, Ryan."

Only a few short weeks ago, my mindset matched Ryan's. Once I learned more about my coworkers, I realized I had no right to ridicule them or their decisions. They welcomed me into their group with open arms, yet I was judging their choices instead of their personalities. I was wrong—both then and now.

"I'm sorry you don't agree with my decision, but it is my choice to make. This is my body, which means I'm the only one who chooses what to do with it."

He scrubs at the stubble on his chin before nodding, once again agreeing with me. He's not happy, but his beliefs on women having the right to choose what they do with their bodies means he'll concede—for now.

After dropping his hand from his face, he lifts his eyes to me. "Are you going to continue walking home like you have every night the past week?"

Hiding my shock that he is more aware of my routine than he first let on, I reply, "Yes."

His hands ball into fists before he asks, "Can I drive you?"

"No," I reply, shaking my head.

I'm not denying his request to be spiteful. I am doing it because he looks tired. His position puts his life in jeopardy every day. If anything happened to him, I'd forever wonder if I was at fault. I've got enough guilt on my plate. I don't need more.

Ryan's chest puffs high as he sucks in a large breath. The rain hasn't let up the past fifteen minutes, but we stand amongst it, not the least bit enticed to seek shelter. I'm happy for the downpour to hide the wetness in my eyes, and Ryan uses it to cool his flaming cheeks.

After what feels like an eternity, Ryan says, "Sorry… let me rephrase it in a way you will understand. I *will* drive you home every night."

The demand in his voice shouldn't be exciting, but it is. He isn't an overly cocky guy, but a lack of confidence has never been his weak spot. He exudes self-assuredness but without the arrogance that usually comes on the side.

"Thanks for the offer—"

The remainder of my sentence rams into my throat by Ryan spinning on his heels and stalking away from me. "Just like I have no right to tell you what to do, Savannah, you can't moderate my decisions. I'll wait for you out back tomorrow."

"Ryan…" I pace closer to him, equally angered and pleased by his determination.

He continues walking, acting as if he didn't hear me.

"Ryan!" I shout, annoyed by him ignoring me.

"Goodnight, Savannah," he says, curling into his driver's seat. He glances at the clock on his dashboard. "Or should I say good morning, considering it is 5 a.m.?"

"You can say whatever you like, I'm still not accepting your offer!" I shout my last six words to ensure he hears them through his now-closed door.

Grinning in a way that heats every inch of my body, he reverses out of the parking lot and drives away.

175

CHAPTER 15

Savannah

"*W*here does he go?" Jet asks while handing me a towel to run over my sweat-drenched head.

I watch Ryan dart across the packed floor of Vipers before answering, "I don't know."

As he's done the past seven days, Ryan arrives seconds before my performance, then leaves after it finishes. Considering I perform three times a night, he's either using his badge to enter without paying the fee, or Pete is lining his pockets with Ryan's hard-earned money.

I don't know which theory annoys me more.

"Maybe you should ask him during your commute home?" Jet suggests, shadowing me to my dressing station, his words breathy from a concealed chuckle.

"That would mean we'd have to communicate with more

than one or two words," I reply before stuffing my cosmetics into my bag.

Jet doesn't hide his laugh this time around. "That would help."

My eye roll looks classier than it should.

As he insinuated last week, Ryan arrives at Vipers every night to pick me up.

Our shameful routine matches our first tussle in the rain— minus gnawing teeth and visits to strangers' houses.

Since I refuse to enter Ryan's patrol vehicle, he forces me into the back seat.

Unfortunately, last night's exchange wasn't solely witnessed by Jet and a handful of waitresses but also by Ryan's partner.

Talk about embarrassing. His partner isn't just pretty. She's downright gorgeous. Fortunately, I spotted the ginormous rock on her ring finger, or the jealousy I've been struggling to rein in the past week would have surfaced more than ever.

Ryan flees the main floor before the silk around my thighs has been removed, but that doesn't stop Viper patrons and staff from approaching him. Although grateful he hasn't accepted any of the offers bestowed upon him, I'm still annoyed.

How many rejections does it take to get the hint?

In Melena's case, the sky is the limit.

She's sitting at fifteen this week alone and still chipping away at Ryan's resolve.

"Prune juice."

I stop tying the laces on my running shoes to lock my eyes with Jet. "Prune juice?"

Not spotting my confusion, he nods. He maintains his

straightforward, carefree composure for two seconds before it comes undone. "Prune juice will take care of the constipated look on your face. Or a dick in your ass. Whatever you prefer."

My mouth gapes. "I'm not constipated."

"So choice B, then," he replies, still laughing.

"I'm not shoving a dick up my ass." I don't know why I'm whispering. The conversations I've heard at Vipers could fill fifty erotic books. "It's not the hole I want filled."

Now it's Jet's turn to be stumped.

He glowers at me, his mouth opening and closing like a fish out of water.

I rib him with my elbow, causing him to gasp in a sharp breath. "Don't act surprised. I'm a woman. I have needs—"

"And now my cock could drill the Arctic," he interrupts, adjusting his crotch.

Unappreciative of my faint giggle, he sneers, "If I didn't appreciate my freedom, I'd stuff your laughter down your throat with my cock." He grips the back of my head before gyrating his hips toward my mouth.

"Such a charmer," I tease, knowing he's only playing.

He can have the pick of any girl, so why would he choose me?

He waits for me to sling my bag over my shoulder before asking, "If you're not going to take me up on my offer, you've got another suitor dying for the same chance."

"I'm not going out with Gerald," I reply, gagging.

Gerald is a regular who's been to more of my shows than Ryan. He seems nice, but dyed combovers and button-up Hawaiian shirts aren't my thing.

Jet flicks two fingers between my brows, demanding the return of my focus. "I'm not talking about Gerald. It is someone much hotter but not quite as handsome as me." He dusts his fingers over his chest.

I roll my eyes. "Well… that could only be one person…"

Jet nods, assuming I've caught on.

I haven't.

"… Pete?"

"What? No!" His voice is so loud it startles my heart as much as my ears. "My god, Savannah. You are lucky you're gorgeous." He whispers my name to ensure those surrounding us don't hear it. "I'm talking about Ryan. The guy who rocks up here every night to drive you home. He isn't doing that to be friendly. He wants inside your panties."

I huff, wishing what he says is true. "Ryan doesn't want to sleep with me. He's been there, done that. He isn't interested. He is just being civil. It is the way he is. He is a gentleman. Nothing will change that."

"A gentleman who wants to fuck you like you've never been fucked." He rocks his hips while making inappropriate moans. "He wants to give you the best sex you've ever had."

I throw my fist into his stomach, winding him. "Once again… been there, done that."

Jet makes a pfft noise. "You said he was a virgin?"

"Yeah, so?"

He cocks a brow. "That means he didn't have a fucking clue what he was doing. He probably didn't find your G spot, much less make you orgasm."

My teeth graze my bottom lip as my mind wanders. Just like

me, Ryan was a virgin, but that didn't stop him from knocking it out of the park. That man knew what to do and *precisely* how to do it. The sex was mind-blowing.

I fan my flaming red cheeks while saying, "Trust me, he knew what he was doing."

I'm prepared to say more, but I don't need to. Jet's wide eyes reveal he believes me.

After shoving a lollipop into his mouth, he asks, "If he was hitting sixes back then, imagine his skills now."

I groan. "Don't say that."

"Why? Tempted?"

I nearly lie, but I swallow my words when I recall how many lies I've told over the past five years.

"More jealous than tempted," I admit.

I want Ryan to be happy, but I hate the idea of him with anyone but me.

"You don't have to be jealous, Savannah. He's there, waiting for you like he's always been."

I wish I had as much confidence in Jet's declaration as he does, but I don't. Ryan hasn't indicated that he dislikes me, but he's not put out any feelers either. He is the most guarded he's ever been. I can't read what he had for dinner, much less gauge his reaction to my resurrection.

I'm flying solo for the first time in the twenty-five years I've known him.

It's a scary, tormented flight.

When I throw my gym bag over my shoulder, Jet asks, "Same time tomorrow?"

My pout morphs onto his mouth when I shake my head. "I

took Saturday off, remember?"

He stares at me like I told him I'm performing open heart surgery with a butter knife and a pair of tin snips.

"I have my performance at Maison's Bordello tomorrow night. Although the possibility of a double payday is appealing, I don't think I can perform four times in one night."

"Oh...."

Jet's reply is not an informative "oh."

It is a worried one.

"Sunday?"

After twanging my bottom lip, he nods. "I'll be here. Will you?"

My frown turns into a smirk. "You haven't gotten rid of me yet."

He half-heartedly nods. "Give him time. He'll soon wear you down."

He doesn't need to say Ryan's name for me to know who he's referencing. Every night Ryan drives me home, Jet's suspicions grow. He's just waiting for me not to arrive the next day.

He has no reason for concern. Ryan doesn't have the means to look after me, and in all honesty, I don't want him to. I love that Ryan is a working-class man. Everything he has, he earned himself. Even when peeved with jealousy, I admire that about him.

"Bye." I kiss Jet's cheek. Abby Rowe may not kiss her friends goodbye, but Savannah Fontane does, even when he makes her ugly green head rear for the first time in a decade.

CHAPTER 16

Savannah

The first person I spot when I exit the back door of Vipers is Ryan. Unlike the past week, he isn't leaning against his patrol car. His knee is cocked and braced on his truck.

The very same truck he owned when he was a teen.

The truck we...

I fan my cheeks, suddenly overheated.

"Night off?" I push off my feet to head Ryan's way.

His foot falls from his truck, his braced stance indicating he's ready to chase me if I run.

"Yep," he replies, eyeing me hesitantly.

The hardness in his eyes weakens when I glide my hand along the overworked curve of his front fender. "She's always had entrancing curves," I murmur on a breathy moan.

I've always loved Ryan's truck.

I'm glad to see he has taken good care of her for the past decade.

"Yeah, she has," he replies, his voice drenched with candor.

When I raise my eyes, he drops his from my skirt-covered backside to his feet.

My smile grows when I notice he's wearing running shoes.

"Come prepared tonight?"

I inwardly cringe. My voice is *way* too husky. I sound like I'm seconds from climaxing. *Damn Jet and his nosey-nancying.*

Now I'm not solely looking at the attractive attributes visible outside Ryan's clothing. I'm thinking about the desirable ones his clothes are hiding.

The chance of dampening my excitement flies out the window when Ryan smirks a boyish grin. It does wicked things to my insides—things I shouldn't be feeling.

"You snooze, you lose," he murmurs, his words as breathless as my lungs.

I tap my tennis shoes together to show I understand his challenge. The scuffs on my stilettos can't be undone, and my walls are slowly crumbling.

Ryan was the first man to break through my walls years ago, so it is logical he is the same one breaking through them again ten years later.

"Why do you show up every night, Ryan?" My voice isn't angry or snarky. I'm not looking for a fight. I am honestly curious to hear his reply. "Your disapproval of my choices was expressed without hesitation last week, so why subject yourself to it over and over again?"

His shoulder touches his ear when he shrugs. "Who am I to judge your choices?"

I'm tempted to shout, "My boyfriend and lover," before I realize he's neither of those things.

I don't even know if he is my friend.

We've spoken more tonight than we have the past week.

Before I can voice a more suitable reply, Ryan's cell buzzes. While keeping one eye on me, he digs it out of his pocket. My thighs press together when a blistering smile stretches across his face.

Damn, I've missed this man's grin.

As quickly as excitement blazed my veins, anger follows it. That smile wasn't elicited by a message from Brax. That's his smile when he's wooing someone out of her panties. I know this because it was the one he always gave me while sliding my panties down my thighs.

My first thought is to slap his phone out of his hand before inflicting my anger on his cheek, but since he suffered a violent childhood, I harness my anger before resorting to the tactic I always use when times get rough.

I run.

With my endeavor to evade Ryan at fever-pitch, I charge for the bush instead of the roadside, reaching it in three heart-thrashing seconds. Because Ryan is distracted returning the message of the person responsible for him grinning like a lovesick idiot, he fails to notice I'm fleeing until I am three to four hundred feet into the scrub.

I realize he's spotted me when he mutters, "For fuck's sake, Savannah."

Peering over my shoulder, I watch him put away his phone before he pushes off his feet to chase me down. It's ludicrous to think I can outrun him, but I sprint like the finish line is in my sights.

The prickly hedges scratch my thighs, but I ignore them, more determined than ever.

Ryan's long strides catch up with me as I reach an opening near the freeway.

I've barely forced out my first set of demands when he opens the passenger door of his truck to throw me inside.

Yes, I said throw, as that is precisely what he does this time.

Luckily for me and my short temper, his truck doesn't have the means to keep me contained like his patrol car does.

Even our exchange being witnessed by over a half dozen spectators doesn't weaken my determination. I charge for the scrub like I'm outrunning an axe murderer, my strides as spirited as my resolve.

Ryan nips at my heels two seconds later. He curls his arm around my waist, hoisting me so far off the ground my shoes run on air.

"You can't outrun me, Savannah. I chase criminals for a living. It's my job," he murmurs into my ear as he walks us back to his truck, his steps not as hurried this time.

My frantic wails come to a shrieking halt. I can't fight him— I'm too busy calming the inane pulse his gritty voice caused to my sex. If the force doesn't work out for Ryan, he should consider book narration. He'd have the readers' panties damp just from reading the copyright notice.

While pinning me to his truck with his body, he opens the

door I slammed shut during my evasion. I'm not going to lie. Not all my breathlessness is from fleeing. Some—*if not all of it*—is from having every inch of his hard body pressed against mine.

He has always had a nice build, but he's added a few pounds of muscle in the past ten years, making his body not just nice but mouthwateringly impressive.

My spine snaps straight as disturbing notion after disturbing notion filters through my head. He was sexting another woman, yet I'm grinding against his crotch like his cock is a metal detector, and I have a treasure chest lodged up my ass.

What the hell is wrong with me?

"Let me go, Ryan," I demand with anger dangling on my vocal cords.

"No," he replies without pause for thought.

He shoves me into the passenger seat of his truck before sprinting for the driver's side door.

With the encouraging cheer of my colleagues, I open the door he just shut and commence sliding out.

I don't even get a foot on the ground before Ryan's impressive body fills the doorframe.

Snarling, I clamber for the driver's side door.

Ryan's torso warms my back two seconds later.

And thus begins a vicious game of cat and mouse.

Our audience grows in size with every back-and-forth exchange. If there wasn't a weird, sick, demented part of me relishing Ryan's resolve, I'd be peeved at the attention. But with playfulness warming my heart and core, my anger is kept at bay.

Ryan's face displays his annoyance, but that isn't the only insight his panty-wetting features reveal. He's also thankful for the challenge. He isn't overly competitive, but he's still a man nonetheless. He loves the chase as much as any red-blooded man. To some men, this type of foray is as good as foreplay.

To some women as well.

I swear my panties have never been so drenched. Last week I argued that my morals hadn't up and left town. Now, I'm not so sure. Am I so desperate for attention that I'm willing to pretend I didn't see what I saw? Wasn't turning a blind eye what got me in this position to begin with?

I'm not doing that again. If I can't be myself around a man I've known since I was four, who can I be honest with?

"Who was she?" I ask, stopping Ryan's trek from the passenger door to the driver's door midstride.

He peers at me, sitting in the middle of his bench seat with confusion slashed across his handsome features. "Who?"

I pray to keep jealousy out of my voice before replying, "The woman you were smiling about earlier. Who is she?"

For once, my prayers are answered.

Ryan remains still, either shocked into silence or striving to weasel out of an awkward situation.

I realize it is neither when he locks his eyes with mine and says, "You, Savannah."

Confusion engulfs me. He's a woeful liar, but when he's looking directly at me, he has no chance of hiding his deceit, so why bother?

"I didn't send you a message." Confusion echoes in my tone.

He smiles, then nods. "I know. But the message wasn't *from* you. It was *about* you."

Spotting my growing bewilderment, he adds, "Izzy wanted to know if I needed backup tonight. I told her I had everything covered." He licks his dry lips, drawing a moan from a female spectator watching our exchange from the sidelines. "I have everything covered, don't I, Savannah?"

Before I can utter a syllable, a female voice purrs, "Oh, yes, you do, *Officer Carter*." She enunciates his name with the same seductiveness I used when coercing him to join the force over a decade ago.

With a snarl, I swing my eyes to the voice. I'm not surprised to discover the seductive purr belongs to Melena.

Utterly oblivious to the half-dozen eyes glowering at her, she twists the rope scarcely concealing her monstrous rack from the public between her thumb and index finger while her hungry eyes burn into Ryan's profile.

I'm five seconds from telling her to row up shit creek without a paddle when the air in my lungs brutally evicts. Since I was distracted issuing a vicious glare to Melena, Ryan snuck up on me unawares.

While whispering in my ear that he has everything covered, he tugs me out of his truck.

Ignoring the excited hollering of my coworkers encouraging me to fight—and the disappointed sigh of Melena—he stomps around the wooden bed of his truck, holds open the door with his foot, then slides into the driver's seat, taking me with him.

Since he's not used to driving with a person sitting on his

lap, his steering wheel digs into my back, and his crotch jabs my ass. It's been over a decade since I've seen his cock, much less felt it, but I am reasonably certain I'm not the only one stimulated by our closeness.

I can't miss the bulge in his jeans.

When I attempt to scoot off Ryan's lap, he yanks me back into my original position. Considering the thickness I'm striving to ignore grows from our battle, I conclude not only is he at half-mast, but his cock is even more enticing than I remembered.

"I can sit in my own seat," I snarl.

I'm not peeved at him. I am not even peeved at myself. I'm pissed at his jeans.

How dare they come between us.

Grunting in lieu of a response, Ryan tugs the seat belt around us before locking it in place. His hot breaths fan my nape when he stabs the key into his ignition to fire up his engine.

My work colleagues' catcalls ring in my ears for the next quarter of a mile, along with the thud of my raring pulse.

I bite on the inside of my cheek when Ryan hits his third pothole for the night. My bite isn't pleasant. It is painful enough that tangy copper stings my taste buds.

The past three minutes have been pure torture. Having Ryan so close but being unable to touch him is the cruelest form of punishment. I can smell him on my skin, taste him on the tip of my tongue, and feel him sitting heavy beneath my ass.

If that isn't already distracting my senses to the point of no return, every bounce of his truck reminds me how perfectly aligned our bodies are.

If I weren't wearing panties, and he wasn't wearing jeans, we'd be...

No, Savannah. Don't go there.

"Pot-ooh-mmm." My warning turns into a throaty moan when the front tire of Ryan's truck hits the pothole with the precision of a marksman.

"You're mean," I mutter in a breathless pant.

I'm not game to look at his face, but I know he's smiling. I can feel it in my bones.

"What? I didn't do anything," he denies for the fourth time, a smirk heard in his words.

My eyes roll skywards. He can deny it until he is blue in the face, but I know he's aiming for every bump in the road. How? Because not only does each collision add to the heat between my legs, but it also makes the thickness in his jeans swell.

"Did you say something, *Savannah*?" Ryan growls my name, sending his voice through my veins like liquid ecstasy, stimulating not just my hot buttons but every goddamn button I own.

"No," I answer, my short reply incapable of hiding my aroused state.

Mortified at the lust-craved idiot I'm portraying, I attempt to scoot off his lap for the fifth time in the past four minutes.

I barely move an inch when Ryan throws his hips forward.

I groan, heightened beyond belief, when the mouth-watering outline protruding from his crotch rubs the sensitive skin between my ass and sex.

I moan, practically purring. I've never been more aroused in my life. My clit is throbbing, and my panties are soaked. I am equally excited and frustrated. I'm not frustrated by Ryan's attention; I'm annoyed my clit doesn't have anything to grind against.

I'm sitting side-straddled, meaning, other than pressing my thighs together, I can't ease the throbbing between my legs.

See—torture.

Pure, unbridled torture.

Groaning in frustration, I burrow my inflamed cheeks into Ryan's neck. Now matters are ten times worse. His scent is more inviting from this vantage point. He smells intoxicating and familiar—a scent I crave more than anything.

"Please stop." The furious pulse raging through his body amplifies the thrumming of my pussy. "I can't do this. I can't be close to you and not..."

I stop talking, mindful I'm crawling into a hole I may never escape. I am dying to taste him again, but I know from experience one taste will never suffice. If I have one, I'll want another, closely followed by another. Is that something Ryan can offer me? Or am I simply praying for a miracle?

Furthermore, is this what I want? I barely survived leaving him the first time. I won't survive a second dose.

"Do what, Savannah?" The raw huskiness of his voice excites me more. "What do you want?"

"Nothing." My disappointed breaths bead condensation on his neck. "I don't want anything."

My knees curve inward when his truck's tires roll over the safety grooves in the roadside. The pleasing vibration lights up every inch of me while also eradicating my hesitation. I'm panting, aroused, and brimming with anticipation of what is about to transpire.

"Ryan..."

"Yes, Savannah," he replies instantly, his voice as rough as mine but a hundred times hotter. It is like ice cream on a hot summer day: heavenly. "What do you need?"

"I need... I want..."

My tongue darts out to clear a bead of sweat from his neck before my brain can command it not to.

Any hang-ups I'm having evaporate when his taste fills my senses.

Even his sweat tastes better than I remembered.

After swiveling his hips to reveal I'm not the only one being led by lust, Ryan says, "Tell me want you want, Savannah."

I contemplate a ladylike way to express my needs.

It is a futile two seconds. "I want you to fuck me." I'm not the least bit embarrassed, too drunk with need to register shame. "I *need* you to fuck me. Please."

My second plea barely leaves my mouth before Ryan drags his truck to the side of the road and frees his cock from its tight restraints. White spots dance in front of my eyes when his engorged crown grazes my aching clit. I'm in so much of a lust haze I didn't even register a change in position. My shuddering

THE WAY WE WERE

knees now straddle Ryan's hips, and my heaving breasts are squashed against his pecs.

After slipping my panties to the side, he guides his cock up and down my glistening slit, coating himself with my arousal.

I grind against him like a nymph, loving that I'm on the brink of ecstasy while still clothed. Ten years have passed since I've felt this crazy ebb and flow sensation—*ten lonely motherfucking years*—but you wouldn't know it.

I'm as giddy as the teenage girl I was once.

Recognizing that I am five seconds from detonating, Ryan nestles the crest of his cock between the folds of my pussy.

When he drives home, I call out, loving the burn of taking a man his size without preparation.

It's been a long time since I've been stretched this wide.

"Fuck, Savannah," Ryan groans, appreciating my pussy clenching around him. "Perfect. Nothing less than perfect."

He doesn't wait for me to acclimate to his girth before withdrawing to the tip of his cock.

His second lunge is more brutal than his first when he rams back in.

I don't mind his aggression. It's hot. For the near year we were together, Ryan never fucked me. We had sex, and we made love, but he couldn't hurt me in or out of the bedroom, so fucking was a no-go zone.

Don't mistake my admission. Nothing he is doing is hurting me.

It feels *way* too good to be anything close to pain.

After securing a grip on my hip, Ryan's other hand weaves through my sweat-drenched hair. His dominant hold aids in guiding me up and down his cock at a speed that drives me wild.

I meet his thrusts even more aggressively, taking what I need without any hesitation. I've been dying for this day for years, so I'm going to relish every perfect second.

"Harder," I breathe out in a moan, my one word barely audible over our combined groans. "Faster. Fuck me, Ryan. Fuck me."

His hot breaths fan my lips when he meets my request with the determination of a madman. His pumps turn frantic, bringing the finish line to within an inch of my spent face.

I brace my hands against the roof of his truck when the crown of his fat cock flicks the sweet spot inside me. The change in position adds even more stimulation to my overflowing plate.

Ryan's mouth-watering pelvic bone smashes into my clit with every grind, and the stubble on his chin grazes my breasts through my thin cotton shirt.

"Sweet Jesus," I pant, my tone spiraling as wildly as my mind.

He rocks his hips forward so effectively that my head smashes against the roof with every thrust. I moan on repeat, loving the craziness of our exchange.

We aren't making love.

We're not even having sex.

We are fucking like two people who can't get enough of each other—because that is precisely who we are.

I snap my eyes shut when a familiar tingle becomes too great to ignore.

Ryan tightens his grip on my hair, wordlessly demanding my focus back to him. As a bead of sweat glides down his cheek, he stares at me.

He doesn't say a word but doesn't need to speak for me to hear his thoughts.

He isn't just claiming my pussy.

He's claiming every inch of me.

"Ohh..." I purr in an eccentric moan when the sensation gripping me turns blinding.

While maintaining Ryan's heavy-hooded watch, I moan through the climax shredding through my body as effortlessly as his promising eyes crumble the wall I built ten years ago.

He grinds into me another four times before my name leaves his mouth in a throaty groan. The heat of his cum coating the walls of my pussy catapults my climax to a never-before-reached level.

There's nothing that could take away from this moment.

Not a single thing.

Not even the flashing of police lights behind us.

CHAPTER 17

Ryan

I slam Savannah's quivering pussy to the base of my cock. I'm not only ensuring she gets every drop of cum still streaming out of my rock-hard shaft. I am guaranteeing the flare of her skirt hides the intimate way our bodies are conjoined from the two officers approaching my window.

Tonight turned out nothing like I had planned. The natural attraction that always bristles between Savannah and me was abundant the past week, but with her spending more time running from me than talking to me, I was certain we wouldn't succumb to our desires for months, if ever.

I shouldn't have fucked her like I did. Even pissed that she puts her body on show multiple times a night for dirty old pervs, I shouldn't have punished her with my cock.

It isn't that I want to hurt her. I just can't control myself around her.

Time hasn't altered the facts. Savannah is my weak spot. Anything she wants, I give her.

That includes my cock.

She wanted me to fuck her. I answered her plea to the T. I gave it my all.

Considering her juices are coating my balls, I'd say she appreciates my dedication.

The walls of Savannah's pussy clamp around my still throbbing cock when an officer taps his baton on my window. With the heat in my cab reaching stifling twenty minutes ago, I cannot identify my colleague through the steam-smeared glass. All I can see is the brim of his hat and his partner's gleaming white teeth.

After drawing Savannah into my chest, I roll down my window as requested. If they weren't aware of what activity we were engaged in, they sure as hell know now.

There's nothing more intoxicating in the world than the smell of raunchy, out-of-control sex.

"You need to move along..." The officer's words stop when his dark gaze locks on my familiar blues. "Carter?"

Benny, a thirty-year veteran at Ravenshoe PD, steps back. He scans my truck as if he's missing vital evidence.

Benny is a good guy. He was one of the rare few who supported me after my father's death.

Even with my mother taking the blame, things were rough for me in the six months following my father's untimely demise —untimely because it should have happened years earlier.

What Regina said all those years ago was true. IA was all over my ass the morning following the dislodgement of my gun. My service pistol killed a man. In my line of work, you can't get worse than that.

Benny and a few good officers like Regina stood by my side the entire time.

It was their dedication to ensure I didn't lose my badge that spurred my commitment to my job over the last ten years. I wanted to make them proud. They said I did when I was awarded my detective role nearly five years ago.

When I first signed up for recruitment, I loathed the idea of being a lawman. Now I fucking love it. My job isn't solely about weeding out the criminals from my town. It is about helping the community thrive. Ravenshoe has gone from an unknown town to a metropolis in the past decade. I like to think part of its growth is compliments of Ravenshoe PD.

By evening the playing field between corruption and legality, we've created a safe, nurturing environment for both families and business-minded people.

With Col Petretti's death last year, the odds are even better. Ravenshoe will continue to grow—especially with a man like Isaac Holt at the helm.

Failing to find anything wrong with my truck, Benny returns his confused eyes to me. "What the hell are you doing out here?"

My lips furl. "Do you *really* need me to spell it out for you, Benny?"

Nate, his recently drafted rookie, chuckles under his breath.

"Nate," I greet, praying he will help a man out. He's young,

THE WAY WE WERE

so he should understand that some things can't wait until you're in the confines of your home.

"Ryan," Nate greets back, doing nothing to aid me.

After glaring at him in warning that I won't forget how he left me hanging, I return my focus to Benny. "We're about to head off."

"Done already?" Nate pipes up, pissing himself laughing. "We only got a call from a concerned motorist ten minutes ago. Shame on you, Ryan. Shame. On. You."

If I didn't feel Savannah's lips curving against my neck, I'd get out of the truck and smack the smile straight off his face.

Benny's eyes dart between Nate, Savannah, and me for several seconds before he finally clues in. "Oh... uh... well... we better let you get back to it."

"He doesn't need more time. Didn't you hear him? He's already done—"

The remainder of Nate's tease rams into his throat when Benny removes his hat to whack it against his stomach. He laughs even harder when he sees how red Benny's cheeks are.

"Don't act bashful, Benny. You heard the rumors about Ryan's fascination with strippers. That's why we've been trawling these parts for the past month. You wanted to see with your own eyes if the rumors were true. Now you're acting too embarrassed to look." He makes a long *pfft* noise with his mouth.

I cuss under my breath at the same time Savannah stiffens. I've known about the rumors circulating at the precinct for days. I would have just preferred for Savannah to remain unaware of them. If she thinks they were started because I was investigating her, tonight's exchange may be a one-night-only affair.

After advising I have five minutes to move or be issued a ticket, Benny heads for his marked police car.

Nate isn't as eager to leave. His eyes scan Savannah's body plastered to mine enough times for the throb in my cock to ascend to my jaw. I'm not only going to issue him every ticket he can imagine on his next day off. I'll scrub his name from Brax's appointment book as well. His back tat will never be finished at the rate he's going.

"All right, all right. Don't bust an artery," Nate murmurs, incapable of ignoring my furious glare for a second longer. "Enjoy your night. It was nice meeting you, Savannah."

You'd swear he issued Savannah a warrant for her arrest for how she stiffens.

Nate has barely climbed into the passenger seat of his patrol car when Savannah clambers off my lap. I groan, hating that her heat no longer surrounds my cock.

"You told them my name," she murmurs more to herself than me.

After throwing down the hem of her skirt and adjusting her disheveled shirt, she locks her wide eyes with me. With our fuck-fest launching my heart rate to a never-before-reached level, my shirt clings to my chest, and my hair is as damp as it is when I exit the shower.

The sex was unexpected, but it was also...whoa...fuck... damn!

When Savannah's attention fails to deviate from my midsection, I follow the direction of her gaze. Her heavy-hooded eyes are narrowed on my cock, the glistening of our combined arousals revealing another fatal flaw of our night.

We didn't use protection.

Fuck.

"You're on the pill, right?"

When I return my eyes to Savannah, she waits for me to hide the evidence of our foolishness in my jeans before shaking her head.

A ball of tension bundles in my throat. "You're not? Why aren't you on the pill? Who isn't on the pill these days?"

"Women not having sex," she fills in, her voice as loud as mine, her eyes just as wide.

The panic in her tone should increase my worry.

It doesn't.

Not. At. All.

She's got enough worry for the both of us, so I have nothing left to give.

Furthermore, her admission that she isn't having sex has me wanting to bang my chest like a macho man. I don't savor the hold she has on me, but I'm glad I am not the only one struggling to contain uncontrollable desires.

"Oh god. This is bad, Ryan. Really, *really* bad."

When Savannah burrows her head into her hands, I say, "It's not that bad. There's a twenty-four-seven drugstore in town. We can get the morning after pill."

My assurance doesn't ease her panic.

If anything, it adds to her worry... and makes her mad—steam billowing from her ears mad!

"Well-rehearsed on one-night stands, are we, *Officer Carter?*"

She sneers my name minus the husky playfulness her colleague used earlier.

I swallow the lump in my throat before shaking my head. "No. I just figured it was the smart thing to do. You don't have to take it if you don't want to. I'd never force you to do anything you don't want."

Her lips quiver as she struggles to govern the moisture in her eyes.

"This isn't about forgetting protection, is it?"

She wouldn't cry about something so insignificant.

The chances of her getting pregnant at this exact moment are slim, but I could never be so lucky to have her tied to me for life.

After raking her teeth over her bottom lip, she shakes her head.

"What is it then? You can tell me anything."

I brush a rogue tear off her cheek, tripling my guarantee without words. Nothing she could say would shock me more than when I walked into Vipers two weeks ago and saw her on the main stage. Even with her honey-colored hair covered by a chocolate wig, I instantly recognized her. A million decades couldn't erase her dimpled grin from my mind, let alone ten painstaking years.

I loathe that Savannah works at Vipers, but I hate that she doesn't trust me even more than that. Alex didn't unearth any additional information on Savannah's whereabouts the past decade than I already knew—she was nonexistent—but the events following our initial contact caused my biggest worry.

The scant information Alex shared about Abby Rowe

changed the course of my investigation. Her record was as sparse as Savannah's the past decade, but it unearthed her employee: Pete Chester, owner of Vipers Strip Club.

That's how I discovered Savannah was using an alias.

If that wasn't daunting enough, I received a call from a US Marshall in Montana within hours of me requesting information on Savannah from Alex. He was also seeking information on a Savannah Fontane that matched Savannah's age and description—though his investigation centered around the previous few years, not a decade.

He explained that the details of his case couldn't be shared, but he would pass on his appreciation for my assistance to my superiors.

It is a pity for him I wasn't born last week.

Although it was unprofessional, I informed him I was working on a cold case that was over a decade old. It wasn't a total lie. Even with no charges being filed, Savannah's name is mentioned in numerous police records from her assistance during Axel's arrest.

My unprofessionalism had karma issuing me a setback with my hearing. The unnamed Marshall's annoyance was so high he slammed his cell onto his desk before disconnecting our call.

When I spotted Savannah outside of Vipers weeks ago, I had a hunch that she was hiding something. After his contact, my confidence grew. I just wish she trusted me enough to confide in me. I broke her trust ten years ago. I learned from my mistake. It won't happen again.

"Talk to me, Savannah. I can't help you if I don't know what's going on," I mutter, using some of her words against her.

She begged me to open up when comforting me after my dad's antics. Rarely did I accept her offer. I can only hope she isn't as stubborn as she's always been.

Her lips twitch, but before a syllable escapes her mouth, police sirens break the silence teeming between us.

"Time to move on, Carter," Benny's deep voice broadcasts over the sirens. "Dispatch is still receiving calls of a suspicious vehicle. They're sending backup to our location."

Not eager for more witnesses to our unexpected reunion, I raise my hand, advising that I heard him before kicking over my motor.

I wait until police lights are no longer flashing in my cab before returning my eyes to Savannah.

Any hope of cracking open her can of worms is lost. Not only is she facing the scenery whizzing by her window, but the massive barrier demolished by our steamy exchange has also returned greater than ever.

The Savannah I know and love has once again vanished, leaving a woman who is only a shadow of the girl she used to be.

CHAPTER 18

Savannah

"*A*re you sure you won't consider another date? The clients loved your routine." Keke, the manager of Maison's pleads while glancing at me with big chocolate eyes. "Our agreed rate isn't set in stone. I have a little leeway. If you agree to increase the length of your performance, I'll increase the purse."

Even if I didn't already have my bags packed, I wouldn't accept her offer.

Jet was right. The clients at Maison's weren't as welcoming of my clothed form as the ones at Vipers. Their requests for me to remove my outfit were louder than the applause that followed my thirty-minute performance.

Thankfully, Maison's security personnel didn't hesitate to

throw out offending members. Even one client whose suit was worth more than I'll make in a year got thrown out after he attempted to slip a hundred-dollar bill into my boyleg panties instead of on the stage.

I shouldn't be shocked by their rudeness.

I've never met anyone who has both money and integrity.

Keke coughs, wordlessly demanding my focus.

"Thank you for the offer, but I'm leaving town first thing tomorrow."

She looks as heartbroken as Ryan did when I fled his car last night. I fucked things up coming back here. After years of hiding, I grew weary.

I thought we'd be safe here.

I was wrong.

I just wish I had realized that before Ryan spotted me. He doesn't deserve to be treated how I'm about to treat him. I wish I could tell him my plans to leave, but I can't. He'll try and coerce me to stay, and that will only make matters worse for both of us.

That isn't an assumption. It is a fact.

"Okay, well, my offer stands if you're ever back this way," Keke informs me, standing from her oversized leather chair.

The weight my chest has been carrying the past sixteen hours slackens when she hands me the three thousand dollars we negotiated weeks ago. It won't get me the car I was hoping for, but it will give me my umpteenth fresh start the past four years.

"Thanks for agreeing to cash. I don't have the means to cash a check." I bop down to stash my lifeline into my gym bag.

Keke smiles, seemingly well-rehearsed on cash-only transactions. "Molten will see you out," she advises, nudging her head to a large Maui man standing guard in the corner of her office. "With the clients being extra rowdy tonight, make sure she gets to her car untouched." Her demand is for Molten, not me.

"Yes, Ma'am," he replies, dipping his chin. "This way." He gestures to the only door in the room.

I gather my gym bag off the floor before shadowing him to the door.

We've barely crossed the threshold when shouted demands to get down rumble into Maison's eighteen-room establishment. Men in riot gear storm into the main arena from all directions. They have assault rifles strapped to their chests and batons in their hands.

I watch the scene unfold like a horrifying action flick. Half-dressed men and women dash for viable exits, their ability to flee thwarted at every turn.

There are more FBI agents than there are civilians.

I jump out of my skin when a roared, "Get on the ground," shatters my eardrums. A man with a face shield and angry snarl stops in front of me. "Get on the ground before I place you there myself."

"I'm not a prostitute. I was just here performing," I stammer out, my nerves at an all-time high.

"Yeah, yeah, sweetheart. We've heard it all before."

My cheek connects harshly with the polished wooden floor when he seizes my shoulder in a firm grip to drop me to the ground.

His movements are so agile I don't have a chance to protest.

"Please, this isn't what it seems. I'm not here illegally," I plead as he zip-ties my hands behind my back.

After ensuring I'm adequately contained, he rolls me onto my back before digging his hands into the pockets of my shorts. A copy of the receipt I handed Pete earlier today when I resigned from Vipers falls onto the polished floor, along with a dozen quarters I had planned to use for laundry last night.

Happy I'm missing any damning evidence, the agent rolls me back onto my stomach. My heart launches into my throat when I scan the surrounding area. The main foyer of Maison's is covered with men and women of all shapes and sizes. They are bound with zip ties like me and are also being searched.

I stop peering at Keke's apologetic face when the man arresting me drops a bundle of hundred dollar bills in front of my nose. "Not a prostitute, hey. You just carry around that much cash for fun." Although you could assume he is asking questions, his tone doesn't convey that.

Before I can deny his assumption, he crouches down in front of me, snags my index finger, and then presses it onto a cool, smooth surface.

"What are you doing?" I ask, panicked.

"You don't have any ID, so I'm scanning your fingerprint through our database," he answers, not the least bit deterred by the worry in my tone.

"You're what?" The hammering of my heart chops up my words.

He positions a small handheld device into my line of sight. It is flicking through numerous matches, searching for me in a country-wide database.

Oh god. This is going to end badly.

Realizing a bullet is the least of my problems right now, I somehow rise to my feet and charge for the Balinese door I entered an hour ago.

My pace is so out of control I'm halfway out of Maison's before the officer realizes I am fleeing. Not even my three-inch heels can slow me down.

"Stop!" several voices shout before they follow it with a warning shot.

"No. No. Please, you have to let me go," I plead when I'm wrestled to the ground. "If he finds me, he will kill me. Please, I'm begging you, you have to let me go."

The pain of a man double my size kneeling on my back fails to register when I spot a pair of ocean-blue eyes across the room. Ryan is standing next to a man with a hard-lined face and blond hair. He's wearing the same riot gear as the officers surrounding me, but he's missing a face mask and FBI credentials.

Just as my arresting officer arches my legs to bind my ankles and wrists together, Ryan locates me. His face whitens as his eyes widen.

With a roar, he charges for me. He darts between a dozen officers in slow motion, the pain on his face matching the strain on mine.

"Get off her!" he roars before ramming the officer with his shoulder.

They land on the floor with a thud. Their brutal collision

gains the attention of every officer in the room, but no one offers assistance. They just stare, as shocked as me.

When Ryan's fists lift from the officer's ribs to his face, the man he was standing next to drags them apart.

Ryan's anger is so white-hot it takes several agents to hold him back. I'm confident the tears streaming down my cheeks are amplifying his aggression, but with my hands bound, I can't clear them.

"Get off me, Alex," Ryan demands, his eyes locked on the blond at his side.

Alex does as instructed but places himself between Ryan and the man he just attacked, who is sitting on the floor, cradling his bleeding nose with his hand.

"Outside," Alex demands, pointing to the door.

When Ryan remains standing proud with his nostrils flaring and fists clenched, Alex yells, "Outside now, or I'll not only arrest her, I will arrest you for assaulting a federal officer." He hooks his thumb to me in the middle of his threat. "Don't test me, Carter," he warns when he spots Ryan's determination. "I am not a man you want to fuck with."

"Take her restraints off first," Ryan demands, jerking his chin to my hands. "She's not a..." He licks his cracked lips, unable to articulate a word I don't want to hear him say. "She's not one of *them*," he settles on, his voice not as confident as I would have liked.

Alex glances into Ryan's massively dilated eyes for several seconds before he commands one of his men to cut the zip ties digging into my wrists.

I know the look Alex is giving Ryan all too well. It is the same one Ryan gave me when he thought I was deceiving him.

Alex doesn't believe him. He thinks I'm a prostitute.

After the zip ties are cut from my wrists, I warily rise to a half-seated position, cautious of the numerous eyes gawking at me. When my movements are conducted without protest, I stand to my feet.

My hesitant steps to Ryan stop when he locks his furious eyes with mine before curtly shaking his head. I don't know if he's requesting me to stay away or doubting the guarantee he just issued Alex.

Whatever it is, it hurts.

"You two outside," Alex says with his stern eyes bouncing between Ryan and the unknown officer. "Everyone else get back to work."

The agents continue staring, their love of drama not contained even while on the clock.

The dead silent space morphs into a bustling hive of activity when Alex snarls, "If I'm made to repeat myself one more time tonight, I'll have you *all* on desk duty by 9 a.m. tomorrow."

Agents dart in all directions, taking witness statements and issuing Miranda rights.

Happy his minions are following his command to the stringent detail, Alex's squinted gaze drifts to me. "If you care about his career at all, I suggest you follow me."

Not giving me a chance to reply, much less request why Ryan's career is in jeopardy, he shifts on his feet and exits the thrumming environment.

I'm nipping at his heels two seconds later.

Whoever invented the quote "ignorance is bliss" is a moron. My watering eyes haven't left Ryan's side since Alex placed me in the back of an unmarked SUV nearly twenty minutes ago. I think I'm under arrest, but I am not certain.

If I could settle my panic for just a second, I'd look into the circumstances of my detainment with more diligence. But until I know Ryan is okay, I must wait.

It feels like the moon circles the planet fifty times before Alex and Ryan head my way. With Ryan's strides not as confident as Alex's, he soon trails behind him.

With a nudge of his head, the locks on the SUV pop up. When Alex opens the back passenger door, I hesitantly climb out.

"You're free to go," Alex advises, his tone low and brimming with anger.

"Me?" I touch my chest. No one is within a hundred feet of us, but I'm still confident I heard him wrong.

Not appreciative of my ditziness, air whizzes out of Alex's nostrils before his eyes drift to Ryan. "Good luck with *that* one." Ryan's anger deepens when he nudges his head at me during the "that" part of his comment.

"One-time only deal, Carter. This will *never* happen again," Alex advises as he returns to the injured man glowering at me.

When they enter Maison's, I shift my eyes to Ryan. "I wasn't—"

"Don't, Savannah. Just fucking don't," he interrupts, his words as dangerous as quicksand.

I bite on the inside of my cheek, praying the pain will stop my tears from falling. His tone reveals he isn't just disappointed in me. He's embarrassed.

That hurts more than anything.

Not wanting him to see the moisture in my eyes, I stay a few feet behind him when we walk to his unmarked patrol car parked half a block down. The sky rumbles above my head, but not a drop of rain falls.

My ass was saved more times than I can count tonight, so clearly all my luck has dried up.

Unlike the past week, Ryan doesn't open my door for me. He violently throws open his door before sliding into the driver's seat.

Even with my heart sitting in my throat, I mimic his movements. Every penny I have is now in possession of the FBI, so I have no other means of getting home.

With Maison's situated on the swanky side of town, the drive to my apartment building is painstakingly long. Even Ryan's love of the gas pedal doesn't make it any shorter.

"I was just performing," I mutter under my breath when the tension grows too thick to ignore. "I'm not a prostitute."

"Goddamn it, Savannah. Will you cut the bullshit?" Ryan slams his hand on the steering wheel during his last sentence. "I nearly lost my job because of you, my fucking freedom, and for what? For you to give me the same excuse you gave every other man in that... that... *brothel* tonight? They all looked at me like I was an idiot. That I'm so blinded by you, I can't see the glaringly obvious right in front of me. They already think you're a stripper, and now... *Fuck*... Now they think I shelled out money for last night."

I try to reply, but I can't. I don't care what his work colleagues think of me. Ryan arrived at Vipers with his partner in tow. If he were truly worried about their opinions, he wouldn't have done that. I'm just shocked at the first half of his outburst. I gave him the same excuse I'd been issuing all night. I didn't alter it at all. I'm treating him as if he is like every other man I've met. But he isn't. Not in the slightest.

"Tell me what to say? I'll say anything you need to hear." My words are choked by a sob sitting in the back of my throat, dying to be released. I hate the way he's looking at me now—like he can't stand the sight of me.

Ryan's chest puffs high before he releases the breath he's holding. "How about the truth? Do you even know what that is anymore?"

The sneer in his tone cuts me to pieces, but it doesn't stop me from saying, "I understand you're upset, but you don't need to be mean."

"I'm not being mean. I am being honest. I don't care what you say or how you say it. There's no way your dad would approve of this, Savannah. He'd be as disappointed in you as I am."

My hands dart up to my chest, certain I've been mortally wounded.

Although my hands come up free of blood, the inside of Ryan's car looks like a massacre. The pain in his eyes... God. It's ripping my heart into a million pieces.

I've only experienced this type of heartache once before.

It was when my father took his final breath.

Ryan's foot slips off the gas pedal when I mumble, "I'm not meaning to hurt you. I'm just trying to protect my little girl from a monster as violent as your father."

CHAPTER 19

Ryan

Savannah swipes her hand across her cheeks as I shadow her down the dimly lit corridor of her apartment building. With her dropping her bombshell just as we arrived, I haven't had a chance to respond.

It is probably for the best. I genuinely don't know what to say.

Savannah has a daughter.

The girl I'd go to the end of the earth to protect has a daughter.

I never saw this coming.

If that isn't daunting enough, the last part of her confession won't stop ringing in my ears. *"I'm trying to protect my daughter from a monster as violent as your father."*

Does that mean what I think it does? Are Savannah and her

daughter being abused? Is that why she's hiding? Because she's afraid?

After jabbing a freshly cut key into a door I've entered many times before, Savannah drifts her watering eyes to mine. I lean into the shadows, praying it will hide my clenched jaw and balled fists from her view.

It does, but nothing can wipe the torment from my eyes.

"Shh," she pleads, pressing her index finger to her lips.

She waits for me to nod before opening the door. I'm sucker punched for the second time in five minutes when we enter Brax's old living room. Regina's disappearing act over the past few weeks now makes sense. She's sleeping on an outdated sofa in the middle of the confined space, nestling a little girl with honey-colored hair into her chest. Reading glasses sit askew on her freckle-covered nose, and a black pistol is hidden under a scatter cushion.

Although grateful she's on the ball with keeping Savannah's daughter safe, seeing her gun tightens the knot in my stomach. This is worse than witnessing Axel backhand Savannah because this isn't just about Savannah anymore. This is about a child— an innocent in any domestic violence situation.

After carefully removing the book dangling precariously on the little girl's chest, Savannah cradles her in her arms. Even if she hadn't confessed she had a daughter, there would be no doubting their connection. The little girl, I'd guess to be three or four, is the spitting image of her mother. When I peer at her dimpled cheeks and pale skin, all I can see is her mother racing down our street on her hot pink bike.

She's adorable—just like her mom.

Savannah barely moves an inch from the couch before Regina's naturally ingrained protective instincts kick in. She snatches Savannah's wrist with one hand as her other creeps across the tacky material in hunt for her gun.

"It's me," Savannah whispers, her voice low enough she doesn't startle her daughter resting on her shoulder, but loud enough to settle Regina's panic...until she spots me standing in the entranceway.

"I'll be right back," Savannah advises. Her eyes are locked on mine, but her words are for Regina. "Be civil. I made her promise."

This time, her plea is for me.

I postpone my interrogation until Savannah disappears down the hall. "How long have you known she has a daughter?" I glare at Regina. "Has she been hiding all this time because she's in fear for her life? And why didn't you tell me about *any* of this the instant you uncovered it!"

My nostrils flare when Regina replies, "She made me promise," deciding to start with my least challenging question. She unsteadily rises to a half-seated position before removing her gun from underneath the pillow to place it on the coffee table.

"I don't give a fuck if she promised you lifetime box seats to the Knicks, you should have told me." Because my voice is barely a whisper, my anger isn't relayed as strongly as I'm hoping.

I am beyond ropeable Regina hid this from me. She knew the hell I walked through ten years ago as she was walking right beside me.

Regina was the first person I called when I discovered Savannah's return to Ravenshoe. How could she not give me the same courtesy? Do our years together on the force mean nothing to her? I thought we were family, or at the very least friends.

She should *not* have kept this from me.

Although I want to continue reprimanding Regina, there are questions I need answered, and I need them answered now.

"Savannah said she's protecting her daughter from a man as violent as my father. Does that mean she's being abused? Is that why she's hiding? Because she's scared?" My tone relays I don't want to hear her reply, but I need to hear it.

Regina swallows several times in a row before murmuring, "If I were to believe Savannah, no." Her dour tone does nothing to ease my anxiety.

"What is your gut telling you?"

She doesn't need to answer me. I can see the truth in her eyes.

The girl of my dreams is a victim of abuse.

Fuck!

I thought handing my badge and gun to Alex tonight was bad. This is ten times worse. How can I keep the girl I promised to protect since I was six safe without a weapon? It isn't impossible, but it isn't easy either.

I stop calculating the many ways I can kill a man with my bare hands when Regina stops in front of me. "If you could pick, what would you prefer? Her keeping her secret? Or her still running from her past?" She nudges her head in the direction Savannah just went. "If I had raised suspicion to my

219

claims, she would have left, you would have never reacquainted, and that little girl still wouldn't know the meaning of family. I hated keeping this from you, but I used what I could to convince Savannah she could trust me. I kept her secret to keep her safe."

I step back, internally wounded by her confession.

When Savannah issues you her trust, you have it for life. She has every reason not to trust me, but why does that apply to Regina?

She once saw her as a mother, not an enemy.

After trailing her tired eyes over my balled hands and ticking jaw, she locks them on my face. "You think you're the only one mad? Tobias didn't just hide Savannah's relocation from me, he lied about it. I asked him on numerous occasions if he had anything to do with her disappearance. He guaranteed me he didn't. I would have never found her if I hadn't occupied my retirement with his old files." The pain in her voice sends ice sliding down my spine. "I gave Tobias the best years of my life, and what did I get in return? Endless lies."

Our heads rocket to the side in sync when a singsong voice says, "That wasn't because he didn't love you, Regina. He lied because I asked him to." Savannah glides across the floor, the weightlessness of her steps not matching the slump of her shoulders. "He wanted to tell you, but I begged him not to. The information Axel and I shared nearly got us killed. I didn't want anyone caught in the crossfire. Especially the people I cared about the most." Her eyes dance between Regina and me—she means both of us. "I'm sorry I tainted your memories of Tobias, Regina, but don't *ever* believe he deceived you on purpose. You were the first person on his mind every morning and the last every night. He loved you. More than you will ever realize. He was the sun, and you were his moon."

Regina's hands sweep her dry cheeks like a madwoman as her eyes drop to her shoes. She's never been good at showing her emotions, but even I know the moon and sun reference is of high significance to her.

"Well... I... uh... better head off. I'm sure you two have a lot to talk about." Regina coughs to clear the nerves from her throat before lifting her watering eyes to Savannah. "Same time tomorrow?"

She nearly loses her battle to hold in her tears when Savannah shakes her head. "We're not safe here anymore. It's time for us to move on."

"What?"

I want to say more, but a set of suitcases at the end of the hall steals my words. There are too many for Savannah to have just packed them. She must have prepared them earlier. I'm just curious if it was before or after we slept together.

My question-seeking steps stop when Regina snatches my wrist. "The more information you obtain, the greater persuasion you will pertain."

I stare at her, unsure how a quote she said to me on my first day at Ravenshoe PD will help me now.

"Until she learns she can bear the unbearable, she will continue running." Her voice is so low, if I couldn't read lips, I wouldn't hear a word she's speaking. "You are a brilliant detective, Ryan, and an even better man. Show Savannah that."

After saying goodbye to Savannah with a quick wave,

Regina's plump lips brush my cheek. I'm stunned by her sociable sendoff. She's not usually a feely-touchy type.

The reasoning behind her impulsiveness becomes apparent when she whispers, "She will listen to you, Ryan, but only after you've listened first. Use what I taught you. Emotions are the best persuasive techniques we have, only second to compassion."

I stand in silence for the next thirty seconds, watching Regina's retreating frame glide down the dimly lit corridor. I understand what she's suggesting. I just don't know if I can do it. This isn't the standard interrogation I've done numerous times in the past decade. This is a woman I've admired for years. She isn't a victim or a criminal. She's my girl.

Any hang-ups I'm having vanish when my gaze collides with Savannah's across the room. Just like Regina's gut has never steered her wrong, neither has my intuition. Savannah isn't just my girl. She is also a victim of domestic violence. The distrust in her eyes relays this without a doubt. How do I know this? Because they are identical to my mother's in every way.

"So you're leaving?" I keep my tone neutral, as Regina suggested.

Savannah's lips crimp before she faintly nods. "I don't want to, but this isn't just about me anymore. Rylee's safety is all that matters. It comes before anything."

Her eyes relay the words she will never say: *"Even you, Ryan."*

Her unspoken pledge doesn't bother me in the slightest. Savannah's daughter should come first. I would have given anything for my mother to put me and Damon above anything just once in our lives. Who knows how differently our lives could have panned out if she had the same dedication Savannah gives her daughter?

I cough to eradicate the lump in my throat before asking, "Your daughter's name is Rylee?"

Although my questions aren't directly associated with Savannah's case, they are just as important. If victims are unaware they're under investigation, they are more likely to talk. Asking simple questions like "Do you have animals?" or "What did you eat for lunch today?" can open doors that were previously closed. Making victims feel comfortable in your presence is of utmost importance.

And, if I'm being honest, I am also eager to discover if the similarities in Savannah's daughter's name and mine are a coincidence or not. The extra thump my heart got when she revealed her little girl's name answers my question on her behalf, but I want Savannah to admit it.

Savannah smiles a traffic-stopping grin before gesturing to her tiny kitchen. "Yes. I think it has a nice ring to it." She lifts her eyes to mine. The pain they held mere seconds ago is now cut in half. "Sometimes I call her Ry. But that's only when she's being mischievous. Which is more times than not lately."

I wait for her to spin away from me before fist-punching the air.

She named her daughter after me.

If that doesn't prove I've been on her mind as much as she's been on mine the past decade, I don't know what will.

After taking in numerous big breaths to calm my manic heart rate, I ask, "How old is Rylee?"

Savannah gathers two mugs from a cupboard above the

SHANDI BOYES

stovetop. "She'll be four next month." The happy glint in her eyes switches to sadness as she murmurs, "I can't believe it has only been four years. When you're hiding, every year feels like ten."

Most detectives would see this as an in to drill her for information, but I'm not like most detectives. I'm the best Ravenshoe has ever witnessed. If I bombard her with questions now, she won't leave tomorrow morning. She'll flee now.

"Rylee looks like you. Did she get any of her dad's features?"

I gather a picture of Savannah and Rylee off the fridge to inspect it more diligently. I've asked that question many times when interacting with victims of domestic violence, but this time it is genuine.

Rylee's similarities to her mother are uncanny.

"No. Thank god," Savannah murmurs under her breath. She places a dash of milk in the coffee she's preparing. "Other than the leaf-shaped birthmark on her neck, Rylee doesn't have any of her father's traits."

I nearly lose my train of thought when I place their picture back on the fridge. There's a faded Polaroid sitting next to the photo of Rylee and Savannah. It is so old the faces are no longer recognizable, but I don't need identifiable marks to unearth its origin. The dimples expose who the fair-haired newborn baby is. It is Savannah. She's being cradled by a woman I'd guess to be in her mid-forties wearing a nurse's uniform. Since she has angled Savannah toward the person snapping the picture, her name badge dangles over Savannah's knitted blanket.

Her name is Ruth.

Even the tenseness of our situation can't stop me from smiling.

That is why Thorn called Savannah Ruth. His brain got a little muddled, but his memories of his newborn daughter remained strong.

After returning their photo to its rightful spot, I sit in the chair Savannah nudged her head at. Although excited about my discovery, there are much more pressing matters I need to face first.

"Rylee has a birthmark?" I ask, getting back to business.

If I weren't staring into a pair of eyes that have graced my dreams every night for the past twenty years, I'd pull out my notepad and jot down all the little tidbits of information Savannah is unknowingly giving me. Mercifully, I have no issues retaining important information. And this is as important to me as it comes.

Smiling, Savannah nods. "Yeah. It's shaped like a maple leaf. Hers is just one-tenth the size of Keifer's."

Her eyes rocket to mine, curious if I picked up on her slip of name.

I act unaffected, even though my brain is working overtime. Not only do I have an identifiable mark to work with, but I also have a name.

I'm tempted to fist pump the air for the second time.

I just hit the detective jackpot.

"Has Regina been watching Rylee long?" I ask, operating like the cool cat I am.

Savannah doesn't buy my nonchalant approach.

She has always been as beautiful as she is smart.

"I didn't invite you into my home to investigate my case, Ryan. I just didn't want to leave with you still being disappointed in me."

"I'm not disappointed in you."

Savannah raises her mug to her mouth, hoping it will hide the roll of her eyes.

It doesn't.

Leaning over, I lower the steamy beverage from her mouth before sealing my hand over her one balled up on the dining table. "I'm not disappointed in you. I am disappointed in myself." When her cute little nose screws up in confusion, I clarify, "I should have known what you were doing wasn't about you. It's not even about me. It was for Rylee."

Her teeth graze her bottom lip as she nods. "It's always been about her, Ryan. Even before she was here."

"Then why aren't you doing everything in your power to keep her safe?"

Anger slips down her face even faster than the tear descending her cheek. "I *am* keeping her safe. I'm doing everything I can to make sure she's safe."

Even hating the pain in her words can't stop me from saying, "No, you're not. You are running instead of tackling the issue head-on. Do what you encouraged me to do for years. Don't keep quiet. Speak up. Seek assistance. Stop the cycle. If not for you, do it for your little girl. She doesn't deserve this life, Savannah."

"You don't know what you're talking about. There's no cycle

to stop." She stands from her chair so quickly it sails back and smacks into the drywall. "I think you should leave," she suggests, moving to the sink to dump her barely touched beverage.

I hate what I'm about to do, but I don't have a choice. Usually, I play good cop while Regina plays bad cop, but since I'm the only person standing in the kitchen, I must play both.

"Did Rylee's dad hit you?" My voice is as rough as my heart thrashing against my ribs.

Keeping her back to me, Savannah shakes her head.

I cautiously step closer, fearful of what her reaction will be.

I'm not scared she's going to lash out.

I am fucking petrified of seeing the truth in her eyes.

"Did he yell at you? Tell you you're not good enough?"

She continues shaking her head, preferring to lie without words.

"Did he threaten to take Rylee away from you if you ever told anyone what he was like?"

She stops shaking her head to gasp in a sharp breath.

"That's abuse, Savannah. He's manipulating you. Sometimes that's more violent than fists. Press charges against him. Throw the book at him. Show him you aren't scared of him—"

"But I *am* scared of him!" she shouts, her voice loud enough I'm afraid she has awoken Rylee.

Savannah must have the same fear, as her eyes dart to the hallway, only returning to me once she's confident the coast is clear. "He'll take her away from me, Ryan. He will take my little girl."

I cautiously step toward her with my hands held out in front of my body to show her I mean her no harm. "No. I would *never* let that happen. That promise I gave you years ago now extends to Rylee. I'll never let anything happen to either of you."

I tug her into my chest when she fails to object to my closeness.

The white undershirt I wear under my riot gear captures her tears.

"I promise you I'll never let him near Rylee. You just need to trust me. Let me in. Let me help you and Rylee. Give me a chance to show you I am the man you remember. I won't let you down, Savannah. I'll never let you drown either."

She hiccups as she struggles to stifle her giggle. Even with tension depriving the air of oxygen, her laughter lassoes a rope around us, tethering me not just to her for eternity but her daughter as well.

I've never met the little girl I am promising to keep safe, but I don't need a formal introduction to know I'll keep my word. If Rylee is even one-tenth of the girl her mother used to be, I'll protect her for eternity because I will love her just as long.

After tightening my arms around Savannah's torso, I drop my lips to her temple. "I'll keep you both safe. I just need you to trust me."

It feels like all of my Christmases come at once when I feel the faintest nod not even two seconds later.

"Yes?" I double-check, mindful my smashing heart might be the cause for her bobbing movements.

"Yes," Savannah murmurs into my chest, freeing me from the torment swallowing me whole while also adding to it.

I let her down ten years ago; I refuse to do it a second time. Failure is not an option.

CHAPTER 20

Ryan

"She did everything right, yet they still did her wrong," Regina says, throwing down the evidence I've amassed on Rylee's father overnight onto Savannah's dining table. "How could they deny that?" She points to Savannah's bruised face on one of the many Polaroid photos nursing staff took when she sought medical attention after a brutal assault. "We know better than anyone there's only one way you get a mark like that, and it sure as hell ain't from falling down the stairs."

Her anger is as palpable as mine was when Savannah handed me these photos. Although grateful she kept evidence of her ex's abuse, seeing the damage firsthand fucking killed me. The face I admired for years is barely recognizable in the faded

THE WAY WE WERE

Polaroid pictures. I would have never believed it was her if it weren't for Savannah's dimples.

Savannah wasn't just abused. She was tortured.

My eyes drift from Savannah sleeping on her couch to Regina. "That's the night she found out she was expecting Rylee. The nursing staff said it was a miracle Rylee survived the assault. In some ways it was. When Kiefer discovered Savannah was pregnant, he kept his hands to himself."

"What about the other Marshalls? What do they have to say for themselves?" Regina asks as she digs through the handwritten notes Savannah kept hidden from Rylee's dad. "Tobias's crew would have never let this slide. There should have been more than one Marshall assigned to her protection. Who was Keifer's superior? Who did he report to?"

I shrug, my mind as jumbled as Regina's. "Savannah said after Tobias died, she didn't see anyone but Keifer. She assumed he kept their location on the down low as a security measure. He told her the fewer people aware of her location, the better. This wasn't a properly run operation, Regina. He had Savannah at his advantage, and he exploited it."

I scrub my hand over my eyes before scooting to the edge of my chair to continue rummaging through the evidence. I'm tired as fuck, but there's no chance of me sleeping. My heart is in a mess, and so is Savannah's case.

Rylee's father is a US Marshall. Although no official evidence has been amassed, he appears to have been assigned to Savannah's protective detail in the weeks leading to Tobias's death.

Although Keifer continued to check in for duty every day

for the past nearly four years Savannah has been running, he has not lodged a single document that includes Savannah's name or one of the many aliases she has had over the years.

He wasn't just hiding her from Col's crew after Tobias died.

He was hiding her from the world.

I stop staring at the long list of names Savannah has been called the past ten years when Regina asks, "How did she get out alive?"

She knows the statistics as well as I do. Over half of the women killed in America each year are related to intimate partner violence. That means they were killed by either a current or former romantic partner. The odds of Savannah getting out were low, yet here she lies, sleeping peacefully years later with the strength of a tigress.

I always knew Savannah was a strong, determined woman, but I admire her even more now. She didn't just accept her fate. She fought it.

Could you imagine the courage it takes to sneak out of a hospital room with a one-day-old baby hidden under your sweater? Savannah knew the odds on households affected by domestic violence. She read every article I gave my mom when we were kids. She knew Rylee's birth would coincide with the return of Keifer's violence. That is why she ran when she did.

By manually adjusting her obstetrician receipts and buying items at the store before immediately refunding them, she amassed over a thousand dollars in the last few months of her pregnancy. It isn't much money when you have a newborn to look after, but she didn't want a glamorous life. She just wanted a non-violent one.

For the first few months, she lived on the money she had stolen, but as Rylee grew, so did Savannah's desperation. She knew Keifer was looking for them, so she had to change her location at least once every two months. That made it hard to secure employment. Not only did she have to trust strangers to care for her baby, but she also had to plead with business owners to keep their payments under the table.

It is lucky Savannah can read people.

She and Rylee lived well below the poverty line the past three years, but they were living, and that was all that mattered... until Savannah's heart had her issuing a plea she never thought she'd give.

There's only one alias Keifer is unaware of: Abby Rowe.

That's how Regina discovered Savannah's return to Ravenshoe two weeks before me. After scouring Tobias's records, she discovered a protocol he had failed to advise his superiors about. He had hidden aliases for every woman he placed into witness protection.

It was a safeguard, their last resort. If their cover was blown, or they were in immediate danger, they only had to use the name Tobias had given them, and he'd find them.

Savannah no longer has Tobias in her life, but she has the next best thing.

She has Regina.

Savannah is too proud to admit she needs help, but the fact she used the alias Tobias advised was only for an emergency situation in the town she was raised in reveals the plea she's too independent to make: *I need help.*

Like she can sense my intrusive stare, Savannah's eyes

slowly flutter open. Although she's only been sleeping for a few hours, she looks well-rested. I doubt she had a solid night's sleep in ages.

"Everything okay?" she mouths, ensuring she doesn't wake up Rylee, who is sleeping on her chest.

I nod, preferring to lie without words.

It's not okay. Not yet. But it will be. Soon.

I'll make sure of it.

The lamp hanging over the sofa Savannah is resting on twinkles in her eyes when I push off my feet and pad to her side. My god, she's a beautiful woman. Brave. Gorgeous. And mine. That's not subjective. It is straight-up honest.

Rylee nuzzles into her mother's chest when I adjust the knitted blanket draped over them. "Go back to sleep. We've got everything handled here."

I can see the controversy in Savannah's eyes, but she still nods, awarding me a trust I've yet to fully gain back. It's not that she believes I will deceive her. She's just wary of everyone.

When Keifer first struck Savannah, she sought assistance at the local sheriff's office, unaware Keifer's brother was the head of their region. When he hit her for the second time, she tried to run as she did four years ago.

She didn't even make it a mile before Keifer arrived at her side.

For every corner Savannah walked, a member of Keifer's family or friends stood on it. No matter whom she sought assistance from, word of her inquiries always got back to Keifer.

That didn't just make matters worse for Savannah. It nearly got her killed.

The horrifying images spread across Savannah's table are the result of her seeking help. As Regina said, she did everything right, yet she was still abused. If it wasn't for the young midwife who stayed by her side when she delivered Rylee, I doubt she'd be free now. She didn't just get out of the hospital unseen. She saved her life.

Once this all settles down, I'm going to shower that midwife with my praise. What she did makes her just as brave as Savannah in my eyes.

After pressing a kiss to Savannah's temple, I run my finger down Rylee's rosy cheek. The heaviness on my chest eases when the little dimple indents further from my touch.

"She couldn't be more like her mother if she tried."

I realize I said my statement out loud when Savannah replies, "You have no idea. You haven't seen her awake yet."

It's the fight of my life not to kiss the cheeky grin off her face, but I hold back the desire—barely. I don't want Rylee's first impression of me to be a lip-sucking-leech, no matter how delectable Savannah's mouth looks.

"Go to sleep," I request again before raking my fingers through her hair in a comforting manner.

Savannah always loved having her hair played with when she was younger. I don't know how often I woke up with strands of her hair wrapped tightly around my fingers, cutting off my circulation. It used to bother me—now I'd give anything to have it again.

I wait for Savannah's chest to rise and fall in a steady

rhythm before returning to my watch station in her kitchen. From where I'm sitting, I can see the living room, the main hall, and the front door. That's why Savannah is sleeping on the sofa instead of her bed. It is the prime spot for me to keep an eye on her.

"Tell me what you want me to do, Ryan. Direct me. Guide me. Take everything I've taught you and flip it on its head," Regina says when I enter the kitchen. "Give me something. Because if you don't, I'm going to drive to Wyoming and pop a bullet between this guy's eyes before the sun sets tomorrow afternoon."

I smirk. I shouldn't be smiling, but considering her thoughts match the ones I've had numerous times in the past three hours, I can't help but smile. If I had my gun, Keifer's breaths would be limited.

"Weren't you the one who told me violence never ends violence?"

Regina glares at me like I've grown a second head. "Yeah, but that was before any of this. He's a US Marshall. He should have been protecting her, not beating her to within an inch of her life." She licks her parched lips before saying, "We need to report this. You know what these men are like. When they lose one target, sometimes they put two in its place. Not only do we need to seek justice for Savannah, but we also need to make sure this isn't happening to anyone else."

I nod, agreeing with her. "But we need to be smart. If he's hiding them like he hid Savannah, and we go in strong, we may never find them."

"We can do this in a way he'll never see coming."

Regina's words aren't as confident as she's hoping, but they don't stop me from asking, "How?"

Her chest rises and falls numerous times before she breathes out, "We use Savannah as bait."

CHAPTER 21

Ryan

I wake up the following day to a pair of bright green eyes gawking at me. Rylee is kneeling next to the sofa I'm sleeping on. Her straight blonde hair is pulled into two even piggy tails, and a curious crinkle is scoured between her brows.

"Hello."

My greeting barely leaves my mouth when she screams blue murder, darts up from the floor, and then bolts across the living room at the speed of a bullet.

Upset that I've frightened her, I quickly shadow her steps. I find her in the kitchen. Her tiny arms are wrapped around Savannah's thigh, and her cheek is buried in her backside. She watches me with a curious sparkle in her eyes when I cautiously approach them.

THE WAY WE WERE

"Don't let her smell your fear, Ryan, or she'll exploit it for all its worth," Savannah warns, unconcerned about the worry in my eyes.

Realizing her cover has been blown, Rylee jumps away from her mother's thigh. She holds her hands in front of her body and roars like a bear.

The squeal she emits when I return her banter sets my hearing forward by at least three decades. My heart smashes my ribs when she races across the kitchen floor to leap into my arms. I'm so unprepared for her attack that I land on my backside with a thud.

My first thought is to wretch her away from me to check her for damage from our collision, but the hearty giggles spilling from her lips stop me.

Rylee's laughter grows when I tickle her ribs before lifting my eyes to Savannah. *"I'm sorry,"* I mouth.

What I said to Savannah last night was wrong. She did everything in her power to save her daughter from living the childhood I did. The fact Rylee is open to waking up with a stranger in her house proves this. She's a well-adjusted almost four-year-old who doesn't have a clue about the danger surrounding her.

She is as perfect as her mother.

It is like no time has passed when Savannah dips her chin, acknowledging she's aware of what my apology is about. She read my eyes—no more words needed.

My hands tear from Rylee's ribs when she demands the use of a bathroom. After clambering onto her feet, she dashes down the hall, holding her crotch.

"Sorry," I apologize again when I notice the small puddle seeping into Rylee's pajama pants.

Laughing, Savannah assists me from the floor. Although her help is more of a hindrance than an aid, I accept her offer. If it keeps her skin on mine, I will never turn it down.

"How did you sleep?" she asks before heading to the hall to check if Rylee needs assistance.

After Rylee assures Savannah that she's a "big girl," Savannah returns her eyes to mine, waiting for an answer.

I don't answer her unless you accept grunting as a form of communication.

Smiling in a way that tightens the front of my pants, Savannah moves back to the sink to finish the breakfast dishes she's washing. I watch her from the side of her tiny kitchen, loving the opportunity to see her in her mothering ways while also reprimanding myself for nodding off.

I had no intention of falling asleep, but the comfort of my gun and badge on my hip must have made my tiredness get the better of me. Although Regina's suggestion of using Savannah as bait was a plausible proposal for an officer of her dedication, I couldn't put Savannah's life at risk.

I only swore to protect her and Rylee a few hours earlier, so I couldn't break my word so quickly. Savannah has had enough promises broken in the past ten years. I'm not willing to add more to her stack.

Thankfully, with my denial, another idea came to mind. Keifer is a US Marshall, so as much as this kills me to admit, taking him down needs a broader skillset than Ravenshoe PD has to offer.

That is where Alex comes into play.

After advising Regina of my earlier tussle with a member of Alex's team, she handled initial contact. Alex was as egotistical as ever, but even he had a hard time stomaching the evidence we presented him. He doesn't even know Savannah, yet he wants to see Keifer pay penance for his horrendous actions.

Thus started my third joint operation with the FBI in the past year and the return of my gun and badge.

You wouldn't think two pieces of metal could mean so much, but they do. They don't just represent that I'm a member of Ravenshoe PD. They display I'm a protector. First to Savannah and Rylee and second to my community.

I don't feel an ounce of guilt admitting I'm putting Savannah before anyone. If it weren't for Savannah's persuasive techniques years ago, I would have never enrolled in the academy, so it is only fitting she is at the top of my list.

"I'm glad to see nothing has changed," Savannah murmurs, returning my focus to the present. She slings a damp tea towel over her shoulder before pacing to stand in front of me. "You still get a little groove right here when deep in thought."

Her thumb rubs the mark etched between my eyes before tracing my quirked brow. Her lingering touch reveals she is as uneager to stop touching me as I'm eager for her to continue.

Once her fingers have graced every inch of my face, her hand falls to her side.

"My turn," I whisper huskily.

After cradling her jaw, my thumb traces the little scar on her left brow. Her face has aged since the last time I studied it, but not in a bad way. The tiny crease in the corner of her eyes makes them dazzle even more brightly, and her dimples give her a youthfulness no amount of time could erase.

She's as beautiful now as she has ever been—*thank fuck.*

I was worried the horrific injuries she sustained during her assault would be evident on her face. They aren't. Her eyes are the only ones left carrying the baggage.

Like the silent pledge I gave years ago about wiping Axel from her mind, I'll also work just as hard to remove Keifer from her memories.

By the time I've finished worshipping her as she deserves, she won't remember the dreadful things he did to her, much less his pathetic name.

After gliding my thumb down Savannah's inflamed cheeks, I brush them over her lips. I've missed studying her mouth nearly as much as I've missed tasting it in the past decade.

I can't believe it's been ten years since I've sampled her lips, yet I still recall its intoxicating palette like it was yesterday. As sweet as her hair coloring but as sinful as vodka.

"Ryan..." Savannah's eyes divulge the rest of her hummed plea: *please kiss me.*

I return her desire-fueled stare as I contemplate her suggestion. I'm dying to kiss her—it's been way too long since her lips have been on mine. We may have fooled around two nights ago, but we didn't kiss. I just don't know if it's an appropriate thing to do with her daughter in the other room.

The last time I was around a baby was when Noah's daughter Maddie was born. If Rylee were a newborn, I'd have no hesitation in granting Savannah's wish. But she's not a baby.

She's old enough to be permanently scarred by the *influence* her mother has over certain regions of my body.

I already tickled her until she peed her pants. I don't want to taint her childhood memories more than I already have.

Before I can announce my worries to Savannah, she balances on her tippy toes to seal her lips over mine. I groan into her mouth.

As predicted, she tastes like heaven.

I keep the swivels of my tongue to a bare minimum, ensuring I can withdraw at any moment.

Yeah, right.

My tongue is so far down Savannah's throat I can confidently declare she still has her tonsils.

Calm down. I'm joking.

I *am* sampling every inch of her mouth like I have ten years of breathing to make up for—because I do—but I'm not doing it in a zombie sucking your brains out via your mouth type of way. I'm matching the lashes of her tongue stroke for stroke while grinding my extended crotch against the heat between her legs.

Our kiss is nowhere near as raunchy as our romp in my truck, but it is a hundred times hotter. There's something profoundly moving about open-mouth kisses. The affection displayed in a kiss can't be replicated in the bedroom. It is the easiest way to show your feelings without additional protection or words. My relationship with Savannah started with a kiss. If I have it my way, it will also end that way.

I stop dragging my tongue along the roof of Savannah's mouth when a deep grunt rumbles through my chest. When the stomping of a foot follows the cranky groan, I reluctantly withdraw from Savannah's sinful mouth. Rylee is standing at our side. Her little hands are spread across her cocked hip, a deep groove between her blond brows.

When she bossily gestures for me to stoop down to her level, I instinctively angle my body to the side.

If she's anything like her mother, I'm anticipating a swift kick to my nether regions.

The wind is knocked from my lungs. It isn't what you are thinking. Rylee isn't just a spitting image of her mother—she also has the same fondness.

After barely pressing her lips to mine, she charges into the living room, giggling like Savannah did when we shared our first kiss.

The girl I've been crushing on since I was four has competition: her nearly four-year-old daughter.

Shit.

CHAPTER 22

Ryan

I rise from my crouched position with my hands held out like I'm under arrest.

Although Savannah finds my cowardly approach amusing, I see a smidge of jealousy in her fiery gaze. "If you break my daughter's heart, Ryan Carter, I'll never forgive you."

Although she uses Rylee as an excuse to issue her threat, I heard the message her stern tone highlighted. She's not worried about Rylee getting hurt. She's petrified of putting her heart on the line.

"I'll never hurt her, Savannah. I promise."

Just like I perceived the underlying message in Savannah's warning, she heard mine in my reply. I secure my first lung-filling gulp of air since her mouth was torn from mine when her lips tug into a smirk.

Her smile makes me want to reacquaint our mouths, but the time displayed on her microwave makes me unable to act on my desires. My unexpected nap has set me back an hour already, and I need at least a day—*if not a year*—to adequately worship Savannah's mouth with the dedication it deserves.

"Is this everything?" I ask Savannah, peering down at the suitcases she packed yesterday morning.

While waiting for Alex to devise our next move, Savannah and Rylee are moving into my apartment. A normal man would be shitting bricks at the idea of having his domain overrun with feminine products.

I'm not a normal man.

In all honesty, I can't wait. In forty-eight hours, ten years of torment has unraveled. I was so angry believing Savannah's lack of contact was because she was a scorned woman. I was wrong—*very* wrong.

And I was man enough to admit it.

I divulged my mistakes to Savannah in great depth at 5 a.m. this morning. She was just as open as me. We shared everything and anything. I even told her what happened the night my dad was killed and confessed to what I said to Chris the day he died.

Within an hour, nothing was left on the table.

Some of the stories shared broke my heart, but the weight our conversation lifted off my shoulders was immense. I truly feel like I can face any obstacle placed in front of me without worry. I'm *that* weightless.

We have a long way to go before the dust of the past decade settles, but having Savannah in my life is as second nature as breathing. She belongs with me. She is my girl.

Savannah huffs, drawing my focus to her heavy scowl. "Yep. My entire life in three little bags. How pathetic am I?"

I catch her wrists and pull her to my body. "Who needs money when you have the world? You're a *mom*, Savannah. There's no greater gift than that."

Her smile grows. "You wouldn't think highly of my mothering skills if you knew the thoughts crossing my mind when Rylee kissed you." With a pout, she peers at Rylee watching cartoons in the living room. "My daughter is crushing on the man I've never stopped loving. This could end disastrously for all involved."

Suddenly, her spine snaps straight and her eyes missile back to mine. I can see a million thoughts streaming through her eyes, but not a syllable seeps from her lips.

Unfortunately, my mouth has no qualms expressing itself. "You *love* me?" I say my L word with an immaturity a man my age shouldn't have.

I swear to god, I feel like I've whizzed back fifteen-plus years to the time I coerced Savannah to kiss me. I pretended to be mortified by the idea, where, in reality, I was dying without her lips on mine. She'd been eating Hershey kisses the thirty minutes prior, acutely reminding me I was a teen boy with teen issues. I thought the throaty moans she released while devouring her treat would be the highlight of my night. It wasn't. The sugary sweetness of her mouth was ten times better.

The air in my lungs evicts in a grunt when Savannah's elbow pops into my ribs. "Don't be a noodle. You're Rylee's first crush, Ry. This is as serious as it comes."

"Why?" I ask, truly lost.

Her teeth graze her bottom lip before she murmurs, "She's never loved a man before. She'll get hurt if you don't love her back."

"Then you've got nothing to worry about."

Her brows furrow as confusion slashes across her face.

"Did you love your dad, Savannah?"

She nods without hesitation. "Very much so. I still do."

I smile. "And did he love you in return?"

"He adored me as much as I adored him," she mumbles, her eyes welling with tears.

"Then who's to say Rylee is crushing on me like you did when you were four?"

The seriousness of our conversation can't stop Savannah's eyes from rolling skywards. "Cocky much, *Officer Carter?*"

She can deny it all she wants. I know she was as smitten with me as I was with her at the same age.

After tugging her a little closer, I say, "Rylee's never had a man in her life, so maybe her kiss was a way of showing you who she wants."

"Who she wants or *what* she wants?" Savannah seeks clarification.

"This isn't an open submission, Savannah. There are no other applicants or an extensive interview process. I was just filling you in on the deets Rylee and I prearranged."

She bites on her cheek to hide her smile. "Is that so?" she murmurs, her hot breath hitting my lips.

"Uh-huh." I bring my mouth closer to hers.

I feel her pulse throb through her body when she asks,

THE WAY WE WERE

"When was this conversation? You only met Rylee twenty minutes ago."

"It was a long time ago," I murmur against her scrumptious lips.

She moans when my tongue can't hold back its desire for a moment longer. It slashes her mouth, nearly drowning out her, "How long ago?"

"When does Rylee turn four?" I nip at her lower lip.

"In thirteen days," she murmurs breathlessly.

"Thirteen days?" I double-check. When she nods, I say, "Then, in thirteen days, our decision was made four years ago. Right around the time you named her after me. You knew she'd be my daughter one day, so you made sure her name suited her title."

Savannah's heavy-hooded gaze snaps from my mouth to my eyes, but she doesn't deny my claims. She can't because she's never been a fan of lying.

CHAPTER 23

Savannah

I think I've died and gone to heaven. Or, at the very least, my heart is sitting in a gooey puddle at my feet.

Ryan just disclosed the exact reason I named Rylee after him. He isn't just a man I've loved for decades. He is my soulmate.

His deceit hurt me, but it wasn't so scarring that it erased the promises we made when we were young. Although Rylee isn't Ryan's daughter, just her having my blood makes her partly his. I belong to Ryan—heart, mind, and body. And from the smitten grin on Rylee's face when she boldly kissed him, I'm realizing I am not the only Fontane under his spell.

One of the reasons I kept Rylee's identity secret from Ryan was because I was worried about the repercussions. I birthed a child with another man, then named her after a man I believed cheated on me.

I don't know about you, but that sounds pretty pathetic to me, much less how Rylee was conceived. The day she was created will forever haunt me, but her beautiful face helped the memory fade so much that it is nothing but a blur.

Keifer didn't rape me, but when you're coerced to do a sexual act for the fear of not being fed for a week, it is nearly the same thing.

But even with the circumstances of Rylee's conception out of my control, I'll always see her as a gift, not a burden. She's been the only one fueling my wish to live for the past four years, so I could never see her as anything less than a miracle.

As the days rolled on, I realized I wasn't just lying to Ryan. I was also lying to myself. Facing a fear head-on is the right thing to do, but when your beliefs are stripped away from you as cruelly as Keifer stripped mine, you doubt everyone, even a man you've known most of your life.

Just like Axel, I disliked Keifer on sight. He was rude to his fellow officers, and he always eyed me in a way that made me uncomfortable. When I expressed my concerns to Tobias, he voiced similar worries.

Keifer was removed from my protective detail the very next day.

I thought that was the last time I'd hear from him.

Unfortunately, that wasn't the case.

After Tobias was killed in an FBI sting gone wrong, Keifer was placed on my protective detail again. Well, so I thought at the time.

When our contact with the department went from weekly updates to being basically non-existent, I started asking questions. Keifer handled my first few inquiries like Tobias always did: "When I know something, you'll know something."

It was only when my father's wedding ring slipped off my thumb did I discover the horrifying truth. A rummage down the side of a leather recliner unearthed a withdrawal slip from a local bank. Usually, that stuff wouldn't interest me, but it wasn't just the excessive amount on the withdrawal that had me choking back spit. My name was attached to one I had not previously used: Keifer's surname.

The first time Keifer struck me was when I revealed what I found. I was astounded. I didn't know whether to laugh or cry. But there was one thing I did know—I wasn't going to put up with his abuse.

I was as naïve as I was young.

Members of Keifer's family thwarted my first and second attempts to flee.

My third, fourth, and fifth endeavors were ruined by his associates.

By my sixth attempt, Keifer was no longer pleased by the challenge.

Could you imagine wishing to die mere hours before being informed you're carrying a life? I taunted Keifer that night as I wanted him to kill me. I didn't want to suffer anymore. He answered my pleas with the accuracy of a deranged man. I nearly lost my life that night, only to discover I was three months pregnant with Rylee the next morning.

Everything changed in an instant.

I nearly killed my daughter—*me.*

That hurt me more than Keifer's fists.

I scribbled my escape plan on a mini notepad a student nurse gave me at the hospital. She was the same nurse who delivered Rylee six months later.

I don't know her name, but I owe her my life.

The first few months on the run were tough, but my dad's quote kept me thriving. There are days where I feel like I've been running for decades, and other days feel like I only fled yesterday. Then there are days like today, where one glance into a pair of blue eyes makes me forget all the horrible things that have happened to me.

I want to pretend I used Abby's name as it was my last resort, but that would be a lie. I was sick of running. I was tired of looking over my shoulder. It was time for Rylee and me to live instead of just surviving. My baby girl deserves the world, and with Ryan's help, I think we can give her that.

The brush of a thumb over my midsection returns my focus to the present. Ryan is glancing down at me, his heavy-hooded gaze as honest as the words he just spoke.

Is it possible to fall in love in less than a nanosecond? Because I swear that's what happened when my eyes first landed on Ryan over twenty-five years ago.

It was only the quickest *boom-boom* of my heart before he somersaulted over his handlebars and broke his arm in two places, but it's never thumped in the same rhythm since that day.

I didn't think any man could outshine my dad.

Ryan did, and he was only a boy at the time.

While my teeth graze my bottom lip, I lock my eyes with Ryan. "Promise me, Ry—"

"I promise," he interrupts, stealing the rest of my words.

I frown, pretending I'm not loving his eagerness. "You don't even know what I was going to ask."

He cocks his dark brow into his glossy locks. "I know, Savannah. Believe me, *I know.*" He runs his index finger down the crinkle in my nose before adding, "And I won't. I learned my lesson. I won't break your heart..." I attempt to interrupt him, which encourages him to speak faster, "And I also won't change...*if* you promise to do the same."

"I promise," I reply as eagerly as he did.

I grin like a loon when he holds out his pinkie for us to seal our pledge. A simple curl of fingers might not seem like much to an outsider, but to me, it's the world. Like me, when Ryan issues you his promise, you have it for life.

A knock sounds at my apartment door before I can show him my gratitude for his pledge. Ryan stops my steps with a quick tug of my arm before lifting his finger to his mouth, signaling me to be quiet.

"Who knows you live here?" he whispers while removing his gun from the top of my fridge.

My heart rate skyrockets. "Other than Regina, no one. Could it be Regina?"

Ryan nods, but the anxiety in his eyes is nowhere near as confident.

I can understand his hesitation. Regina knows I'm cautious about security, so she usually calls before arriving.

Just as Ryan crouches down to gain Rylee's attention, a loud bang rockets through my eardrums. Wood splintering is closely followed by a silver canister rolling across my living room floor.

Ryan swings his head to me in sickening slow motion.

"Get down!" he screams before charging for Rylee.

The blast from the canister knocks me on my ass, causing my head to hit the dining table on my way down. I cradle my throbbing skull in my hands as blinding lights and smoke fill my apartment. I sit, stunned, for barely ten seconds, but it is long enough for guilt to set in.

My daughter is in another room, being protected by a man she only met thirty minutes ago.

Fighting through nauseating wooziness, I crawl into the living room on my hands and knees. My ears are ringing from the blast, and smoke is burning my eyes, but it doesn't encumber my senses enough to miss the terrifying visual in front of me. Even with his midsection rounder than the last time I saw him and a sprinkling of grays on his temples, I have no trouble recognizing the man standing in my living room.

It is Keifer—the monster from my nightmares.

He has Rylee clutched in his arms, and his pistol is braced on her right temple. Ryan is standing across from them with blood gushing from a large gash above his right brow and his gun directed between Keifer's brows.

"Mommy," Rylee cries, struggling to get out of her father's clutches.

"It's okay, baby, it's okay," I assure her, crawling closer. My words are barely heard through the panic constricting my throat, but Rylee understands them. Not only do her tears stop, but so do the big shakes hampering her tiny body.

"Drop your weapon, or I'll shoot her," Keifer warns Ryan with his country twang on full display.

"No," Ryan replies, shocking me with his calm, non-affected tone.

A madman has my baby at his mercy; how can he be so calm?

"Please don't," I beg when Keifer's anger gets the better of him. He digs the barrel of his gun so profoundly into Rylee's temple fresh tears roll down her ashen cheeks.

"Do you want your daughter to die, Savannah? Do you want her blood on your hands!" Keifer glares at me like I'm a piece of shit under his shoe.

"No," I reply, shaking my head so fiercely that my brain rattles in my skull. "Just let her go, Keifer, please."

My plea reveals what Ryan already knew.

He's facing my demon head-on.

"Then tell him to lower his gun." Keifer's demand is so loud I wouldn't be shocked to discover half the block heard it.

My eyes bounce between Ryan and Keifer as my mind scrambles for a response. I know Ryan would never place Rylee's life at risk, but trust has been an issue for me all my adult life.

My heart wallops into my ribs when I lock my eyes with Ryan and demand, "Please lower your gun."

"No, Savannah. I can take him out. He'll be dead before his finger gets near the trigger."

As if bombarded with stupidity from Ryan's pledge, Keifer's

index finger curls around the trigger of his gun before he slowly inches it back. He compresses it until it is halfway cocked.

"No, no, please, no," I beg with tears streaming down my face. "She's your daughter too, Keifer. Do you really want to kill your own blood?"

"Yes, she's my daughter, yet you still took her away from me!" he roars, sending spit flying out of his mouth.

"Mommy," Rylee cries, her voice as broken as my heart feels.

Keifer clutches her more firmly, stealing the rest of her words with a tight compression.

"It's okay, baby. You'll be okay, I promise."

After assuring her she is safe with just my eyes, I raise them to Keifer. I can hear Ryan continuously pleading with him to stand down, but I can't make out all the words he is saying. The image of my baby being held captive by the man I fear more than anyone isn't just affecting my hearing. It is threatening my very sanity.

"Please, Keifer. I'll do anything you want. Just let her go. She didn't do anything wrong. It was me. I stole her from you. I kept her hidden. If you want to blame anyone, blame me."

Keifer's finger remains clamped on the trigger, but the cleft between his brows is nowhere near as deep. I'm getting through to him.

"You don't want Rylee; you've never wanted kids. But you want me." His eyes snap to mine during my last sentence. I flatten my hands against my thudding chest. Its mad beat triples when I ask, "Do you still want me, Keifer? Am I still what you need?"

SHANDI BOYES

"Savannah, don't," Ryan warns, recognizing what I'm doing. His voice relays he isn't happy about my decision, but he also understands nothing is above me when it comes to protecting Rylee.

When Keifer's glassy brown gaze answers my question on his behalf, I say, "Let Rylee go, then we can get out of here."

Ryan's thighs stiffen as he tightens his grip on the butt of his gun. If my plan works out as I'm hoping, the instant Keifer releases Rylee from his grip, Ryan will pounce.

Unfortunately, Keifer is as smart as he is violent.

"Disarm him first." He nudges his head to Ryan.

"No," Ryan replies, his response more for me than Keifer. "This is your last warning. I will shoot you if you do not heed my caution. This is *not* a negotiation."

I crawl closer to Rylee when Keifer grips her so tightly that a painful wheeze parts her blue-tinged lips. He's clutching her so constrictively that her lungs are struggling to fill with oxygen.

"Please," I beg, turning my focus to Ryan. "She's my baby, Ryan. Please don't pick me over her."

His eyes only drop to mine for a second, but it is long enough for him to see the honesty in them. I'll never forgive him if his failure to stand down results in Rylee getting injured.

Peering into the eyes of a man I'll never stop loving, I assure him, "He won't hurt me." *Because you won't let him.* My last guarantee is issued without words.

Ryan is a protector, and I'm a nurturer. It is the way we are.

While murmuring profanity under his breath, Ryan lowers his gun. An egotistical grin stretches across Keifer's face when Ryan unclicks the chamber from the butt and slides the two separated pieces across the floor. When Keifer nudges his head for me to collect Ryan's gun, I do as requested, albeit hesitantly.

"Now let Rylee go," I demand, my confident words not betraying the shaking encumbering every inch of me.

Keifer's evil eyes bounce between Ryan and me for several terrifying seconds. Just when I think he will deny my request, he drops Rylee from his grasp and fists my hair in a firm grip. The roots of my hair pull from my scalp when he drags me into the position in which he was holding Rylee. His pistol notches into my temple as his death clutch steals the air from my lungs.

Although I'm terrified, I am also relieved. Rylee has her little arms curled around Ryan's thigh. He will keep her safe.

"If you attempt to follow us, I will kill her." Keifer's tone leaves no doubt about his threat.

As I am dragged out of the place I've only called home for two months by my hair, I mouth to Ryan and Rylee that I love them while silently praying my tear-stained face won't be the last memory they have of me.

CHAPTER 24

Ryan

My eyes drop from one tear-stained face to another. "It's okay, Rylee. Your mom is going to be okay. I promise."

She accepts my guarantee with the same assurance I took Savannah's earlier.

Keifer won't hurt her—because I won't let him.

Ignoring the crazy beat of my heart, I dig my cell phone out of my pocket before scooping Rylee into my arms. She's so warm, the sweat slicking my skin sizzles when I draw her into my chest to calm her panicked shuddering.

The 9-1-1 dispatch officer connects my call at the same time I reach the door Savannah was just hauled through. After checking the corridor is clear of any threat, I go to Mrs. Daphne's apartment. She's Ravenshoe's collective grandmother.

Nearly every child in this town has been babysat by Mrs. Daphne at some stage in his or her life.

"My name is Ryan Carter. We have a 134 in progress at an apartment block on Wren Street. The suspect is wearing black trousers, a navy blue collared shirt, and a faded baseball cap. He's armed and considered highly dangerous..."

My hurried words skid to a stop when my eyes lock in on a flurry of honey-colored hair. Savannah is being shoved into the passenger seat of a white sedan via the driver's side door. Keifer's vehicle is mounted on the curb, showcasing his desperation has reached fever-pitch.

The panic burning my esophagus grows. Smart criminals are a menace to society, but unhinged ones usually only harm those closest to them.

When Keifer cranks his ignition, I increase my speed. "Suspect is driving a white Chrysler. The last three digits of the number plate are 382. He's heading north on Wren. His victim is a Caucasian female wearing white denim shorts and a pink sweater."

With one hand holding a crying Rylee to my chest and the other caressing my cell, I alert Mrs. Daphne of my presence by kicking her door. She answers not even two seconds later. One look at my face tells her everything she needs to know.

"It's okay, baby girl, come on," Mrs. Daphne coerces Rylee, who is clutching my neck for dear life, fighting to stay with me.

I hate her being torn from me, kicking and screaming, but I know she's safe with Mrs. Daphne. Her mother's safety isn't as easily guaranteed.

After pressing my lips to Rylee's flaming red face in silent promise that I will return with her mom, I charge down the corridor. My pulse is pounding my eardrums so fiercely that I can barely hear the instructions the 9-1-1 officer is giving me, but I don't miss the most vital part of her information—Keifer's location.

With years of training under my belt and even more years of admiration, I dive into the driver's seat of my patrol car, stab my key into the ignition, and floor the gas. My car rockets out of the parking lot of Savannah's building as my cell connects to my command's Bluetooth.

"Right on Turner," the operator's instructions are mixed with the helicopter hovering above my head.

They've brought in the big guns.

"North on Taite."

Gratitude for Regina's love of pursuit pumps into me when I take the corner like a maniac. A handful of pedestrians ignorant of my siren can't ignore my horn when I slam my hand down on it. They race onto the sidewalk, their eyes as wide as mine, their fists clenched just as tightly.

The features of Ravenshoe I've grown to adore the past decade whizz past my window in a blur. My speed is so excessive the front tires on my patrol car struggle to hold onto the asphalt. I'm practically soaring.

"West on Mercer."

I slam my foot on the brake and skid to a stop mere inches from Mercer Avenue. After taking a second to ensure my abrupt pause hasn't caused an accident, I shift my foot from the brake to the gas pedal. I'm flooded with painful memories when my extreme speed along Mercer Lane doesn't impede my notice of the many tourist signs dotted along the way. They are all for the man-made wonder I haven't visited since a horrifying day nearly eleven years ago: Bronte's Peak.

When the operator advises that Keifer has turned east on Wesley, I realize what he's doing. He isn't fleeing with Savannah. He's taking her to hell with him. But his hell isn't filled with fiery flames and ashes—it's a bed of water.

He's returning Savannah to her deepest, darkest nightmare.

"Direct emergency first responders to the base of Bronte's Peak. Instruct them to bring police divers."

Dust hinders my vision when I drag my car off the roadside. I careen down the valley on the outskirts of Bronte's Peak as if my mode of transport is a four-wheel drive.

I can only hope my intuition isn't hindered by the pain shredding my heart to pieces because if it is, I didn't just risk Savannah's life—I took it.

"Move, move, move!" I scream at a group of tourists scaling the volatile rock surface, hoping to capture a superstar unaware. Noah has lived on the cliffs of Bronte's Peak for the past six months. Not only is he living the dream. He's living the life neither of his brothers got to live. To say I'm proud of that man is an understatement. He didn't just break the cycle of domestic violence in his family. He smashed it out of the park.

When the tourists scamper out of the way, I release my foot from the brake. I don't need to place it on the gas pedal. The natural decline of the cliff edge guides my speed.

Blisters form on my palm as I struggle to keep control of my vehicle in the loose sand. Recognizing that my sinking tires are slowing me down, I throw open my door and continue my trek on foot. My heart rate is dangerously high, but nothing can slow my speed, not even the sirens I hear growing closer with every thump of my feet.

My intuition is proven spot on when a loud boom rumbles through my chest a mere nanosecond before a white sedan sails over my head like a plane soaring in the sky.

With my heart in my throat, I charge down the wooden jetty filled with tourists. They stare at Keifer's car flying through the air with their mouths hanging open as if they're at a stunt show in Hollywood Studios.

"I'm hijacking your boat," I advise a fisherman at the end of the jetty.

Not giving him the chance to protest, I grab him by the scruff of his shirt and throw him away from the wheel.

Keifer's car barely breaks through the water when I race toward them. Salt water splashes my cheeks as I scan the water's edge, seeking any signs of movement. I know why I haven't been oceanside in years. It smells as horrible as it always has.

But this is different from the last time I swam these waters. Savannah knows how to swim, so her chances of survival have drastically improved... right?

Right.

Then why do I have a horrible feeling twisting my stomach?

CHAPTER 25

Savannah

The impact of Keifer's car hitting the barricade at the crest of Bronte's Peak dislodges his weapon from his grasp. While we sail through the air, I prepare for impact.

I'm not talking about the ocean.

I'm referring to my fist connecting with Keifer's jaw.

I knew the instant he turned down Taite what he was planning to do. He had read my record. He knew how much I hated this place, so this was the perfect spot for him to seek revenge.

This event isn't a kidnapping.

It is an attempted murder/suicide.

When I first sailed over this gorge years ago, I was confident I was going to die. I should have never underestimated Ryan.

He doesn't understand the word defeat. He didn't just save my life that night. He restored my faith in humanity.

I can only hope he achieves the same outcome today.

My body launches forward when we crash into the ocean with a bone-shuddering crunch. Hitting water at the rate we were traveling is the equivalent of crashing into a concrete wall. It steals the air from my lungs and sends pain hurtling through my chest and stomach.

But it doesn't alter my plan of attack.

After slamming my elbow into Keifer's ribs, my hand jack-knifes up, punching him right in the nose. He grunts before retaliating to my violence with the same amount of force. White spots dance in front of my eyes when his clenched knuckles rattle my teeth.

His viciousness intensifies my flight and fight mode. After slinging my seat belt off, I spring to a crouched position and then throw out my leg. Although I'm aiming to inflict harm to him, I also use his face as a springboard to escape the water flooding into his vehicle at a rate faster than my heart is pumping blood.

I'm halfway out the window when Keifer seizes my ankle and drags me backward. Recognizing the hard top design of his vehicle is sending us to the bed of the ocean faster than Axel's convertible did, I suck in three deep breaths to replenish my lungs with air before I'm swamped by water.

My assumption about Keifer's plans is proven dead accurate when he doesn't attempt to flee his rapidly sinking car. He holds me captive by my legs as bubbles of air trickle from his nose.

I struggle with all my might, not willing to go down without a fight. I didn't spend years ensuring Ryan didn't become a statistic of domestic violence to become one myself.

My fight agitates Keifer more. With the aggressiveness I've always seen in his eyes, he grips my nape before throwing my head forward. My forehead connects with the dashboard so fiercely the crystal blue water instantly turns murky.

Dizzy and profusely bleeding, I attempt to gasp in much-needed air.

All my lungs take in is water.

As I struggle through my body's convulsive reaction to the horrible-tasting water gushing into my lungs, I dig my nails into Keifer's hand.

The harder I battle, the greater my wooziness becomes.

Before I know it, blackness takes over.

"Thirteen... fourteen... fifteen," a voice from above grunts as my chest caves inwards. "Come on, Savannah. We're not going down this road again. Fight, baby. Do it for Rylee. She's waiting for you."

The heaviness on my chest elevates when a pair of lips seal over mine, replenishing my lungs with much-needed air.

One lung-filling gulp is quickly followed by another.

Arching my back, I suck in a mangled breath as tears prick my eyes. The salty water I swallowed during my near-drowning gargles in the back of my throat, almost drowning me for a second time.

"That's it, Savannah. Come on."

I'm rolled onto my side and whacked on my back before I can see who is saving me. I don't need to see my savior's face to know who he is. His heavenly gruff voice and delicious lips tell me everything I need to know. Ryan has once again dragged me from the bottom of the ocean, saving me in more ways than he will ever know.

When my eyes slowly flutter open, it dawns on me I'm not the only person he has saved. Keifer is hogtied on the sand next to me. The blood dripping from a split on his left brow reveals he's alive—*unfortunately*—and the arrogance in his eyes is doused with every unsteady breath I take. He wanted me dead so badly he'd happily go to jail to witness it.

It's a pity he underestimated Ryan's determination.

I'll never make the same mistake twice.

EPILOGUE

Ryan

Four Months Later. . .

*T*he worry my shoulders have been carrying all night lifts when Rylee's dimples pop off her face from my finger tracing her cheek. She mumbles incoherently under her breath before slipping her stuffed bunny under her chin.

With the sun peeking through her hot pink curtains, I switch off her underwater-themed nightlight and then head for the door. The nightlight was Savannah's idea. With her fear of drowning passed on to Rylee, she's hoping the introduction of water in her everyday life will help when we tackle swimming lessons next week.

I don't like her chances. Rylee is as stubborn as her mother. It is lucky I love her just as much as I did Savannah at the same age. The first few weeks were rocky. Rylee was not impressed when I palmed her off to Mrs. Daphne. She didn't speak to me for days, not even when I decorated the spare room in my apartment head to toe with stuffed animals and hideous pink bedspreads and cushions.

That is one way Rylee and Savannah are different. Rylee loves the girly stuff. She likes having her nails painted with bright pink polish, and if makeup is involved, she's there with bells on.

That's how I won her over. After sharing my dilemma with Izzy, she gave me some tips she used with Callie, her sister/somewhat daughter. Callie was smitten with Isaac, but she wasn't too keen on Izzy at the start. By utilizing the same persuasive techniques she shared with me, Izzy soon won Callie over.

Izzy's advice was as solid as a gold nugget, because not only did I get back in Rylee's good graces, I won over her mother as well. It was a win-win situation. I need an army when it comes to combatting Savannah's stubbornness. Thankfully, Rylee accepted the rank with honor. She helped coerce Savannah into following our original plan we created the morning of Keifer's unexpected arrival, citing the park next to my building as her reason for wanting to move.

It wasn't the basis for her relocation. Rylee is as smart as she is cute. She knew her mom wanted to say yes. She was just too worried about what people would think to stick it to the naysayers.

Rylee doesn't have that hang-up.

Although Keifer is no longer an issue, he didn't factor into our original plan. I had a decade of labored breathing to make up for. If Savannah had denied my suggestion, she wouldn't have just dented my ego; my lungs would have suffered too.

Mercifully, Savannah gave in without too much convincing. Thank god. If I were forced to use the persuasiveness I know she can't fend off, I may have scarred Rylee for life.

I already tickled her until she peed her pants, then dumped her on a stranger all within an hour, I didn't want to scar her any more than I already had.

Savannah stops cuddling her pillow when she notices me entering our bedroom. The tiredness on her face matches mine. The past few months have been tough on all of us, but the brunt has been carried by Savannah. The woman I have admired since she was a girl took my admiration to a never-to-be-reached-again level last month. She not only faced her fears head-on, she looked into the eyes of a monster as she testified about the horrific things he did to her.

There was not a dry eye in the courtroom when Savannah left the witness stand.

Even my eyes were wet.

After a short trial, Keifer was sentenced to twenty-five-years to life. The counts against him are so astronomical the chances of him ever being patrolled are slim to none. I was hoping the DA would push for the death penalty. That is the only reason I advised the fisherman surrounding me that there was another person in the car when I pulled Savannah from her watery grave for the second time in my life.

Fatal flaws by both Savannah and me four months ago were the cause of her near demise. With the tenseness of our night,

Savannah forgot about the FBI agent scanning her fingerprint in the nationwide database. Then, with my mind fritzing from all the disturbing information Savannah bombarded me with, I forgot about my call from the US Marshall two weeks earlier.

Keifer added two plus two, and he reached four.

That is how he tracked Savannah's location so quickly.

Fortunately for me, Savannah never goes down without a fight.

After tugging off my jacket and loosening my tie, I crawl into bed. My sixteen-hour shift made me want to chase sleep nearly three hours ago. If it wasn't for a break in Brax's case, I would have succumbed to the petitions of my heavy eyelids. Three armed men jumped an employee of the tattoo parlor Brax is a part owner. They fled with only minor possessions, but I can't settle my curiosity in his case. Brax is my brother from another mother, but that's not why I can't hand off his case to officers below me. My intuition is telling me this is my case. I just haven't figured out why yet.

"How's Brax? Did you find the people responsible?" Savannah's knees straddle my hips as her hands tackle the buttons of my dress shirt.

She's not teasing me. She's merely comforting me like she always does in a crisis.

It is a pity my cock didn't get the memo.

The instant her breath fans my neck, I become acutely aware my body hasn't figured out that I'm no longer a teenage boy with teenage issues. I swear to god, Savannah only needs to do a half-hearted hum, and my cock thickens to the point I could bounce a nickel off it.

Considering the circumstances of my night, this is wrong of me to admit, but Savannah and I tested the nickel theory.

Don't do it.

It doesn't hurt, but the laughing that follows the nickel's bounce may sting your ego.

It did mine.

Lucky for me, Savannah's lips soothed the sting in the best way possible. Even with her skills being as rusty as my truck when I brought her, she gives better head than any woman I know.

Recalling where I've been the last four hours, I adjust the thickness in my pants before drawing Savannah off my chest so I can see her eyes. I need them to quell the unease swirling in my gut. I've only had this feeling twice before. It was the two times I had Savannah's life in my hands.

"Was Brax hurt?" Savannah questions, confused by the deep groove between my brows.

I shake my head. "No. It's just..." A sigh finishes my sentence. "Something about this case is off."

She chews on the corner of her lip, making her look as youthful as she does in my memories. "You don't think it's a standard mugging?"

I shake my head again. "Have you heard from Damon lately?"

The quick squeeze of her thighs answers my question on her behalf.

Cocking my head to the side, I arch a brow. "You didn't give him money again, did you?"

Guilt grows in Savannah's eyes before she shakes her head. "Jet said that's the worst thing I could do."

"It is. If you're not going to listen to my advice, you should listen to Jet."

Miraculously, I keep jealousy out of my tone. That's a first. Savannah only sees Jet as a friend. Jet returns her friendship, but I'm confident if I weren't in the picture, he'd be happy to fill my spot.

"Where did you see Damon?"

"Outside that little bakery in town. He wanted to talk to Rylee." Savannah lifts her too-easy-to-forgive eyes to me. "He asked about you. He misses you, Ry."

I want to believe her, but I know that isn't the case. Damon didn't just break the promise we made over a decade ago. He crumbled it to pieces. He is more like our father than he's ever been, but that doesn't mean I don't love him. Just like Chris, I'll never give up on him. I just need him to put forth the same effort.

I run my hand down Savannah's back, loving the boost of color it gives to her cheeks. "Did you give Damon the brochure I gave you?"

Her teeth graze her bottom lip as she nods. "He said your mom already gave it to him."

"Ma gave him a drug counseling brochure?" Shock resonates in my tone.

Savannah smiles, wiping away my shit day in an instant. "Yeah. She's getting better, Ryan. Maybe not at a pace suitable for everyone, but a step forward is better than a step back." Her smile doubles, tripling the growth in my pants.

"Did Brax tell you where he was planning to take Clara last night?"

The zeal in her voice shocks me. I haven't heard her tone this high in months. Well, except when she's screaming my name in ecstasy, but since I'm trying to ignore the rock in my pants, I'll pretend I'm shocked.

When I shake my head, Savannah reveals, "Back to his apartment."

My mouth gapes. "Brax doesn't take girls back to his apartment. That is the very first rule on his long list of many."

"I know," she squeals, her voice piercing my eardrums. "That's why I asked Mrs. Daphne for proof. Clementine had to show her how to work the camera on her phone, but there's no doubt Brax had a girl in his arms last night."

She leans over to snag her cell off the bedside table to show me the proof firsthand. When she slams down onto my lap, we both freeze for a moment. If I weren't wearing trousers, and she wasn't wearing panties, we'd be...

No, don't go there, Ryan. You are a grown man having an *adult* conversation with a woman you plan to marry one day.

You are not an out-of-control teen.

Even Savannah thrusting a picture of Brax into my peripheral vision doesn't dampen my excitement. The girl of my dreams is right here, directly in front of me.

I'd be a fool not to take advantage of the situation.

Faster than Savannah can snap her fingers, I swipe her wrists out from underneath her. She topples onto the mattress with a giggle, her fall softened by my outstretched hands.

I'd never hurt her... not in a million years.

"Kiss me," I demand, narrowing my mouth toward hers.

The pout she makes shouldn't turn me on, but it does.

"I'm not kissing you, Ryan. I have horrible morning breath." She folds her arms under her breasts, thrusting her glorious tits that have grown a little bigger over the past three months into my line of sight.

"Kiss me," I demand again, tickling her, my fingers running more over the generous mounds on her chest than her actual ribs.

She arches her back.

It is more for show than annoyance.

"Ryan!" she squeals when I up the ante. "I swear to god, if you make me pee my pants, I won't speak to you for a week."

"I've had worst," I jest, laughing.

I continue my onslaught, loving that it seems like we've stepped back in time.

When I am with Savannah, I truly feel free of burden. I will always feel guilty for what happened to Chris. What I said to him when he killed himself will stay with me for eternity, but with Savannah's help, I've realized Chris never intended to be here for the long haul. He wanted an out. I gave him one—it just wasn't in the manner I had believed.

He didn't want to leave his brother, so by me promising to look after Noah, he finally felt at peace with his decision.

Was it the right one for him to make? No. Never. But I'm glad he has found peace.

I'm drawn from my thoughts when a pair of smaller hands join my campaign in tickling Savannah into submission. Rylee bombards her mother's ribs, making sure she doesn't press too hard on the little curve peeking out of Savannah's pajamas.

The beautiful roundness of her stomach proves that wishes can come true. You've just got to put in the hard work first because whether you have millions in your bank account or not even two nickels to rub together, life isn't easy. You have to fight for everything you want. That includes love.

After placing a kiss on the two-letter name scrawled on Savannah's lower left hip, I continue tickling her ribs. Savannah claims she got her "Ry" tattoo in the weeks following Rylee's birth as a commemoration, but she's as bad at lying as she is at saying no to Rylee. She would have gotten her whole name if it were solely for Rylee. It represents me as well.

By the time I'm hunched over with a stomach cramp from laughing so hard, Savannah's face is as red as a beetroot. Happiness isn't the cause of her inflamed cheeks, though. She looks moments away from murdering someone.

As she charges into the bathroom like a woman on a mission, my eyes swing to Rylee. "I think we made Mommy mad."

Rylee grins an adorable dimpled smile before nodding.

"Should we make her something yummy for breakfast to make up for it?"

Her smile turns blinding.

"All right, jump on." She leaps onto my back before my offer is fully issued.

"What do you think your little brother will let mommy hold down this morning?" I ask Rylee as we giddy up into my kitchen.

"Hmm..." When I place her on the kitchen counter, she taps her index finger on her pursed lips. "Fruit Loops?"

My brows furrow. "Do you think Fruit Loops will stop Mommy from being sick?"

My deep tone is smothered with uncertainty. Savannah has a hard time keeping down toast, so I don't think she'll fare well with sugary cereal and full cream milk.

Rylee shakes her head. "No, but the toilet will look pretty after she vomits."

I throw my head back and laugh.

Stick me with a fork, ladies and gentlemen.

I am fucking done.

If I hadn't already worked this out months ago, there's no doubting it now. Not only is Savannah Fontane, the prettiest and most entrancing woman in Ravenshoe, but my god, so is her daughter.

"Please be careful," Savannah begs while handing me the canister of coffee she made when I announced a break in Brax's case required me to return after only an hour of sleep. "Do you think you'll see Brax today?"

I nod. "I'll update him on what Nate discovered before heading to the office. Why?"

She tries not to smile. She shouldn't have bothered. Her dimples give away when she's smiling even without her lips moving. "Can you give him this for me?" She doesn't hide her grin when she hands me a white paper bag.

Her shit-eating smirk morphs onto my face when I peer into the bag.

There's a twelve-pack of magnum condoms nestled in the middle.

"You were over the moon when you discovered I was pregnant. I have a feeling Brax might not be so eager to join the parenting club just yet."

I laugh. "I think he'd shit bricks."

"Most men would," Savannah agrees, smiling.

I inch my mouth closer to hers. "Lucky for you, I'm anything but normal."

Any reply she's planning to give is halted by the lash of my tongue against her lips. My god—as sweet as honey and as sinful as vodka. Savannah's intoxicating palate would make a sane man insane and a sober man drunk.

I stop refilling my lungs with air when a grunt sounds through my ears. The stomping of a foot closely follows it. Not needing further instructions, I bob down to Rylee's height so she can issue me the same farewell kiss she has given me every day for nearly four months.

"Bye, Daddy," she whispers, her farewell as perfect to my ears as the first hundred times she's called me her dad. She curls her arms around my neck to squeeze me tightly. "Be careful." She stutters her last word, her fret as high as her mother's when I am on duty.

Although the massive settlement the state will pay Savannah means I could soon live like a king, I have no intentions of resigning from my position at Ravenshoe PD. What Regina said all those years ago was true. I was born for this job. I just

279

needed to pull my head out of my ass to see it. Savannah understands this. That's why she's never mentioned me leaving. It is only Rylee who doesn't understand why I can't stay home and play Barbie dolls with her all day. The extended paternity leave I plan to take when her brother is born will hopefully quench her desires for a few months.

After drawing Rylee into my chest, I assure her, "Don't fret, sweetheart. Daddy has been waiting for your mommy for a very long time. I'm not going anywhere anytime soon. And neither are you."

RAVENSHOE GOSSIP

STORY BY: TRACY MCCLANE
SOURCES: UNKNOWN
PHOTO: RYLEE CARTER

TOWN HERO ENDS CHALLENGING YEAR ON A HIGH!

Ravenshoe Police Officer and beloved local, Ryan Carter (30), is set to marry childhood sweetheart, Savannah Fontane (30) in an intimate wedding on the cliffs of Bronte's Peak later this evening. The couple's two children, Rylee (5) and Christopher (6 mths) will be a part of the ritzy celebrations. With members of the wedding party being much-loved residents of the Ravenshoe area, the guest lists has been reported to be in the high- to mid-three hundreds.

Ryan is a decorated officer who received a medal of honor for his risky rescue on the banks of Bronte's Peak fifteen months ago. After being shot by his brother, Damon (28) in a domestic altercation twelve months ago, Ryan began a long and bumpy road to recovery. His fiancée was at his side every step of the way.

Forever an advocate for domestic violence victims, Ryan testified on behalf of his brother at his trial. He requested for the judge to be lenient on the basis that victims of domestic violence also include other family members subjected to repercussions of the abuse. The Judge heard his plea. After serving his bail period in a minimum security prison, Damon Carter was sentenced to two years of extensive rehabilitation at a center in Kentucky. Although he was initially included on the guest list for today's celebration, at last report, he will not be attending the festivities.

I am sure you will join Ravenshoe Gossip in wishing Ryan and Savannah the best of luck today. Their wedding has been many years in the making.

RAVENSHOE NEWS   EDITION: 034

NEWS ARTICLE

Town Hero Ends Challenging Year on a High.

Ravenshoe Police Officer and beloved local, Ryan Carter (30), is set to marry childhood sweetheart, Savannah Fontane (30) in an intimate wedding on the cliffs of Bronte's Peak later this evening. The couple's two children, Rylee (5) and Christopher (6 mths) will be a part of the ritzy celebrations. With members of the wedding party being much-loved residents of the Ravenshoe area, the guest lists has been reported to be in the high- to mid-three hundreds.

Ryan is a decorated officer who received a medal of honor for his risky rescue on the banks of Bronte's Peak fifteen months ago. After being shot by his brother, Damon (28) in a domestic altercation twelve months ago, Ryan began a long and bumpy road to recovery. His fiancée was at his side every step of the way.

Forever an advocate for domestic violence victims, Ryan testified on behalf of his brother at his trial. He requested for the judge to be lenient on the basis that victims of domestic violence also include other family members subjected to repercussions of the abuse. The Judge heard his plea. After serving his bail period in a minimum security prison, Damon Carter was sentenced to two years of extensive rehabilitation at a center in Kentucky. Although he was initially included on the guest list for today's celebration, at last report, he will not be attending the festivities.

I am sure you will join Ravenshoe Gossip in wishing Ryan and Savannah the best of luck today. Their wedding has been many years in the making.

The End

The next book in the Enigma series is Cormack! His book is called <u>Sugar and Spice</u>. It is available NOW!

Facebook: facebook.com/authorshandi

Instagram: instagram.com/authorshandi

Email: authorshandi@gmail.com

Reader's Group: bit.ly/ShandiBookBabes

Website: authorshandi.com

Newsletter: https://www.subscribepage.com/AuthorShandi

Hunter, Hugo, Cormack, Hawke, Ryan, Rico & Brax stories have already been released, Brandon, Regan and all the other great characters of Ravenshoe will be getting their own stories at some point during 2020.

If you enjoyed this book - please leave a review.

ACKNOWLEDGMENTS

Thank you to the following individuals who without their contributions and support this book would not have been written.

First to my husband Chris—my rock, my boo! I love you!

Second to my mum Carolyn Wallace. You support is endless!

Third to my editor, Krista. Thank you for making my manuscripts nice and shiny. Love your work!

Fourth, to Bec, for listening to my ramblings. AKA—spoiler alerts! Let's take this industry by storm!

And last, but not at all least, my beautiful readers. You guys ROCK! I love every blood one of you!

My first book was originally written to be shared amongst my friends, in a hope that others may enjoy the story I created, but with the support of the people mentioned earlier, I self-published my stories to share with others. I hope you enjoy them!

Please remember to leave a review of my book.

Cheers

Shandi xx

ALSO BY SHANDI BOYES

Denotes Standalone Books

Perception Series

Saving Noah *

Fighting Jacob *

Taming Nick *

Redeeming Slater *

Saving Emily

Wrapped Up with Rise Up

Protecting Nicole *

Enigma

Enigma

Unraveling an Enigma

Enigma The Mystery Unmasked

Enigma: The Final Chapter

Beneath The Secrets

Beneath The Sheets

Spy Thy Neighbor *

The Opposite Effect *

I Married a Mob Boss *

Second Shot *

The Way We Are

The Way We Were

Sugar and Spice *

Lady In Waiting

Man in Queue

Couple on Hold

Enigma: The Wedding

Silent Vigilante

Hushed Guardian

Quiet Protector

Enigma: An Isaac Retelling

Enigma Bonus Scenes (Two free chapters)

Twisted Lies *

Bound Series

Chains

Links

Bound

Restrain

The Misfits *

Nanny Dispute *

Russian Mob Chronicles

Nikolai: A Mafia Prince Romance

Nikolai: Taking Back What's Mine

Nikolai: What's Left of Me

Nikolai: Mine to Protect

Asher: My Russian Revenge *

Nikolai: Through the Devil's Eyes

Trey *

The Italian Cartel

Dimitri

Roxanne

Reign

Mafia Ties (Novella)

Maddox

Demi

Ox

Rocco *

Clover *

Smith *

RomCom Standalones

Just Playin' *

Ain't Happenin' *

The Drop Zone *

Very Unlikely *

False Start *

Short Stories - Newsletter Downloads

Christmas Trio *

Falling For A Stranger *

One Night Only Series

Hotshot Boss *

Hotshot Neighbor *

The Bobrov Bratva Series

Wicked Intentions *

Sinful Intentions *

Devious Intentions *

Deadly Intentions *